The Road Goes On Forever

The Road Goes On Forever

Jake Hessman

iUniverse, Inc.
New York   Bloomington

The Road Goes On Forever

iUniverse books may be ordered through booksellers or by contacting:

iUniverse
1663 Liberty Drive
Bloomington, IN 47403
www.iuniverse.com
1-800-Authors (1-800-288-4677)

ISBN: 978-1-4502-3908-0 (sc)
ISBN: 978-1-4502-3907-3 (dj)
ISBN: 978-1-4502-3906-6 (ebk)

Library of Congress Control Number: 2010909470

Printed in the United States of America

iUniverse rev. date: 06/28/2010

For my family. Both of them.

"The road goes on forever and the party never ends."

- Robert Earl Keen Jr.

Author's Note

This book began as a series of notes, thoughts you might say. It was a system of organizing ideas, complaints, and dreams at a time when the options before me were innumerable. There is much confusion involved when you have no motivation to move in any one particular direction but feel the need to always move forward.

In time, these hypothetical ideas of what I would do, which direction would I go if there were no obligations either personal or financial bearing down on me, became the latter half of what you have before you. The question of 'what would I do if...' seems to be easy to answer but the more a scenario is studied the more difficult an answer may become. This is one of many hypothetical answers which arose from that confusing time. How would you answer?

I hope you enjoy.

Jake Hessman

May 23, 2010

To everyone who put in their two cents, thank you.

Mother, I know my eccentricities may surprise you from time to time but you're unconditional support is an invaluable resource when I begin to doubt by own insanity.

Angela, I would like to apologize for all the late night calls, random messages, and putting you through the chaos that is my creative process. I hope you enjoyed it and may we suffer through it all again soon.

LG, without you there would be no book. I appreciate every lesson you have taught me, whether you intended them or not. Thank you.

Prologue

Ramone turned off the cracked and ragged black top, heading east into the brilliance of the rising sun toward Coupland Studios, as the sign directed. Reaching across the weathered dashboard of his '57 Chevy step-side, his crooked fingers latched onto a pair of sunglasses and slid them on. Large lenses and a cross bar, the same style he'd worn for the last fifty years. With a glance in the rearview mirror, the usually subdued old Mexican caught a smile seeing the large trail of red dust billowing up behind him. The truck, his old companion, was referred to as Loretta. He'd named her after an ex-girlfriend from back in grammar school. His wife of 52 years did not know this. It would remain that way if he wanted to live to see another season pass. Loretta was well worn, maybe a little beat up, but she was mechanically sound. Together they danced down the half mile drive with just enough bounce through the hills to keep his coffee thermos from making full contact with his lips and rinsing his gray mustache thoroughly.

Chris Coupland, the patron of Coupland Studios, was a young man, only a few years out of the university. He had an average height, stocky build; to Ramone he looked like the average young gringo, except for his eyes. He had this ghostly blue gaze that seemed as if it could burn holes through walls and entrance any woman sorry enough to fall under their spell. It made Ramone wonder occasionally if there wasn't a ghost alive in the young man. Senior Coupland was very laid back; excitement still grabbed him on occasion though, when he was fully engrossed in some project. Ramone could see in him that something burned bright. His mind rarely if ever rested. Sometimes he talked a lot, sometimes not. There were collective rumors around the community regarding the circumstances that brought him here, yet Ramone, who knew him best, elected to remain absent from all conjecture.

As Loretta pulled over the last hill, Ramone could see the lights were already glowing in the Studio. The truck coasted down the last hundred yards and came to a stop in his usual spot, just along the side of the drive, parallel to the barn, halfway down the south side. A thought occurred to the old man. In the few years he had worked at the Studio, not one time had he been the first one to work. It was just the two of them, and sure, the boss lived a stone's throw away just across the lawn that separated the house to the south from the Studio. Early or late it did not matter what time he finally arrived, the boss was already scheming for the day, chores done, horses fed and the radio blasting some gringo twang. Ramone never cared much for the music that was played, but every once and a long while a song would come up that struck his fancy. This morning was no different. The young man was already standing atop an old boat they had been refinishing. The craft sat on its bracing in the middle of the yard. The attention paid to this particular project was sporadic at best throughout the last two years. It was close now though. Chris stood to wave as the truck shut down.

Taking his time to exit, Ramone thought about Senior Coupland. He had arrived several years ago, from somewhere up north. Ramone could not remember exactly from where and did not care or feel the need to ask. He was an impressive man for such a young age. The boss did not act it or show it, but being a man of many generations Ramone could tell he was a person of much wealth, in more than one manner. There had been several projects that built the foundation of his financial fortune. One book had been published and several of their projects had sold or been patented. His knowledge though, Ramone did not know where it came from. He spent hours upon hours pondering over the most random thoughts and ideas. Senior Coupland carried himself in a way the old Mexican had seen in only a few people before, men he'd met in his past. He didn't know how much money they had, but they were wealthy also and carried themselves as such, with class and charity that few in their shoes would have been able to fill.

Surveying the scene Ramone noticed how much the place was changing. He had spent his life working this land. He was born just off to the east some seventy odd years ago to a ranch hand and his housewife. He had been raised here, educated here, and worked here. When the boss came through and bought up the old place, Ramone was very pleased. He was surprised though when Senior Coupland had asked him to stay with the land to work as an extra pair of hands. Why he'd been selected over many other younger men who were also familiar with the place, he did not know. He had his theories, but that was all. His family was not so confident about the change. They thought he should retire and move to Lubbock with his youngest daughter and her family but to Ramone that would be emasculating. He was born here, and he was stubborn enough to let his days pass here until there were no more. In return for his services he was paid very well, better than he'd been paid as a working cowboy. Come to think of it, this job was easy, this was his retirement.

The rusted door of the '57 groaned with intense objection as Ramone pushed on the cracked vinyl. The morning was always rough on both of them. The old man made similar sounds as he forced his knees to extend as he stepped out. His baby screamed back when he slammed the door shut. Standing there eyeballing Loretta, Ramone wondered who would succumb to old age first, he or the truck. It was a neck and neck race they had fought through their many years together. He ran his callused hands along the rim of the bed as he walked beside her. Several flakes of paint fell off under his fingertips along the way. The cancer on her was growing, it was a lost cause.

Ramone's seasoned boots stirred the dirt as his heels drug in stride across the drive toward the boat. Crossing onto the lawn, the blades of grass brushed the dust clear from his soles. Senior Coupland looked up and gave the Mexican a nod and returned to the project at hand.

This particular morning the boss was attaching a custom built brass railing to the twenty-foot vessel. The railing had been the crowning achievement of several months spent studying metallurgy. Ramone was proud of the final result. The elder walked out into the middle of the yard, beside the boat a radio blared. There were sketches and numbers he could not decipher scattered on pages strewn across the boat and lawn alike, weighted down by an assortment of bottles, mugs, and rocks. Page after page sprawled across the scene, some stacked in order while others were tossed to the side in no discernable pattern. Ramone may not have known exactly what the boss's intentions were, but he understood what Chris expected of him. There was an unspoken understanding between these two men. They may have been separated by generations, cultures and numerous beliefs, yet there was still that understanding which neither one spoke of but recognized the first time they met. This was an odd find for either man. Their minds functioned on the same wavelength; it was uncanny from time to time.

Chris (Intro)

C hris looked up as the old Mexican approached. He had chosen
Ramone to stay when he bought this place because he saw
something of a quiet wisdom in the old man. Knowing himself, Chris
understood his own flaws and though try as he might, he had trouble
dealing with them. His passions often drove him over the edge, and he
would need a calm steady head to keep his feet grounded and moving in
a productive direction. Ramone conducted himself in this manner and
Chris appreciated the ways he pushed him to finish one thing without
taking off on a new tangent, though it was often unsuccessful.

Chris gently set down the bracket he was holding and took a seat
on the edge of the boat, dangling his feet in the morning light. Sliding
his fingers through his hair he realized it had been several months since
his last cut. That was just one more thing to get done in the next 48
hours. With a deep breath and a click of his heels, Ramone looked up
as Chris asked, "What say you?"

With a long sip of the Columbian brew from his thermos, which
had cooled beyond his taste by this point and a lick of his mustache,
the reply came in its own time, of course. "Sailing is still running, is
it not?"

Chris looked into those dark eyes sunk in below his heavy brow
and gave a quizzical look, not analyzing his remark but rethinking his
own true intentions. Questions rolled over as ice would over a tongue,

none of which had a correct or incorrect answer. This was the keystone of Ramone's wisdom. He had the ability to present a problem from different angles and perspectives causing Chris to rethink his solution over and over from differing points of view. Typically such comments from the elder man were neither right nor wrong but rhetorical, bringing previously unseen aspects of any situation to light. "My intentions are not what you think my old friend."

"Senior, you have a bad habit of assuming that everyone knows what you are up to, what kind of ace you have up your sleeve, sometimes I'm right and sometimes I'm wrong. Either way, you never clarify whether these are correct or incorrect, so I'm left to fend for myself and unless told otherwise I will follow my perceptions with the assumption that I am correct."

"Usually you are correct old man." Chris stated, nodding in agreement with Ramone's statement, still with no clarification as to why he was sitting atop a boat in the desert of West Texas, days away from any sea.

Ramone stood stoic, looking over the assortment of documents spread across the ground as Chris jumped down and began to pace. He walked down to the bow, back to the stern and around again, seven steps in each pass. He repeated this cycle many times. Eventually he made his way back to stand next to the Mexican, who had not moved from his post. The old man bested him in height by several inches even though he had been shrinking along his spine for several years. Chris could only imagine the stature he had held in his prime. "Ramone, I'd like to learn how to sail."

"It seems my assumptions are correct so far." He stated adding a little sarcasm. "Why, is my next question?"

Chris thought of the best way to answer that would not draw further questioning or criticism, "Because I don't know how."

"What do you plan on doing? Sailing right out across the plains past the Rio Grande?"

Chris smiled, Ramone was in a good mood as usual, that always made the day pass a little quicker. "I'm sure as hell gonna try. Just to prove to you it can be done." Chris replied. Changing the subject he asked, "Would you mind spraying one of the 'Taxi Chairs' again? I got distracted last night and sanded one of them down to the primer. It has to be ready before I leave tomorrow morning."

"Si`, no problem," came the answer, it was always the answer. Ramone made his way toward the old hay barn that now housed so many pieces of furniture and the machinery that produced them. As he was passing out of sight, Chris squatted down next to the boat and began laying down graphite on one of the pages. Erasing some, adding more, this was how Chris worked. It would be a solid hour before he was done sketching, and several years before he finished this particular project. This is how their days passed.

West Texas

~~

This Monday was fairly uneventful; it was mostly spent discussing new projects amongst the young designer and the old ranch hand, while putting the finishing touches on pieces that would be taken to Austin tomorrow. Chris had been given an opportunity from an old friend to present several selections of his work in the state capitol. Lance, the orchestrator, had moved to the Lone Star State after graduating college a year behind Chris and made himself known in the local art and design scene. Several months ago, on his way to Colorado he'd stopped by and fallen in love with the furniture that had kept Chris and Ramone busy. Upon his return home Lance made the calls needed and setup a premier for Coupland Studios. The show would contain a broad cross section of everything they'd done, from ashtrays to armoires. Chris wasn't looking forward to the show, but he'd used the opportunity to draw everyone together for a few days. Since leaving school many of their old friends had drifted apart with careers and families, but this week they would be down for the opening. One in particular he hadn't seen in years.

The heat rose with the sun. The craftsmen worked tirelessly, but even as Ramone pulled away, headed home for the day, there was still much to be done. Chris needed a break and strolled to the house searching for dinner. He walked across the lawn, past the boat, now covered, and up onto porch. The front door, a solid oak piece with inlaid glass panes, was one of the first things he'd produced here. It was heavy and sturdy, perfectly balanced, the ornate piece swung open with the slightest of effort. Opening into a smaller than average gathering room with a staircase rising to his left, he stepped through admiring the high copper ceilings and the cracked lathe and plaster walls that gave this house so much of its character. Only a few rooms had yet to suffer remodeling, but this one was under debate. Should it be patched and shined, or should he strip it all down and refinish the entire space? That was a question he'd tackle at a later date. A door-less opening led into the dining room which had been completely refinished. The bamboo floors and custom built sideboard gave it a unique look in contrast to the traditional front room. Still further in, past a double swinging door propped open with books, was the kitchen. Standing in front of the fridge, Chris stood perplexed. There wasn't much to eat and none of it looked appetizing at the time. He reached for an amber bottle. Sometimes dinner came in the liquid state.

With a beer in hand, Chris returned to the tin roof front porch and sat on the park bench he'd been left by the previous owner and propped his dusty old boots on the railing. His head leaned back against the cement board siding that had been hung his first autumn in the house. Taking a long drink he felt the bubbles on the back of his tongue and tasted the malted grains. It was so good he took a second, the chill of the brew working itself through his inside. Chris was comfortable here, the weather, the distance, the scenery, it was all just as he liked it. Nothing impressive mind you, only a small, half renovated, half weathered, two level three bedroom, ranch house. It had just received central air two years ago. Chris could remember his first summer here vividly. It was miserable. Waking up in the middle of the night drenched in sweat. No number of fans could alleviate the curse either. The house sat on a few hundred acres. There were exactly fourteen trees located within his property line, two windmills, and Ramone's assorted livestock. There were twenty plus head of cattle, two fillies, and assorted poultry to give it his best guess. The Studio, some forty yards away was large enough to handle all their equipment and space needed for finishing, as well as storage of all the pieces built on speculation.

The dust blew hard on most days, the summers were intense enough to send anyone in their right mind packing, and the winters were equally as bitter but seasons ended. The horizon though, was never ending. No matter where you looked, from the right vantage point you could see forever. It may not have been the end of the world, but you could almost see it by the time you arrived out here. Chris liked the feeling of absolute freedom that such an extensive skyline brought. The most important aspects though were the house and shop; they stood as prize jewels, works in progress.

Sitting beneath the old tin roof Chris gazed up, noting several holes that would have to be looked after soon. The evening breeze brought a cooling effect to his damp skin that was dearly appreciated after the long day. Even now, here in his own world, his mind still raced. It never slowed really, unless forced into the blinding fog of alcohol, which was the case more often than Chris would be comfortable admitting to a stranger. The sun was still a good hour away from settling in for the night, but it still hung low enough, off to the west and slightly south, that the beaten brim of his sweat lined and sun bleached old hat needed to be cranked down another notch.

The stereo in the Studio played on, though at this distance Chris could make out a few distinct lines.

"The rays of light through the Shiner Bock bottle make me wanna turn the key and put down the throttle, get lost down thirty-five."

The modern poet is a forgotten artist amongst America's mainstream music these days. The melancholy words of this troubadour were once an anthem for a lost man. Chris didn't feel like he'd actually found what he was looking for yet, or if he ever would, but now these lyrics acted as a catalyst reaching back to a nostalgic scene.

"'Cause I know I can make it there on a twelve pack and a prayer... no matter how big the storms, I know I can find me a place that's warm.

The sun's shining somewhere in Texas, I hope it's shining on her, somewhere down in Texas."

No longer a dream, now a reality, the poet didn't lie, the sun did shine. Was it the dream of Texas that brought him here or the dream of her?

Chris shook it off. There was no time for those thoughts, not now. Tomorrow was a big day, Austin, and there was more work to do. It would make for a long night but he didn't worry. It would all buff out in the end.

Dingo, a three-year old Aussie Shepherd he'd kept from several litters out of his old shepherd Duke, strolled across the front yard. The last remnant of the toughest old dog he'd ever known. They'd looked almost identical, that's why Dingo had been selected above all the others. The bitch belonged to a local artist, much like himself. The dog was shaggy and dirty. He was just as miserable as every other poor creature unlucky enough to find themselves caught in the summer heat. Dingo still hung around though, loyalty ran deep between them. There had never been another dog so odd for its breed. Even his father was hard working and easily excited but not this one. Dingo was so indifferent to the world around him it was shocking. It wasn't but a few weeks ago, while lying next to the door, a rare, massive thunderhead rolled through the county tormenting every living thing within sixty miles of the house. Chris had seen the clouds building early in the day as he moved to and from the Studio. If they continued on their path, he knew it would be a wild evening. By late in the afternoon the sky had begun to darken and the wind picked up, as would be expected. Standing in the front doorway watching the pending storm, Chris noticed several beefs wandering down the road just as the rain began to fall in massive bombs. They had broken through a line just north of the house and were trying to head out the storm. Bursting through the front door Chris unintentionally pushed his companion aside taking out after the livestock. Almost an hour later, with the animals corralled and himself thoroughly soaked, Chris returned to find Dingo unmoved. The canine simply acknowledged the crazy man's return with a slight lift of the head and remained right where he lay, half piled on top of the boots next to the door, wedged against the old park bench. He did not give a damn at all. Chris was jealous.

Dingo slowly made his way up the front porch, strolling around Chris's right side, passed underneath the bench sniffing his way around eventually emerging just to his left. He circled himself twice and sat just out of his master's reach and joined him in surveying the front yard. The dog looked as if he were guarding his territory. Though if anything were to take after the hens he would probably just as likely help the scavenger corner the poultry as soon as he would defend them, but neither would be the case. Dingo would sit on the porch and just watch. He was one hell of a watch dog; there was no action behind him, just watching.

The evenings out here in no man's land were a beautiful sight according to Chris. A person must have the right mindset to really appreciate it but about the only sight more breathtaking than the ending of the day was the beginning. Unfortunately the only time Chris seemed to catch the beauty of it was if he hadn't slept the night before. If that was the case then there was usually much whiskey involved also. He could settle for dusk, for now. The windmill he purposely neglected to fix loped in the distance. The clouds passed gracefully on the wind. Nothing else moved. A lone swallow passed overhead and disappeared behind the house.

Lost in the peaceful scene Chris sat amongst a sea of ideas and dreams. Tomorrow was Austin, and Austin meant friends and strangers. Friends were fine, strangers though, well those he did not want to see. He didn't mind visiting the metropolis on rare occasions, if it was unplanned and unannounced. Not that he felt like hiding anything, but the element of surprise was something he'd always cherished. Give them something they don't expect, throw a monkey wrench in their gears to keep things exciting. This attitude was reflected in most of his work also, some of which could be shocking to a few of the finer pallets. Unfortunately though, tomorrow's visit had been widely announced for some time now. The newspapers in the region had run varying articles on some of his work, in one article that he'd seen, referred to it as 'a shocking collision of tradition and lack of tact.' He didn't care. His work was not made to be put up on a pedestal. Either way, Hope's paper had run a small notice, and he trusted she was planning on making the drive in from Dallas. He'd put the tickets in the mail late last week, they should get to her office in time.

"C'mon Dingo, let's get."

The dog responded, hearing his name, but only looked at Chris with utter disregard for his actions or commands. As Chris shifted to stand, his boot scraped along the rail breaking free even more pieces of the flaky, dry paint that was in dire need of attention. The sun faded white bits gently floated to the decking when a sudden gust of the building breeze lifted them airborne, mixing with the dust in the air and headed out. They crossed over the low slung branch of the oak tree in front of the house and made an abrupt change turning southbound toward old Mexico. Chris doubted if they'd make it that far, hell they'd probably never get past the fence line, but it was his optimistic nature to imagine they would. The young man was a hopeless dreamer, always had been. Stepping around the dog, the dried leather soles of his boots scuffed softly against the hardwood of the porch. Three steps and he was down to ground level. Past the grassy lawn and kicking up dirt as he moved across the drive that ran all the way between the house and studio, making a roundabout in between, and continuing on into the pasture, Chris was off to the Studio to wrap everything up. Within a few strides he could feel the small rocks pushing up through the bottom of his feet; they reminded him just how old and sore his body was. Chiseled through hard work and long hours, the darkness of his skin was a testament to the sheer number of hours he'd put in around here. Who was he kidding, at twenty nine he had a long way to go and he was definitely not as durable as he was at twenty-two, but then again, what would forty bring?

Across the road and around the northwestern corner of the Studio he stepped through the nine foot, front doors still standing open to let the breeze work its way through. As darkness was just beginning to set in, Chris reached around the large door to his left and flipped the switch kicking on the dormant lights. The space lit up with great brilliance. He'd spent a lot of time selecting the correct lighting to ensure that even at night his colors would remain true to Mother Nature. Toward the rear of the large space, along the wall to his right, up on the stage, just outside the bathroom stood a large, white 1950's refrigerator with 'Devil's Door' painted across the front. This helped ease the nerves of some of his God fearing clients when they came to visit. They may not agree with his habit but if he acknowledged the evil spirit's presence they let it be. Unfortunately it was the spirits contained within the ice box that he feared more. Chris mounted the steps up to the stage and swung open the fridge, the light had long burnt out, but he knew exactly where to find what he was looking for. Reaching in, he pulled out another bottle and pried it open with a lighter. This was the sole reason he still carried one.

Returning to the main floor, road soda in hand, he checked the chairs he'd left on the other side of the Studio in the spray booth to off-gas. Still tacky, they would have to be loaded last. Setting the bottle down, he took to unmasking a desk that should be complete if everything had gone right with the last round of finish. The rest of the night passed as the stereo pumped out tunes to keep him company. Dingo came and went, taking his fill of beer when the opportunity arose. After packing the last of the chairs that were to be hauled eastward into the morning sun once it broke free of the night's dark grasp, Chris loaded the late model Ford he'd backed up to the front doors. As the hours ticked away and work toiled onward the bottles fell faster and faster. Finally, well into the early hours of a new day, Chris made the return journey back across the drive to the house. Not yet ready to call it a night he joined the dog on the back deck this time. He picked a hammock and lay rocking under a canopy of stars.

A.M.

~~

The morning light came a little too early for his taste. Chris's mind was still fuzzy from the night before. Everything that had to be done was taken care of, he could recall that much. Since he was not expected in Austin before five in the evening, the young man took his time to rise. He looked over and saw Dingo lying on the floor beside him soaking up the yellow rays that cut through the darkness. He was on his back, legs stretched to the heavens half cocked like a crescent moon, tail wagging. How could a dog be that comfortable on a tile floor?

"Well, we missed the bed again, dog," Chris groaned as he sat upright at the breakfast table. It was a small, unfinished shaker style table just under the only northwesterly window in the kitchen. It was just before eight in the morning, and Marlene should be by soon to pick up Dingo for the week. She was a great sitter having several pets of varying breeds of her own. She also had two of Dingo's litter mates so it worked out well for everyone. Marlene was a good woman, young, strong and beautiful, but she was up and ready to go before the rooster out in the yard, and Chris usually was not. This did not mean he didn't get up; he just did not do it with her enthusiasm. Reaching out for an epic stretch to start the day, his back popped violently.

Marlene had been a comforting friend when he first moved here. In time they had their passions, and she'd proposed on more than one occasion, but Chris didn't need a woman like that. Not her anyway. He was just as comfortable to take care of the lust and be on his way, many times returning home. Occasionally she would stay with him when it was convenient enough for her, but she always left long before he rose. This didn't bother him one bit. He was better left to his own vices. Chris vaguely remembered speaking to her late last night as he rubbed the sleep from his eyes. That meant there would be hell to pay this morning.

One more stretch and a solid yawn, he stomped his wooden heels on the floor to stand. The table was scattered with four bottles, though there were bound to be more littered throughout the property. Chris rubbed his boot down Dingo's long side causing the canine to roll quickly to his feet. Dragging his heels on the tile and his hands along the wall he made his way through the house and up the stairs, he began stripping off the old dirty threads from the day before. Naked, he strolled down the hall back to the main level to the one working bathroom. It was the first room he had refinished. The first few months Chris lived here were warm enough he could hose himself down outside before Ramone showed up for work. It didn't bother him, and there was no one within eyesight to offend, so why not.

Inside the bathroom stood a beautiful pedestal sink he had designed and commissioned a local potter to produce. It stood under its own weight below a large vanity mirror on a long, fluted base. There were no exposed pipes as the p-trap had been installed below the floor, and the faucet with its handles came straight out of the wall. It was an interesting contrast to the 1920-something high tank commode he'd found at a flea market in Santa Fe. He grabbed the toiletries needed from the cabinet just inside the door as he passed. Toothbrush in his mouth he climbed into the oversized ball-and-claw cast iron tub. Paste dripping from his lips he reached down and cranked both handles to the left. The anticipation made his heart race. It always took the cold water a half a second to fill the pipe before bursting out of the rain style shower head. Unfortunately it took the hot water much longer to catch up from the heater, he had counted the seconds several times.

Those five seconds where the longest, most frigid feeling he'd ever experienced. The brief shot though was just what he needed to wake up. If he wasn't sober yet, the adrenaline would cover it for now. As the water burst forth, he let out a scream that startled the dog on the other side of the house. His toothbrush fell into the tub. Shivering for just a short while, Chris reached down, picked it up and finished brushing. After a good scrubbing and a quick shave, he was ready to go. Marlene was picking up beer bottles when he walked out to start the coffee. He had no modesty and made no effort to cover himself. She'd seen him naked before.

"Long night last night?" Marlene asked trash bag in hand standing on the back patio. She'd already made it through the kitchen and was working her way outward. Chris set up his coffee maker and filled the reservoir to the top. "Yeah, Dingo and I had to get some things finished before we could call it a night," he said hitting the on switch. Marlene turned away from him picking up bottle after bottle. When all the glass containers were bagged she crossed the roundabout and tossed the large white sack in the recycling bin behind the Studio. As she clasped the kitchen door behind her Chris passed through the swinging door from the dining room. He was kind enough to put on some shorts. "Austin huh?" she asked.

"Yeah, I'm leavin' within the hour, soon as I can get my bags packed." He replied pouring a mug of the black crack. "You want some?" Chris asked, gesturing toward her with the pitcher in hand.

"No, thank you," came the answer as she sat down, her jeans didn't seem like they'd take the stresses, but they held solid. She brushed her hair back with her hand. "When you coming back?"

Mid sip he acknowledged the question with a nod and savored the morning drink, "Two days."

Chris stood, back against the sink, legs crossed. Marlene sat at the table fingering the stack of mail piled up against the wall. He could see clearly that something was on her mind. Finally she asked, "She's going to be there, isn't she?"

Chris knew exactly who the young lady seated across the room was wondering about. He'd told her all about the ghost he'd been chasing, or running from depending on who you talked to. He nodded, "I think so, I sent her tickets and everyone else is going to be there."

"You aren't hoping?" She inquired knowing his affection for this woman, one she hadn't met but did not really care for already. Something had gone wrong, real wrong a few years back but Marlene never brought herself to ask why he still held on so tight.

"Thanks for watching Dingo by the way," Chris said rolling the mug in his hands. He was avoiding the subject. He never discussed it unless he was drunk, which was not as often as it used to be. "I have to get ready; you know your way around." Chris stepped across the room and set his ceramic mug down on the table. "Thanks, again."

Chris packed with great efficiency. His bags were in the rear seat of the truck by the time Marlene pulled her old Dodge around on her way out. She pressed down on the horn and gave a heavy wave out the window as she passed by. Dingo rode in the bed with one of his brothers, each one hanging over their respective sides of the cab.

After inspecting the packing job he'd performed in the wee hours of the morning, making sure everything was secure, he started the Ford. One last trip into the Studio to leave a note for Ramone, and Chris was on the road ahead of time. The first five hours should be smooth; it was the last couple state highways that tried his patience.

Hope (Intro)

Hope sat in the front window of her downtown, high-rise apartment looking out across the Dallas skyline. She was all of five minutes out of bed and her first pot of coffee hadn't finished just yet. She didn't need it anyway; sleep had been rough the last few nights. She pulled her auburn hair back and tied it with a white hair tie; a few strands fell free immediately. She ran her left hand up across her face and tucking them behind her ear. Bringing her hand back down, she wrapped it around her bare knees, pulled up to her chest and gripped her other arm already embracing her tan legs. The bottom half of her robe lay bunched around her hips. She sat there surveying the scene. The sun that was already baking West Texas was just above the lowest level of surrounding structures, she squinted in its brilliant orange glow. This was the first day it hadn't rained in over a week. Sometimes it was a downpour and others only a light sprinkle. So far this year everything had remained moist since spring. Going into late summer now, the sight of a clear sky was sorely overdue. The recent weather did nothing to help her mood. The people down below were running to or from places they most likely did not want to be. She could see them down there, scurrying around, Hope felt like she would rather be running aimlessly than running in the direction she was now headed. Nettle, her feline friend, rubbed along her backside and curled around to stretch out alongside her, soaking up the morning light with the distressed young woman. Hope had heard at one time that people with pets lived longer. Seeing the lean, athletic fur ball lying next to her, she could see why. She was beautiful and peaceful. A low purr came as her response to the sunlight as she stretched again revealing her claws. The dark green eyes of the cat almost matched Hope's, glimmering in the morning sun.

Where was Jon? This was the fourth time in the last week he had pulled a no show, eighth time this month. The last few he had claimed he was working, and she believed him. His position as a project engineer was very demanding on his time, but it had never been this demanding. His firm had slowed down recently, but Jon was very talented and they gave him all he could handle. Most recently his team had been working on a high rise in Denver that would be going up next year. From the last update she got, Hope figured it should have been done by now. What would he say this time? Was he drunk, in jail maybe? She deserved better than this.

Hope looked around, she and Jon had done well for themselves. She didn't need him, she didn't depend on him. They were together as equals, or so she thought. The pad was a luxurious one. She scanned over the living room and kitchen, all she could see from her vantage point. It was a beautiful pallet she'd picked out for the place. Her natural taste for interior decoration paid off well. Not a dime was spared in the effort. She loved it all. They had lived here for three years and a comfortable three years it was.

Hope finally felt like she'd made it. She grew up in an industrial town north of Oklahoma. It wasn't bad. She had a loving family, her parents eventually divorced, but it was all for the better. They never had the best, but she never went without. Through the typical rebel child phase of adolescence she dreamed of heading to a city and getting away from the dirty alleys, shady restaurants and meth dens back home to the bright lights and fine foods somewhere bigger and better. College was fun, a break from home, though not far enough for her tastes. It was just a means to an end. An end of her time served as a rural bumpkin. Initially the city had been rough. The job, living conditions, money, they almost broke her. She debated leaving, but now she was glad she persevered. Here, now, with Jon, she finally felt like she'd made it. Her dreams were coming true, until lately. Suddenly she felt like the rug was being pulled out from under her again. Once before she'd been crushed by a man and swore it would never happen again. Ironically, he was still around. She would see him tonight and didn't know how to feel about it just yet.

A voice came from the hallway and she quickly turned, expecting to hear a key slide into the door. It did not. The voice faded away as the stranger made his way down the hall. Hope exhaled in frustration. She reached over to the occasional table beside the couch and picked up her phone. She flipped open the palm sized device and checked her messages, still nothing. Quickly closing the cell, she gripped it tightly as her arm wrapped around her again and she rested her chin on her knees.

Work was only a few blocks away, but with the deluge of thoughts on her mind and the events of the day weighing heavily she had almost forgotten the time. The large clock on the wall told her it was almost nine; she had to be to work in an hour. If she didn't get started now she would be late. If Jon was out drinking all night he would have to remedy his hangover by himself, it's the least he deserved anyway. Hope could not afford to take another day off to chase him down if she was to leave for the next few days. Friends would be gathering from all over and it would help take her mind off the current predicament.

Hope released her grip on her legs and let one arm slide down to stroke the cat lying next to her. The long slow breathing was palpable as her fingers ran perpendicular to the furry stripes. She swung one leg down to the floor followed by the second and stood leaving the feline to its own accord. Her feet slid over the hardwood floor they had just refinished. She could barely feel the grain of the planks beneath her. The contractor had done an amazing job. Hope untied her robe and dropped it just inside the bathroom door. Leaning into the shower she adjusted the temperature of the water turned the central handle to divert the flow.

Stepping in she let the warm water soak her hair as she rolled her neck from side to side in an attempt to work out the stiffness of last night. Waiting up for Jon was taking its toll, and her tense muscles reflected this. Standing there, water coating her entire body her emotions burst to the surface. For the first time in a long time she cried, it hadn't shown yet and now it all came at once. Between sobs she wiped the water from her eyes and rubbed the back of her neck. In one last eruption she hit the tiled wall so hard that she briefly wondered if a bone had been broken. She had been on edge for so long and had buried it all.

With the scent of body wash still heavy in the humid air, Hope cut off the water and stepped from the shower still dripping wet. The towel she pulled from the wall did well to absorb what it could as she worked her way down to her toes. She wrapped herself and stepped to the mirror. Picking up her phone, she checked it one more time; nothing. The fog of the looking glass began to fade away. Hope stared into her own emerald green eyes; a million thoughts rolling through her mind but only one was standing out, 'how had this gone all wrong?' This was not the way things were supposed to be. She was supposed to be happy. Jon was supposed to support her and tell her how much he loved her and how proud he was of her. The sweat began to bead up on her forehead. Instead he elected to spend his time working. This would be the second time a man had chosen work over her. Still, she worried about him.

If Jon had elected to stay and work, at least he could have called. Maybe he was passed out somewhere. She had no clue. The worst case scenario came to mind as she stood there, watching herself physically lose color. What if Jon were stretched across some coroner's slab? She shook her head to jar the idea loose.

Drying her hair with a fresh towel she picked up her phone again. If Jon had been out drinking, Alan would have been with him.

The phone rang once, twice, four times. Finally the line clicked on the other end. A long pause and some shuffling with a little cursing is all she heard from the phone. "Alan?" pause, "Alan, pick up your phone," another ruffle of the sheets and she could hear a grizzly voice, barely audible, across the line. "Alan here."

With her sweet drawl carrying a cautious tone, "Alan, it's Hope, is Jon with you?"

The voice on the other end cleared, "Jon? No, I left him at the Ballroom last night, it was umm... I don't know, sometime around eleven." The Ballroom meant that they had been out drinking. Maybe he was in the drunk tank down at the P.D. Alan's mind seemed to be finally waking up. "Did he not make it home last night?"

Hope thought of the best way to answer this query, "Well, no. He hasn't been home in three nights now. I haven't been able to get a hold of him. He would call if something was wrong, wouldn't he?"

"Yeah, well, they do give you at least one phone call in jail, even if you're piss drunk and use it to order Chinese food."

Alan was right; he would have called for bail money if that was the problem. Alright that theory was flushed. The hung-over associate continued, "Look Hope, Jon probably just walked back to the office to sleep it off. He can crawl there from the Ballroom. Cheap bastard never wants to pay for a cab." This was true; he continued, "If I hear from him, you'll be the first to know, okay?"

"Okay, thanks, Alan."

"No problem, good night Hope." He uttered, lost in the haze.

Hope hung up and set the phone back on the vanity. She gripped the edge of the sink with both hands and took a few deep breaths. As her head slung lower, the towel wrapped around her hair started to slide off. She ripped it off, tossing it aside. She tried to put it all behind her for now. Turning on the radio, she began her daily dance with the blow-dryer. In no time, she was ready to go. Heading out the door she left a note on the table for Jon, if he were to make it home before she did. Same as she had done the morning before, and the morning before that. Both previous notes where gone when she returned at the end of the day, she wondered if today would be any different.

Nine to Three

Taking the stairs down two at a time Hope landed solidly on the ground floor of her apartment building and headed out through the lobby. The doorman, Norm, gave her a large smile and a nod as he opened the door, "Good morning, Miss Hope." His greeting was always the same.

"Thank you, Norm," Hope replied as she hurried by. The late model Pontiac sat on the far side of the two lane road, exactly where she had left it the night before. Hope checked both directions as she crossed the street. Traffic was noticeably less crowded than when she had left her post at the window, before jumping in the shower. A few quick steps and she was seated behind the wheel. With a glance in the side view mirror, the Pontiac pulled away from the curb. It was a short five minute drive from home, fifteen minutes by foot on a good day, but she was running late, no time to walk today.

Rounding down into the sub-level parking, Hope pulled into her assigned stall. The office was on the third floor; she took the stairs up the entire way. This was a habit that developed in regards to her limited time spent at the gym. Plus, it was a good way to get the blood flowing in the morning, second only to sex. Hope was not fond of sitting around desks and conference tables all day so she would take whatever exercise she could get.

Her current position at the newspaper was not what she had planned on upon graduation, but it was a paycheck. It would do until she figured out where she wanted to go. Entering the third floor lobby she was greeted by several co-workers. Exchanging small talk, Hope made her way down to her desk. Amongst the paperwork was an envelope. It lay on top of several CD's and assorted files that had to be looked after throughout the day. The return address was titled Coupland Studios. This was expected.

Hope had not asked for anything from anyone, but there were unsolicited gratuities whenever Chris was around. She was given tickets to any event that he was involved in. He'd worked hard and spent his money liberally on charities, art programs in several urban areas, music programs, and university donations, amongst other things. Though for the last few years, when he had been to Dallas three times, Hope had managed to avoid him on all three occasions. This would be the exception.

She finally felt comfortable seeing him again. Their last meeting was not so bright, besides they would be amongst friends. She cut into the white wrapping and retrieved two tickets to the Coupland Studios opening at a gallery in Austin, tomorrow night. He always sent at least two tickets and had made it clear every time that Jon was always invited though Hope knew better than to put those two men in the same room. Chris could be very sly at making someone feel uncomfortable, and Jon had a short fuse. It would be a bad combination. Thankfully she'd already made arrangements with Lacey to ride down together. Her old friend flew in this afternoon.

Chris had tried for so long now to convince her that she almost believed him. Their past was a rough one. It was a history that she would rather move on from but could never seem to forget. It had been harder on both of them than either had predicted. Along the way Lacey had been her support. Every time she broke down Lacey was there for her, through the long nights and many tears, she was there.

Hope stuffed the tickets into her purse and slid the whole bag under her desk. Flipping through the files that scattered across her desk, the memories were pushed back as she focused on the tasks at hand. There were meetings and deadlines. All of which had to be completed on time and with due attention.

Hope's day drug on and on. She went from one meeting, to her desk, and back to other meetings. She gave her reports objecting vehemently to the direction the paper was currently headed.

"As you can see our advertisements have begun to take over the latter sections of the paper. There may be money in them all but if there's no content behind the publication then there will be no readers to view the ads." Hope sat back reviewing her statement. She had made the same argument more or less in the last four meetings and had made no progress. This should be common sense to most people, but management was in dire straits. The print industry was suffering, and the wounds were starting to show. There had been cutbacks made every quarter for the last year. Over sixty of the lower level employees had been laid off during that time. It was frustrating; ad space was the last thing she wanted to deal with right now. The sales department got first swing at layout, and her articles had to work around the money makers. In Hope's opinion, people didn't pick up a paper for the specials that the local hardware store was running or which bar had the best beer special for the weekend. Hope wanted to produce something that would be in demand for the content, and the boys upstairs were screwing everything up. Having one boss was bad enough but having to report to four was a pain in the ass. With a couple glasses of wine, she would tell anyone exactly how she felt. She also believed that for every ten employees who lost their job, one manager should go as well, if asked. This corporation was about to get the best of her and she could feel her teeth grinding as she had to sit and listen to someone else tell her why things should be this way or that. Finally she lost interest, and anticipation for her friend's arrival and the impending trip began to build. Chris was nowhere near yet, not that she knew of. Longing for something to pass the time she noticed a hunger and contemplated taking an early lunch. Scratch that, skip lunch and get the hell out of here as soon as possible.

Three o'clock had never taken so long to roll around but with all the needs of the week taken care of Hope was out the door for the next few days and had no plans of returning anytime before she must. The rest of the week was to be a time of friends and family. The first of which was scheduled to arrive in half an hour, and Hope was going to be late.

Lacey (Intro)

B y the time she made it onto the interstate headed north toward Irving and the airport, Hope's phone was ringing. Lacey's picture appeared on the screen, "Hello."

"Hey *chick-a,* where are you, I've been on the ground for twenty minutes." That was one voice she could never forget. Lacey was ready to go, and she was not the patient type.

"I'm on my way, meet me out front of the terminal."

Hope and Lacey had not known each other as long as some, she was a later addition to the crew, but they had instantly found a connection. In college both were wild and rambunctious. Hope had worked at the bar, the same bar they had all worked at one time or another, for over a year when Lacey transferred in from another school. Lacey was short, sassy and full of opinions that she felt everyone needed to know. A beautiful blonde, she was a mothering type always looking out for or taking care of others. Sometimes her love was rough, honest and to the point, but it was always spot-on. Many people had joked that she had scared her husband into marrying her for fear of physical violence. They were a dynamic couple; unfortunately Mac was not able to make the trip this time.

There was no other woman who could pack more personality in a five foot-two frame. There Lacey sat, atop her largest piece of luggage, which was almost as big as she was. Three other bags surrounded her improvised pedestal. She could pack enough for several weeks just to make it through a few days. Puffing on a cigarette, wearing sunglasses covering the upper half of her face and hair as big as Texas itself, she leapt up when the car came into view.

Hope had to smile, it was a funny sight. She pulled up to the curb and almost forgot to throw the car into park before jumping out. There were big smiles and bigger hugs as the two girlfriends greeted each other. Each one inspected the other making compliments, commenting on any change in hair, shoe style or breast size. Looking over the mass of bags piled out front of the terminal she asked, "Did you bring enough stuff? How *will* you find something to wear?" putting an extra sarcastic drawl on the 'will'.

"Grab a bag, let's get the hell outa' here; I've been sitting around too long already."

Hope was thankful she had packed the night before; Lacey was not in the waiting mood. Together they flew down the interstate, back through downtown Dallas and beyond, past Waco and even further south into Austin. Along the way they discussed everything and nothing in particular. By the time they arrived, the clouds were building in an attempt to choke out the evening sun.

Neal (Intro)

A fter dropping the last few pieces off at the gallery Chris crossed the river from the south heading into downtown along Congress Avenue. His phone called to him, he answered, "This is Chris."

"This is Neal, where you at son?" came the familiar voice. Neal referred to Chris, three years his junior, as 'son' frequently. Chris had chosen Neal as his business manager to oversee the day to day leg work of patents, publishing and promotion, because of his business connections throughout the Midwest. His background was in business and his passion was food. The two had met as line cooks at the bar, and it was a favorable acquaintance for both. Though Neal soon left, he would reappear in a short time when Kathy became the ball and chain he so admired.

"I'm just turning off Congress and headed your way. What's up?"

Neal, audibly chewing on something muttered above the foodstuffs in his craw, "Rugby just called. Said he had an accident. I'm going to your room to check things out."

"Well, I'm just pulling up; I'll meet you in the lobby." Chris said and slapped his phone closed. Grabbing his two bags he jumped out and tossed the keys of the Ford to the valet and strode inside. His boots rapped on the beautifully polished stone floor as he crossed the lobby approaching the front desk. The nice young lady who manned the computer checked him in and gave him several messages. Most of which were from his publisher, and one package. This had to be the test print of his latest book. The last message, handwritten in a very feminine script amused him.

"If you would answer your phone I wouldn't have to hunt you down at your motel. Call me.

Jackson"

The rep from his publisher was an annoying character and one he didn't care to deal with unless he had to. Chris had actually gone so far as to block his phone number several months back. Now it was all e-mail and messages posted through services like that provided at the motel. Chris threw a few of the notes away while still scanning over others. He tore open the brown package and tossed the paper in right behind the notes. The ding of the elevator brought his eyes up. As the doors slid open Neal came into sight, before Chris, in all his glory stood his business manager. The designer gave him a once over.

Neal was Indian by genetics, dot, not feather. As the only minority amongst the family he was referred to as the 'brown guy' and often mentioned of himself as such. He stood just slightly taller than Chris but weighed significantly more. He was not obese or unhealthy by any means, but he was a stocky man. Neal stood in the elevator by himself, clad only in dress socks, not exactly matching, a pair of cargo shorts and a white tank top under shirt. This was not surprising.

Chris stepped onto the elevator beside his friend and business partner saying nothing. Neal made no attempt at speaking with a mouth full of what looked like a ham sandwich. His obsession with meat and veggies stuffed between two pieces of bread amazed many people close to the Indian. It is not a remarkable feat for the brown guy to put away a dozen sandwiches in a day. He always had something to eat or drink in his hands.

The elevator doors closed and the machine carried the pair up twelve stories with not a single word said between them. As business directed, they spoke on almost a daily basis, sometimes personal but almost always professionally oriented. There was not a cheerful, long time gone, greeting since they had such an open line of communication. As the elevator came to a halt and the doors opened Chris stepped into the hallway finally speaking, "Is that mustard on your shirt?" he asked walking away.

Neal looked down. It seems that some of his late afternoon/evening snack had rubbed off. "Looks like it." He stated matter-of-factly. "Hum," he grunted disregarding the stain, following Chris into the hallway. The low nap carpet gave a soft shuffle to his bare feet and they both strolled down the long hallway toward the suite on the end.

Covering the small bit of business that had developed in the last 24 hours Chris mentioned, "The final format of the new book looks good. I think we'll go with it. When you get back home will you be sure to call the marketing firm and see that they are ready to pull the trigger when we say go?"

"No problem. As soon as I get back to the office I'll touch base with them," Neal replied with a half of a bite left rolling over his tongue.

"You mean as soon as you get back to your guest room?"

Finishing his last few bites of sandwich Neal mumbled with a shrug, "Whatever works."

"So, you said Rugby had an accident. What happened?"

Neal strolled just ahead of Chris and rounded the door into the suite first. "He got his woody caught in a door," he noted just as he turned into the room and out of sight.

Rugby (Intro)

Rugby came out of the bedroom to the left of the door completely nude. Over his groin he held a large bag of ice. "Evening gentlemen, where are the broads?" He was rather hirsute and it stretched from his chest to his ankles. One trait he was very proud of.

Chris was not surprised at Rugby's current state. They had lived together in college and he was used to the gratuitous nudity and attention seemed to always direct toward his manhood.

With a small bit of sandwich still sitting in his left cheek Neal nodded, "they're getting ready. Uh, are you going to explain why you're naked?"

"That needs no explanation," Chris noted, "but the ice looks like a good story." He had to forcefully hold back his laughter at the situation.

Rugby began the retelling of events that left both Chris and Neal in tears leaning on each other for support. "Well, see, I was going to brew some coffee when I first got here, right? So I'm standing in front of the sink and one of the doors of the cabinet below was open. When I reached up to grab the pot I guess I leaned in and my thing was hanging between the doors, now the further I reached up the further I leaned in. Before I knew it I could feel the door closing on my junk. So my natural reaction was to jerk backwards. When I did, my knees bent forward and slammed the door closed with a certain piece of my anatomy in the way." Rugby took a deep breath and shook his head. "Man, I tell you what, *that hurt.* I let out a yell and fell to my knees. Eventually I gathered the willpower to pull myself off the floor. I've spent the last half hour curled up in the fetal position in my room."

Chris could not believe it. Incidents like this seemed to happen to Rugby with more frequency than most men. Of course that came with the territory of letting things hang loose as he did.

"Wait... wait... wait," Chris couldn't breathe between fits of laughter. When he finally gathered himself and the pain in his sides faded enough where he could talk, he had no sympathy for his old friend.

"Dude, that sucks," was all that came from Neal while gasping for breath. "Put some shorts on."

"In hindsight, *yeah,* that sounds like a good theory, but I don't really think they would have helped in this situation."

Chris finally gave up his attempt at standing and sat down in the middle of the room, laughing for some time. His face was on fire and his body began to ache.

"I know man, it'll be a good story eventually, but it still hurts to laugh about it yet. You should see the damage it left, gnarly right?" Rugby offered.

This friendship was an odd one. Physically Chris and Rugby were about the same size, average height and weight, and they had similar views socially, but that's where the similarities ended. How they ever became so close was something neither could pinpoint. They had different backgrounds, different educations, Chris was a farm boy and Rugby a hippie, but they always had a good time.

Eventually Rugby went to get dressed, and Chris picked himself up off the floor with the help of Neal. Tears still in his eyes, he went to his room and unpacked while the brown guy returned to his own. The girls should be ready by now. They would all meet up later for drinks after the day's business was done.

Kathy (Intro)

After checking in at the plush hotel on the river they settled into their room. Their bags, when emptied, almost filled the closet space provided. Hope never understood why Lacey insisted that they must unpack everything and have everything put away before anything else. She lay across the bed while Lacey worked to prep herself for a public appearance. This was a surprisingly quick process, Lacey was very efficient. It was the rest of the details that took her forever to get ready. The phone beside the bed, below the golden touch lamp rang breaking the constant hum of the hair dryer. The sheer volume of it startled her. Hope rolled over and answered with a curious, "Hello."

"Hey, it's Neal, just checking to see that the phone worked. We're just across the hall."

Hope did not understand the logic of this, "Why don't you just come over then?"

"'Cause I'm naked and that my friend would be considered public indecency."

Hope remembered why these boys all got along and there was never a dull moment around them. "Well, whenever you're ready, come on over."

They said goodbye and Hope sat up. She took a deep breath and sat gazing at the closet across the room. She scanned over her wardrobe again and again trying to decide what to wear. As she zipped up a yellow, cotton dress there was a rap at the door.

"Get that!" Lacey yelled over the noise coming from the bathroom.

With her bare feet shuffling across the carpet Hope went to the door. Through the peep in the door she could see Kathy standing in the hallway. "What do you want?" She yelled at her old friend on the other side.

"Just open the door, woman!" Kathy exclaimed. Hope turned the handle but before she could fully open the door Kathy pushed her way through stepping directly into the bathroom. "I have to borrow your facilities."

"Don't you have a bathroom in your room?" Hope questioned.

Lacey seconded, "Yeah, why can't you use yours? I'm trying to do work here."

Kathy explained as she let out a sigh of relief, "Brown guy, Indian food; I'm not following that."

Hope laughed from outside the bathroom as she heard the toilet flush. Kathy was a high strung gymnastics coach. She always had something to do. She was the organizer. Of the three girls, Kathy stood slightly taller than the duo that drove in from Dallas. Her voice was smoky and seductive, a sharp contrast to Lacey. Hope had not bonded as close to her as she had with Lacey, but they were still family.

"You damn Texans and your heat." Kathy exclaimed fanning herself, "I don't know how you do it." She lived up north in Kansas City with Neal.

Hope smiled, "My first summer here was miserable, but you get used to it."

Kathy was the last addition to the family. Ironically Neal had already graduated and left town before Kathy came around but through frequent return trips they both became familiar friends. Only after Kathy had graduated and moved to KC did they begin dating. They were going on nine years together now, and of all Hope's friends they were next in line to get married. Rumor had it that Neal had entertained the idea but never spoke of it. Kathy did not push the issue.

Hope stood in front of a mirror as Kathy came out of the bathroom running her hand through her short brown hair. "It's good to see you," she said, hugging Hope from behind. Smiling in the mirror Kathy's dimples always made Hope grin.

"So what's the plan?" Hope questioned.

"Well, as soon as you two are ready, I say we go get something to eat. Chris and Rugby are going to catch up with us later after they find Lance. Other than that I have no plans."

"Fish tacos," Lacey offered leaning out of the bathroom.

Kathy looked back and gave a shrug, "I don't care honey, it's whatever y'all want."

Hope laughed, "Did you just drop a 'y'all' in there?"

"When in Rome sweetie," came the smoky response. "I'll get Neal."

When they had all finished with their business and gathered in the hallway the small group headed out for the night. It would be many hours and drinks before they returned.

Business

~~~~~~

Yelling across the suite, Chris questioned his disabled roommate. "Rugby, you ready yet?"

"As soon as I get up the courage to pull these pants up," he called back.

"Do you need a hand?" Chris offered with a laugh.

"No thanks man, I can handle my own business."

"Alright but we're going to be late, we got to go."

"Lance is never on time anyway," Rugby yelled back from across the suite as Chris strolled into the living area separating their rooms. His friend had a point. Lance was never on time, and Chris was sure that tonight would be no different. Eventually Rugby appeared from his room buttoning his shirt, walking a little more gingerly than usual with knees spread. Chris laughed at the sight.

Leading the way out into the hall and eventually down to the lobby and out the front door, Chris' boots made good time through the hotel. They had a dinner meeting with Lance, the initiator of this entire show, and the curator of The Gallery, whom Chris did not know yet, where the show was to premier tomorrow night. When Chris and Rugby finally found the restaurant, they spotted Lance immediately. He was on the far side of the patio out front of the establishment speaking to a small crowd.

Lance was an interesting character. He was the first waiter they'd ever had at the bar. Given his natural disposition, he really had to convince the boss to give him the job. He was tall, just over six foot, good looking and well dressed with thin dark hair. He was everything Chris was not. He was outspoken, flamboyant and extremely energetic, almost hyperactive. He stepped away from the crowd when the boys came into view, "Hello cupcake," came his usual greeting. Lance was what people often referred to as 'a bird of a different feather.'

"I'm shocked, I figured we'd beat you here," Chris jabbed.

"These people don't waste their time on just anyone, and they have cheap crafts of sangria." Chris smiled, Lance was an honest character.

"Well, *by god then*," Rugby exclaimed, "*show me to the bar!*"

As Rugby headed into the crowd Lance turned his attention back to the designer, "Now, Chris, we have dinner reservations with three reporters, one from the Statesman and two from an online…"

Chris cut him off, "I don't care Lance, I'll answer their questions and I know it's good for publicity, but I just don't care."

"Well, be nice, that's all I ask."

"I will, I just want to get tonight over with."

Lance poked him in the chest as he passed by heading deeper into the patio "I know what you're worried about and you need to stop right now mister."

"I'm not worried about her showing up."

"Lie to yourself sweetheart, but you can't lie to me." Lance turned to the crowd, "*Rugby*, wrong way."

The meeting was typical. Question, answer, question, answer, Lance did as much of the talking as Chris. This neither surprised nor offended the designer. Rugby critiqued the food, as was his style, which resulted in a rather positive acclaim. Chris, too, was fond of the fusion of styles. Lance ate little, watching his figure, and all three departed just after sundown leaving their guests to discuss amongst themselves.

Breathtaking

⁓

The three men stood on the opposite side of Guadalupe waiting for a break in traffic as the sky began to let loose the moisture swept up from the gulf. Chris thought the drops felt sweet compared to the dry winds back home. It had always amazed him how two parts of the same territory could have such different weather patterns, though it was a very large territory. None the less, he took in the moment as long as he could, for it would be the last bit of calm he may see for a while. The friends who awaited their arrival were not the subdued sort. As the last foreseeable car passed they took to the road skipping all the puddles they could. Lance was being particularly careful. Rugby hit a few that splashed back on the two who followed him. Chris didn't care; he was still focused on the group sitting just inside the front window.

On the sidewalk, under the protective awning, keeping them from soaking completely through, Rugby and Lance went straight in the door shaking off what they could. Chris stopped short of the door, looking in. Everyone was there. Neal and Kathy were seated next to each other facing away from the window. They had made the twelve hour drive south just for this occasion. He was thankful. It was a long drive, one he'd made many times and knew it was not easy. Lacey was already at the head of the table talking with her exaggerated gestures. Several were not making the trip apparently, but he was thankful for those who had. One was still missing though. As the table rose to greet his two dinner partners, Chris scanned the room looking for her. He hadn't been told of her absence, but then again no one had spoken of her arrival either. Maybe she had decided against coming to town.

Chris gave his hair a vigorous rub, shaking the excess water free as he opened the front door and turned right. Everyone congregated at the head of the table to exchange hugs and greetings. These friends had been sorely missed. As everyone took their seats, Chris looked over the bar once more. The long room was very similar to the joint where they had all worked and met through back at school. The high ceiling was dark and the lighting gave the feeling of a large recess you could lose yourself in. The bar ran along the opposite wall covering almost half the length of the space. Just past the wait station at the end of the bar a staircase led to the balcony which wrapped around two sides. His eyes came back to the table where he picked a seat toward the end of the group leaving three spots open.

As everyone settled in, the waitress made her rounds taking drink orders. Neal had his whiskey, Kathy was satisfied with her beer for now, and Lacey had a rather large, empty margarita in front of her, Lance ordered rum, and Rugby would have scotch and Chris settled on rye. When the young blonde headed for the bar, orders taken, questions began to fly from every direction but few of them settled in on Chris.

The moment he'd almost decided she hadn't come, he saw her. Looking up from his vantage point, he barely recognized Hope's figure. She had changed. She looked more athletic now than she ever had before. The tone in her legs moved up past the curves of her hips which swung in forming the perfect hourglass figure as her chest curved out. He could see the definition in her arms. He'd never seen her look more beautifully. Her hair was shorter and darker than he remembered. Her face had lost that round, youthful beauty he'd always loved. She had grown into the woman he always knew she would. Hope took another step onto the landing halfway down the staircase as it turned in toward the room.

Entrance

~~~~

She had been in the restroom for a short while trying to gather herself for the inevitable. Earlier in the evening, for some reason she had spent a little more time making sure not a hair was out of place and a little more time choosing her dress for the night. She'd poured over three choices. The first was a plaid, strapless piece that looked fun. 'Too cute,' she'd thought. The second was a red dress with a slit up the side. It was leftover from a cocktail party she'd attended several months before. Hope thought it might be too spicy. She didn't want to look like she was trying for anything, she wasn't, or so she thought. Finally Hope decided on a lavender cotton dress. It fit her well and covered from her knees to the edge of her shoulders. It was cut a little lower in front than she'd wanted, but it fit so well it would do. Hope hated herself for this. How could any one person have this kind of influence on her? After all wasn't it Chris who drove her away? His insecurities created the rift that had separated them. For so long he'd been there but when the time came down to act on everything they had planned and longed for, he backed out. What the hell was she thinking, he'd tried many times since they parted ways to get her attention, but there was no consoling. Lines had been drawn and the bridges they had crossed lay in ashes. Still here she was trying to impress him. She could never let herself love him again, Hope knew this and still she wanted him to want her.

As Hope stepped down and rounded the corner of the landing she noticed Chris sitting there amongst old friends, his chair leaned back on its hind legs. Their eyes locked. He had apparently noticed her long before she had returned the attention. Chris looked to her longingly, he looked completely taking aback, lost in wanted dreams as was his style. They were one part of him that she never fully understood. Suddenly seeing him now, seeing the impact she held made her heart race. She thought back to a time when he was all she ever wanted. Now, he was almost a stranger. She had made it so. The night would be an eventful one, a fact she was certain of but the specifics of how or why still eluded her. Stepping down toward the table Hope wondered what her world would be like now if he only could have swallowed his pride, if he could have seen what she was capable of.

Flashback #1 (Meeting)

The bullshit rose and fell as often as the glasses. Voices drowned out voices, which in turn were trumped by laughter. The stories came back as if piecing together a night lost in a drunken haze upon a sea of inebriation. Floating along this river of the tales, Chris's mind was drifting away; in a slip of consciousness his eyes caught Hope's. Her radiant emeralds flashed with a heat he had not seen in anyone since. He could not decipher if it was passion or fury that fueled them, but he leaned toward the latter. Not seeing anything coming toward him, Chris slipped away from the table, if only mentally, to a time gone, back across the years that now separated the two ex-lovers.

Before careers, before salaries or money, the brethren sitting around that table once enjoyed a camaraderie that was founded by work, built by common habits and cemented by a love for life. No one knew what actions they had communally put into motion, but before anyone realized it they were all inseparable. If you asked, no one could say when exactly they had become a family. Many had come and gone, some were distant and others closer. Of everyone sitting around this table, Hope was the only one Chris could remember from the first moment they met.

It had been a typical Thursday night not quite ten years ago. After his shift, Chris pulled a stool up to the lengthy bar that ran along the north wall. The space was long and narrow. The interior scattered with neon signs and memorabilia of the University. There were five tables separating the L-shaped bar from the seven booths which formed an elongated C along the south wall. To the west was the front door and large windows where the neon light reflected against the dark night. Opposite the wall of glass, in the back, was the kitchen and restrooms partitioned from the seating by a single pool table surrounded by signage and televisions. It was a small place; by standing room only you might fit one hundred patrons, but that was only on rare occasions. The customer base was built on returns. The same core group frequented the place on a nightly basis and everyone, over time, became family.

Sitting at the bar, alone, he was surrounded by the regulars. Julie, a waitress who'd manned the lunch shift since the first day they had opened for business a year and a half ago called over to him, "Chris, come here."

She was seated by the front door in a booth perpendicular to the front windows along the west wall. With her were two others he had yet to meet, all three of them employees. The two strangers had only been there a short while longer than Chris. Only three months on the job, he hadn't yet met the entire staff. Julie was the only one he knew, though not well. He joined the party, glass in hand, sitting next to Julie facing the two co-workers. One of the two girls seated across the table caught his attention.

Hope, as Chris came to know, was a lovely girl. She had a beautiful smile that stirred the coldest of hearts, a caring sense of humor no one could resist, and a body that caught every eye. Hers was a classic beauty, a rare combination between the physical and intellectual. It was a very uncommon blend to find in their generation. She belonged amongst the ranks of Garland and Hepburn. Hope was young but not naïve. Chris, beyond the lust of a lively college student, was floored by her wit and humor. There was never a dull moment in her presence.

They were all good people. Memorable though they may have been, the other two who sat with them that night would drift away in time, but Hope would always remain in the forefront of his mind. The night passed as any other night, customers came and went and drinks provided the lubrication as laughter spread. The weight of the world outside had yet to chip away at the four sitting in the front window.

The months flew by. With disregard for the world that carried on without them, they all lived for the moment, reveling in their youth. Class was class and grades could be dealt with at the end of every semester. Work though, was more than work at this bar. Nowhere could you find a more eager group to see their coworkers. The list of people who applied, signed on and soon after quit, grew at a very regular pace for the first year. Every so often though, one stuck as another left. The summer Julie turned in her towel, Lacey signed on. Shortly after Neal left, Lance showed up and refused to leave until they gave him a position. Right about the time Rob, the limey British bastard left, which was a shame, no one cleaned the kitchen quite as well; Kathy came around to pick up a few shifts. It was a constant rotation but within two years of Chris's arrival they had solidified. Hope, Lacey, and Kathy anchored the wait staff. Rugby kept the kitchen in order with Brett and Will, while Chris jumped between flipping burgers and selling beer. Individually they may have been polite, quiet and respectful individuals, but together they were a crazed, deranged force to be reckoned with. They ran off several potential employees, intimidated a few customers and generally had their way when it was consensual amongst the majority.

When the initial staff started to rotate out of service and new blood was introduced, those who remained from the early days, namely Hope, Rugby, Lacey, and Chris, became more closely associated. Others assimilated quickly, and before long they were living together, working together and playing together. Everyone was broke, and no one seemed to care, they knew no different. They were young, independent and full of energy. There was never a dull moment. To Chris, these friends were closer to him now than his family seven hours away, they were his new family.

Well into their second year, as the ranks began to swell once again, Hope and Chris remained drawn together. Many afternoons were spent on the patio of one saloon or another discussing family, school, or whatever seemed to be on their nerves at the time. Their past was uncannily similar. Both came from broken families. Each had a tense relationship with their fathers and an older sibling they hadn't always gotten along with. The ability to understand each other's grief built the foundation of a bond that would only be broken by the most extreme of circumstances. Through sickness, distress amongst friends, and death, they saw it all side by side. One spring afternoon they sat, beer in hand, skipping class in the sunlight of an unseasonably nice February afternoon. The wooden table felt warm under Chris's fingertips. Beneath her sunglasses, he could not see Hope's eyes but knew they drifted from corner to corner of the picket fence surrounding them. She was nervous. She was not happy with her current relationship. She had been with this man for three years, but for the last two it had been long distance. He was in her home town, several hours away. Though she visited often, he had not been to see her in almost half a year. It was taking its toll. Chris had his own issues to deal with, but he listened intently. Occasionally his mind drifted away to the waitress who weighed heavy on his own mind. The conversation volleyed back and forth, from the long distance boyfriend to the tormenting waitress. By the end of the afternoon, not walking straight but seeing clearer than before, they had both decided to jump into the single's pool. It would be an easier move for Hope, a phone call, one trip to return some things left behind, and it was over. For Chris though, this made his job a little awkward. They did work together after all. It would take several months, but over time things would smooth out between them. He had Hope there the entire time. She acted as his voice of reason when things became difficult, the buffer when he lost his temper. She was always there for him. In time, one day, in the company of all their friends, everything between them would change. Facing death can radically alter anyone's perspective.

The Last Word

Back in Austin, Chris fell to reality, jolted from his world to theirs by laughter as Rugby recounted the horrible events he had endured at the hotel earlier in the day and the damage it left. As he sat amongst friends, family if you asked anyone amongst them, they all took their turn telling stories of forgotten nights. They were all back at their bar, if only in thought. The atmosphere lost its tension and there was no mention of past fights, feelings hurt or friends lost, save for one duel. This was the one which no one dared to mention. Everyone was aware of it; the smell of sulfur seemed to hang over Chris and Hope. Seated on opposing sides of the table, a few chairs working as a buffer, they avoided each other's gaze, instead electing to focus entirely on whoever was the narrator at that particular moment. On occasion though, when either party was unfortunate enough to be caught in a stolen glance, the knots swelled, and nerves, still raw even after all these years, burned. They were cordial, but beyond that neither knew what to say. Hope spoke of work and friends in the city. Everyone laughed, even Chris, at her revelry of the chaos which surrounded her. He still loved her. She was a caring woman who understood him and knew more of his skeletons than anyone else ever would again. She had always been there when he needed her, and he had failed to return the attention she showered upon him. She showed no sign of returning any affection this evening.

Watches made their laps with the passing time, and no one noticed. No one wanted to acknowledge that the sun would come around eventually. Late into the night Chris swallowed his pride and gave a formal greeting to his ex-lover across the table. She was receptive and more open than the young man would have ever guessed. In time the table began to rotate with trips to the bar or jukebox. In a lull of conversation full of liquid courage Chris finally spoke his mind, as gentle as Kentucky rye whiskey would let him. "I'd like to talk, just you and I. No guilt trips, no drama, just catching up."

Rugby returned just as the offer was laid out on the table. He immediately returned to the bar from which he came. Hope stood with a deep sigh, she spoke, "Goodnight, Chris"

Chris did not want to plead, he already felt like a fool, deservedly so, "Sit, stay."

Hope gave him a look of annoyance and flashed Rugby a smile as he watched from a distance not knowing if he should intervene and try to prevent the impending train wreck or not. Hope shook her head at him seeing the dilemma wrinkling his brow. Pulling her chair back to the table she asked, "Why do you have to do this?"

Neither one of them made a move to close the unusually large distance between them. It was needed to facilitate such a conversation. Chris stared at the glass in his hand, rolling it around softly, "Because you owe me."

"I don't owe you anything," Hope snapped with more ferocity than intended.

Chris threw his reply quicker and with a vicious tone beyond what he had meant, though it still carried a timid feeling, "Like hell, you left me standing in the cold on New Year's Day, with no real explanation, not even so much as a tear. Then you go on to ignore me for nine months, complete cold shoulder. And the two times we've run into each other since then you act like nothing ever happened. You've made it very clear things could never return to the way they were before. I don't agree, but I've accepted it. Still, I have no closure, no reason as to why things went the way they did. I could have chased you, but we had already been through so much. I respected your wishes even if they went against everything I wanted. I wanted so badly to pursue you, to prove you had made the wrong decision but I couldn't even get a hold of you for so long. I wanted to stay in touch, you meant so much to me beyond a failed relationship, but you wrote me off. I've let it be until now. So tell me," he paused to catch a deep breath, " why so cold?"

Hope sat back in her chair. This was more than she expected first rattle out of the box. He never really beat around the bush anyway; she should have seen it coming. She took a long drink before answering. "What do you want me to say? Do you want to hear about the nights I couldn't stop crying? Do you want to know how I almost lost my job because I couldn't hold myself together?" Hope could feel her face getting red with anger. "I would love to sit here and tell you all about how I cursed myself, about all the time I spent haunted. Every time you called, I had to shut my phone off to keep from answering. Do you think I just walked away and never looked back? I loved you, but I wasn't going to go through the same punishment over and over again like I did before. You had two chances, that's more than anyone else. Every time you were too busy to focus on me, it ripped my heart out and that was the eternal cycle we were riding. I had to make a clean break from you. We were too close and leaving everything behind was the only way I could get over it."

Chris was shocked. This was more direct than he'd expected. "Hope, I'm sorry, I guess I never saw it that way. Look, if…" She cut him short.

"Chris, no, you always have the last word. You have to; it's just who you are, but not this time. You thought I was weak because I didn't want to stand on my own. Just because I didn't want to did not mean I couldn't."

Enough said, Hope stood and walked away from the table not even saying goodbye. She was right. It hurt, but it seared the wounds shut. Hope left with Rugby and Lacey, headed for where, Chris did not care.

Neal, in charge of the jukebox finally made his selection. Chris, brow beaten, watched from the table wondering what was next on the playlist. Ten seconds into it and he knew.

"So tonight, so I lied... are you the now or never kind? In a day and day love I'm gonna be gone for good again."

"Nice choice asshole!" Chris yelled in the brown guy's general direction. Neal, in the fog of drunkenness smiled back and extended a thumb up in response.

"Are you willing to be had? Are you cool with just tonight? Here's a toast to all those who hear me all too well."

Kathy came back from the bar with drink in hand, "Hey buddy, how's it going?"

"Here's to the nights we felt alive. Here's to the tears you knew you'd cry. Here's to goodbye tomorrow's gone and come too soon."

"Shit," Chris mumbled above the music.

In the depths of the breakup when no light was in sight, Kathy was always there. Rugby was by far Chris' closest confidant in the world, but Kathy was always the rational light that could show the true colors of life no matter how opaque Chris' view may become. When Chris saw the perfect woman slipping away in the first few months after the breakup, Kathy was there to bring him back to reality. She could prove that no matter how close Chris and Hope had been, no matter how perfect she seemed to him, everyone was still human. Kathy was the catalyst to recovery. Without her Chris couldn't imagine where he'd be right now.

"Well, that's not what I expected, but I'm always the optimist," Chris said trying to smile as he sipped on a fresh glass.

"You know, Chris, this probably isn't the best time or place to bring up old wounds."

"Seemed right at the time," he responded.

"Oh yeah, and what's your lifetime average for perfect timing?" Kathy posed.

"Well, I'd be an all star in baseball, but it's well under five hundred."

Kathy smiled, "Okay, so let's go with the average and assume that you're wrong now, so don't let it eat at you. It was a kneejerk reaction. She doesn't hate you, but I'm betting she has just as much pent up as you do, you have to understand that."

Chris nodded as a small smile grew across his face, "Thanks Kathy, for every time you pulled me back up, thank you."

"No problem sugar, I have to get Neal to bed or he's going to be worthless. I'll see you in the morning," She said.

As Kathy stood she leaned in and kissed the young man on the cheek. Chris smiled and watched as the pair made their way outside. After finishing one last drink, he stood precariously, and surveyed the empty glasses and bottles as a smile appeared. That night brought a deep sleep and not once did the apprehension of tomorrow's show surface.

The Morning Of (Hope)

The morning brought an orange haze over the city, the humidity holding a veil across the skyline, the beauty of downtown shimmering in the shallow light. This was the twelfth day in a row Hope had woken with the sun. It was a habit not built on choice but a result of her mind spinning tirelessly, even as her body shut down.

The morning also brought a hangover. Hope lay with company this morning though, an almost unfamiliar feeling. Sleeping next to her was her best friend. A sight sorely missed. Hope looked over in humor, Lacey, in the same shirt she'd worn the night before, no pants, face buried in a pillow. She slept, snoring, typical 'morning after' pose. Hope was no belle at the moment either, and she could feel it. Her head pounded, and her tongue stuck to the top of her mouth. Her teeth felt fuzzy. It disgusted her. 'Water, water would be amazing,' she thought. She rose and stretched, making her way to the bathroom. When the faucet roared to life with more pressure than necessary, spraying water across her waist, the snoring immediately stopped. Lacey bounced out of bed and strolled in to meet Hope near the sink. "*Wow*," she exclaimed, rubbing her eyes, seeing both of them both in the mirror, "Which way to the beauty pageant? J.B.F hair and I didn't even get any last night."

Hope couldn't help but laugh.

"So let's assume I can't remember how we got home last night. What happened?"

"Not much." Hope took a long drink and passed the cup to her short friend, "Chris wanted to talk."

"Wait, wait, wait, I thought we discussed this already. He's a good man and a great friend, but he's a miserable lover," Lacey reminded her companion, "you know this. You told me yourself on the drive down here."

Hope looked at her with disdain, toothbrush working vigorously to remove the sweaters from her teeth. "Of course I know," came the garbled response. Removing the toothbrush and spitting the excess down the sink to make her point even more clear, "I made the call a long time ago, and I'm not going back. He knows that. I guess he just needed a reminder."

Staring into the mirror Hope brushed the loose hair from her face and took a deep breath. Lacey stripped down, tossing a towel over the shower curtain she stepped into the shower. As the small bathroom began to fill with the steam, she leaned out from behind the curtain. "He's had seven years to *'clarify'* these things. *Seven!* We're all doing very well, and we don't need any new drama. Look at me," she said as Hope turned to lean back on the sink, arms crossed. Lacey looked her squarely in the eye and repeated, "No new drama!"

Hope cocked her head to the side and smiled, and squinted accordingly, "I think I can handle this." That said, Lacey gave her a stern look and turned back to her shower. Hope returned to the mirror, watching intently, wondering if she truly was able to deal with what may come out of the upcoming day. Slowly the fog rolled down the glass eventually blurring her reflection all together. As she walked out of the bathroom, a knock came from the door. Pulling on a pair of shorts, she strolled over peering through the hole in the door. It opened to reveal Neal, in all his morning glory. Sliding the chain out of its slot, she turned the handle and opened the door. Leaning on the handle Hope greeted the stout Indian, "Nice PJ's."

Neal stood in the hallway clad in plaid boxers and a white tank top undershirt ordained in a stain she could not identify. "I'm all class," he said opening his arms.

"And oh, how you show it," Hope replied shaking her head, "You have a little something… right, just, there," she drifted off pointing to his right side.

"Banana. No worries." Neal stated as he wiped the smear from his waistline.

The laughter was mutual. "So, what's up, Neal?"

"Well, Kathy and I were thinking brunch. There's a little place around the corner if y'all are hungry."

"Lacey's still in the shower, then it's my turn. Give us an hour. Come over whenever you're ready."

"Deal," Neal accepted crossing the hall to his open door. Inside Kathy was barely audible, rocking along with the radio.

Hope heard him yell as he entered the room, "Baby, they'll be ready in an hour and a half," he shut the door as he stepped in. He was right. Lacey would be on her own schedule. Hope closed the door as the waterfall in the bathroom stopped.

The blonde emerged from the bathroom, still dripping wet, wrapped in a towel, Hope asked in passing as she headed to take her turn, "We have a lunch date in an hour. Will you call the boys?"

Head tilted to one side then the other, bouncing up and down, draining the water from her ears Lacey replied, "Sure."

While Hope showered Lacey picked up her cell and called Rugby from the speaker phone. The speaker responded with a very guttural greeting. "Good morning?" Rugby was never a morning person.

"Hey, sleepy head, you boys need to get up, we're going to lunch in an hour."

Rugby's mind was still glazed over, "Yeah."

"I'll call you again in five minutes."

"Yeah," and with that, the line went dead.

The Morning Of (Chris)

Chris woke fighting his natural tendency to rise early. The large bed provided enough room to roll around long enough to get the blood flowing, and he finally surrendered to the day. He strolled to Rugby's room, his sweat pants dragging across the marble floors. The stone felt cold under his bare feet, it was an unusual sensation. His home was not made of such cold, hard surfaces. Chris never understood why people would choose a material so bitter and lifeless to surround themselves with. He yawned pulling his arms behind his back and brought his fist down hard on the door. It swung open. Rugby's white ass was not a greeting he'd hoped for. "Dude, get up."

No answer.

Chris let him be, leaving the door open he turned his attention toward the kitchenette. Rugby would get up when he wanted. He searched the cabinets for coffee, recalling the tragedy from the day before, Chris was sure to check his position before pulling down the canister. He filled the brewpot and set it to run while he brushed his teeth. The smell was amazing. Even the complimentary coffee in this place was top of the line. He picked up his shirt and jeans from the night before. They smelled like booze, no surprise there.

After a shower and shave he pulled on a pair of jeans and walked out into the morning glory, blazing through the windows, onto the balcony. It was later than he'd thought. His new book would keep him company, along with a cup of joe, and a local morning show on the radio, overlooking downtown. The duo on the radio used to be a staple of life when he lived here. Even out west, through the glory of the internet, he still followed their show when he could. Chris sorely missed this city. It had been years since he moved away and every time he came back it made the vigor of youth beat through his veins. If there was ever a city for him, it was Austin, Texas. The first few hours of the morning passed quickly. Lost in his work Chris barely noticed the sun rotating above him. Halfway through the eighty-thousand plus words, he heard Bob Marley singing from inside the suite. Rugby answered his phone, but Chris was unable to hear the conversation. It didn't sound like much. He placed his book on the occasional table beside the empty mug and stepped through the curtains to check on his slumbering friend.

Rugby was lying with his head propped up, now partially covered by a sheet. He was scratching his hairy chest. His lips smacked a few times before he spoke with eyes barely open. "*Good God*! This bed sure beats the futon mattress I have back home."

Chris leaned on the doorway with a new mug, held out to the man lying before him, "You still haven't gotten a frame for that dirty old thing?"

The coffee smelled enticing, but Rugby couldn't bring himself to crawl out of the comfort where he laid. "It's worked well for me so far."

"That thing has got to be crusty by now."

Laughing through the sandpaper in his throat, "Nah, I burn my sheets on a regular basis."

"Nice. So who called?"

"That was Lacey, we're supposed to meet in their room for lunch in an hour."

"It's only ten o'clock," Chris said with a questioning tone.

"Lunch, brunch, whatever man, we have an hour."

Chris shook the mug in his direction, "I'm ready, c'mon sunshine, let's go."

"Coffee and a cigarette to exorcise the daemons of last night, the natural remedy," Rugby offered as he sat up with visible effort. Chris stepped to the bed and handed him the mug. Turning away he went back to the balcony to finish what he could in the new book.

The two suitemates were the first to arrive at the ladies' room. The girls were dealing with mirrors and blow dryers so the boys laid out across the bed, searching the TV for anything entertaining. Chris avoided looking at Hope as she passed and instead focused on the local sports network. Soon after Kathy and Neal knocked, they came in and joined the other two on the bed. With the addition of Hope they were now packed five deep across the bed. This is how things went amongst them all. When they were together, there was no distance between them. Chris could see now they were still the family he'd known.

Lacey was the last to call 'ready' and they all raced down the stairs and out into the street.

The Day Of

T he café was a short stroll across the four-lane and around the corner. It was a small Americana style place; black and white checkered floor, silver stools surrounded the soda bar, neon lights ran the length of the trim and everything in between. They sat at the largest table in the house. The waitress came around to take drink orders. She went around the table and water seemed to be the general consensus, until Rugby that is.

"I'll have a bloody mary," he said leaning back in his chair, "and a glass of water."

Everyone thought the same thing but it was Hope who spoke up, "Really…" she paused for emphasis, *"Really?"*

"Hair of the dog, sister."

Chris seemed to entertain the idea and added to his original order, "That sounds good, I'll have one too, heavy on the juice." The waitress nodded. She spun around and left for the kitchen.

Chris looked over the crowd and smiled. The scene reminded him of 'Sunday Funday.' Every Sunday for almost three years, they always got together. It was the one day of the week when the bar industry was slow enough that those who pulled their weight could get the whole day off and relax together. It often involved the boys cooking while the women took care of the entertainment. The location rotated week to week but it was always the same environment. There was only one person missing.

Cindy Coupland would always frequent their gatherings, especially on Sundays. Chris's mother acted as the matriarch of this band of cohorts. Even in his mother's absence they were together again, if only just for today.

Chris had tried desperately to convince his mother to attend the gallery opening but she insisted that there were matters of business that needed attending to. She was currently in Denver negotiating a contract on behalf of Coupland Studios for the production of a new patent they had filed for.

When the meal was finished and tickets paid they all walked out into the blazing heat of the Texas summer sun. The asphalt was already radiating heat that almost melted through his boots. Chris immediately put on a pair of sunglasses that were as dark as a welder's mask. It seemed that as the temperature rose, nerves cooled. While they all strolled out into the parking lot, Hope finally spoke directly to him. "You know I always hated those glasses. No one can see where you're looking."

Chris caught a glimpse of her out of the corner of his eye, following the curve of her figure, "That's half the point. If I didn't look like a tool, I'd wear them all night too."

"You're already a tool, so what's the worry?" Hope offered sarcastically.

Chris smiled, nodding; things might get back to normal someday, but for today, he would accept any attention he could garner with great appreciation. The day passed quickly, engrossed in the comfort and compassion of the family.

Apprehension

Chris's hands were shaking. Just about the time they had arrived back at the hotel it had begun. The nerves, the apprehension, it all finally caught up with him. Everyone else was sleeping the evening away, but Chris had to leave early. They would all meet up again at the show. The damn tie would not come out like it should. Too long, too short, his hands would not do his bidding. He was on edge. This first show was scheduled to start in two hours.

The radio in the small suite called to him.

"We call them fools who have to dance within the flame, who chance the sorrow and the shame that always come with getting burned."

"Thanks, Garth," Chris offered to the radio.

Without the help of the Austin Art Council, none of this would have been possible. Chris had never considered his work as pieces of art. They were simply products to him, furniture, lighting elements, plate ware, he called it anything but art. His joy came from making things with his hands, something from nothing or even found goods for that matter. For a long time now that had been his focus, staying up in the Studio all night was his therapy. The show tonight was not his idea; Lance was the one at fault. It seemed that Lance had turned from country boy to art guru in the liberal Mecca that is Austin, Texas. A knock at the door announced his arrival.

"Good evening, cupcake."

Chris didn't know how this nickname came to be, but it had been this way for years. Lance came straight in and grabbed the tie, now mangled around Chris's neck. He continued, "Okay, are you ready? Do you know who's going to be out tonight?"

"Rugby if he doesn't keep his zipper up."

Lance gave a weak laugh, "True, but seriously, these people are here for you, we're going to introduce you to the world."

"Lance, I moved to the middle of nowhere for a reason."

With his usual flair, "When you were slinging drinks for a living, you loved the attention, I know you did."

Chris smiled slightly, "That was a long time ago, and I was not exposing myself to the public. I think I'd be more comfortable showing the world my man-hammer."

"Oh, now don't flatter yourself, I've asked around, I know. Come on now, we have to get going."

Lance took his arm, and they swung out into the hallway. Ten paces toward the elevators, and Chris swung back in the opposite direction. His heels immediately slid to a stop on the carpet. The effort was frivolous, Lance had him within reach and was not letting go; another about face and they were on their way. The elevator music was an instrumental cover of 'St. Elmo's Fire' by John Parr, sickening. Lance left the timid designer standing in the lobby with the orders to sit and stay. Chris seriously thought that if he made a break for it he could disappear before Lance got back. The thought slowly faded as the black SUV pulled up to the sliding doors out front. Lance had to honk several times before Chris decided it would be better to attend the gallery opening than sit here and listen to instrumental covers that poured out of the speakers.

Lance pulled up alongside South Congress in front of the gallery. It was a narrow space, just over thirty feet wide, with a centrally located door in the façade, which was almost all glass from the ground up. Chris exited the vehicle into the dusk of late evening, stepping up the sidewalk and there in front of him, framed for pedestrians and critics alike, was his dining set. It was an Antoine Predock inspired piece, it was very orthogonal and the exposed layers of plywood revealed the structure. The natural colors of the maple veneer seemed to glow in the lamplights that had just begun to overtake the darkness. It was his personal favorite of everything that had been chosen to bring to town.

An elderly man standing just outside the door, smoking, caught his attention. The secondhand smelled amazing. It had been years, since college, when he'd had his last smoke. There was nothing better than a solid nicotine buzz after a whiskey, rye preferably. The gentleman noticed him and struck up a conversation.

"Here for the opening?"

Chris nodded, "Yeah, it could be an interesting evening."

The stranger showed agreement and took a small pull from the cancer stick. "I've never seen any pieces like this. Is it really art?" His statement agreed with Chris's own thoughts. The stranger continued, "Who am I to say, but it is nice to see some new blood on the market. Stirs things up a little bit you know? This guy, Coupland, though," he paused to fill his lungs again. "I think this Coupland guy plays too much on the shock value of things, he's lost sight of the subtleties. What do you think?"

Chris stuck his hands in his pockets and cocked his head to the side and thought for a second, pretending to study the piece. Finally he replied to the critique, "I think a monkey with a protractor could come up with the same basic vocabulary as this style."

As Chris spoke Lance strolled by, back from parking the SUV, heading into the gallery. Chris gave the stranger a pat on the shoulder as he passed grabbing one last hint of smoke rolling off the stubby cigarette. "Thanks for the insight and secondhand, I needed it, trust me."

Stepping into the gallery was what Chris imagined an alternate reality felt like. The pieces, his pieces, which he and Ramone had designed and assembled in a dusty studio four hundred miles west of here, were now on display in an incredibly sterile environment. If only Ramone could see this. Chris had offered to pay his way, but he'd refused. This was way off the reservation for him, but Chris adapted well. After a quick once over to inspect the layout and a few formal introductions, the designer went directly to the rear reception where the wet bar stood, awaiting his attention.

The Show

Chris stood at the rear of the long gallery space, next to the bar, watching the staff move throughout the assortment of pieces. With just enough time to drain his glass of all liquor, the people began to flow in. Shaking hands, listening to both praise and criticism, Chris attempted to remain as anonymous as possible. Friends showed, as they'd planned. They would be his safety vest against drowning in the tsunami of onlookers. Kathy and Neal were the first familiar faces he saw. Greetings were exchanged, and Chris thanked them heavily for keeping him afloat. Right behind them were Lacey, Rugby, and Hope. Good god, Hope in a black evening dress. She was ravishing. It was low cut with the shoulders pulled together in back. It cascaded gently down her figure to just above the floor. Her auburn hair, loosely tied back, fell over her exposed shoulder. She was glowing.

Chris laughed at himself and gave his head a slight shake, a feeble attempt to correct his thoughts. Champagne in hand she stood like a beacon in the night. The crowd parted for her as she gracefully crossed the room, she walked like she owned the place. This event was more of her style anyway. Chris was unsure of how to handle the situation, but with a class all her own, Hope took the lead. She walked to him, gave a small hug, and complimented on how much she looked forward to the show. Chris gave a slight nod and thanked her. Each party stole a longer embrace than was expected, holding firm, letting the sea of people around them disappear if only for a moment. It was their moment. When they parted Chris spoke under the white noise of the crowd.

"Hope," he stammered for a second, "I'm sorry about last night," he looked down as his left foot, cocked on the outer edge of its sole, rubbed along a groove in the tile floor. "I didn't mean to…"

"Don't worry about it," she beat him to the punch. "We can make amends later, you should enjoy this."

"Later, yeah, okay," he smiled.

Her hand held fast on his arm as she maneuvered around him through the crowd. Lance pulled Chris in the opposite direction guiding him around the hall for even more introductions. As he moved further away, Chris caught a quick glance over his shoulder at that black dress. Hope tried to pretend that she didn't notice but Lacey could read her red lips too easily.

Not wanting to drift too far from the bar, Neal and Rugby stuck to the rear of the party. Surrounded by larger pieces, a dark armoire with strategically lit, etched lexan panels played lead blocker against the masses. Rugby took a sip, "Poor bastard," he said lifting his glass in the direction of the designer as Chris looked back, envious. "I can think of a few things he'd probably rather be doing right now and I would be happy to join him."

Neal chuckled, "Open bar man! Enjoy the show. There have to be enough bored women here to keep you entertained for at least one night."

Playing on the sarcasm, Rugby countered, "I don't know Neal. I tried to exhaust myself last night but when she was all worn out, the hooker just gave me my money back…" he paused for a drink, "I swear."

Neal couldn't contain himself, he stepped away to ease the pain in his sides, "I need a drink if the shit's getting this deep."

At the front of the house a rapping of a champagne flute got everyone's attention. Lance took a stand atop one of the shorter pedestals.

"Excuse me, everyone," pause for dramatic effect, "I would like to apologize for anything my speech deprived friend may not say this evening, but we are all very appreciative of your attention… and money. Also, I would like to extend my highest gratitude to the association for lending us the gallery space for a few weeks. I could not think of a better canvas with which to unveil our newest addition to the Austin art community. Now, Chris, come up here and say something nice, if you would please."

Chris knew it was coming. His throat choked up as he slowly mounted the impromptu stage. Clearing his windpipe he spoke timidly, "I never really expected this when I first set up Coupland Studios. Originally this was a hobby just to pass the time. This work gave me something to do. Contrary to what my dear friend believes, I'm not in this for the fortune and fame. He can have all the fame, and any fortune generated throughout the show will be split between the art association and local charities. With that in mind, I would also like to thank the association, and to Lance, thank you for making this happen, it is a great opportunity and without your ambition and hard work none of this would have happened. Everyone, please enjoy yourselves, and thank you for coming out this evening."

A round of applause saw Chris off the pedestal. At least the masses seemed to be having a good time. For the designer, his nerves had yet to cool.

Hope and Lacey were admiring a bamboo bed set, discussing the interweaving grains of Asian Grass that formed the replacement for the box springs. Chris was unnoticed as he approached from behind. "And how are my two favorite ladies doing this evening?" Both girls turned to face him. They always seemed to dress alike. One blonde, the other brunette but beyond that, they were generally interchangeable. They could easily pass as sisters. Lacey looked excited about the event as she spouted off the pieces she liked.

"That corner lamp is great, the post looks medieval, it's very interesting but my favorite by far is the pedestal sink in the bathroom setup."

"That one is actually a replica of the sink in my bathroom back home."

In typical Lacey fashion it was not all praise and glory, she was always an honest one, sometimes to a fault. "But what are those things?" she asked pointing to a pair of chairs located just beyond the bathroom display. "It looks like a lazy boy ate a taxi and that's what was left the next day."

"Aw, thanks sweetheart, but that's actually a very close assumption, they're scrapped together from an old yellow taxi. They were more of an extreme take on an aesthetic theory, not fine art. Think: Theoretical Furniture."

As the night rolled on, Chris had a chance to speak with everyone, and the overall review was positive. As the gallery was closing and patrons made their way out, Chris shook hands and exchanged hugs with those he knew well.

When the crowd began to thin, Chris met up with Rugby and Neal. The two were still anchoring the back end of the gallery, "So do we have any plan for afterhours?" Chris asked.

Neal, who had been obviously testing the patience of the bartender, said, "Sixth Street, definitely. Definitely Sixth Street."

"You'll have to check with the girls to be sure, we just do as we're told," Rugby added.

"Good plan," Chris nodded in agreement. "Hey Rain Man, you got something on your suit," he noted slapping Neal on the shoulder.

The brown guy looked down, sure enough, it seems part of an appetizer had landed on his lapel. "*Damnitt,* and this is my good suit!"

Chris left the duo to their vices and began shaking hands as visitors left. Arrangements were made to meet up on Sixth Street for the after party. As Hope passed by on her way out, she slipped him a note. Surprised, Chris put it in his pocket, not wanting to reveal its secrets, both in fear and anticipation of what it might hold.

Flashback #2 (The Split)

Sitting on the curb alongside South Congress Avenue, beer in hand, waiting on Lance, his ride, to stop socializing, Chris thought back to when this whole journey had begun. He had never planned on being a designer. For the longest time he always thought he'd build houses, but when that industry fell through shortly after graduation and still reeling from a breakup, he had been lost.

Five years ago, on New Year's Eve, he and Hope had just returned from visiting their families over the holidays. The entire trip had been a rough one. Chris had never been very good at reading subtle hints and signals, it was a problem. He was like an open book, very honest and almost anyone could read him. Hope once told him he wore his heart on his sleeve and she was right, though he didn't want to hear it. On this day, in the middle of a bitter end of the year cold front, he noticed. Hope had not been very subtle about it. The drive south, after gifts had been exchanged and everyone said goodbye, Hope had avoided any conversation about them and she'd been that way for several days. When they arrived at her apartment in Dallas that evening, she went straight for the shower. Chris joined her as soon as the bags were unloaded. She stood with her back to him, the water running through her hair. When she did not turn to meet him he knew that something was amiss, the holidays should have been a joyous time. Standing there that evening Chris finally asked the inevitable, "You've been cold lately, what gives?"

Hope was trying to avoid the conversation until later but could hold back no more. "I didn't want to do this now. I wanted to wait until after the holidays, but I don't think this is going to work out. I've been trying to tell you for a while but you never notice me anymore."

Chris knew this woman well enough to understand that this was a decision already made. Chris stood before her as she finally spun on her heels to meet him eye to eye. Naked, both physically and emotionally he didn't know what to say, neither of them did. Hope stepped through the curtain grabbing a towel from the wall next to the stall. Chris quickly washed off and followed her lead. Still recovering from the impact of her statement he sought out the only thought he could muster, "This isn't even up for discussion is it?"

Hope looked at him, her hair still dripping wet. It hung lifeless, reflecting the emotions that both of them felt. Her beautiful green eyes were somber and weighed heavily with sorrow, but she said nothing.

Chris, even as dense as he was, could read her now, nodding he answered his own question, "You've already made up your mind."

Hope took a deep breath, holding it as long as she could in an attempt to hold back her emotions. Given the recent turn of events she defended herself, "I've been trying to tell you for weeks but you wouldn't listen, you never do. You're always caught up in something that's more important than I am." She took another deep breath feeling the energy in her on the brink of eruption. "I wanted to use this holiday trip as a gauge of where we stood. I've talked to my family about it all, and I don't think we're going in the right direction."

Chris shook his head not wanting to believe what he was hearing, "I came here for you. I left everything back home and moved here for you. We were looking at houses, making plans. What do you mean not in the right direction?"

"You come up here and we play house on the weekends, but what is that doing for us. You complain that you're not happy where you're at, and I know you couldn't be happy in Dallas, and that spills over into our relationship. What am I supposed to do about it? I can't help you if you don't know what's wrong. You're a dreamer, Chris, I'm not, and that is driving us in different directions."

In the long term picture of everything, she was right. She was always right. Hope could read him better than anyone.

They cancelled their plans for the night and opted to spend it with each other but little was said. The evening passed, there was a countdown and they watched the ball drop over the big apple and back home at the little apple, the start of a new beginning, but there was no kiss at midnight. They made love that night, and it only brought her tears and made Chris nauseous.

Chris could not sleep much and for good reason. His mind, which was typically in high gear at all times, was well into overdrive that night. As soon as the sun rose, so did he. His bags were packed by the time Hope woke up. While she prepared for work, Chris started his truck and her little car to get them both warmed up. He stood outside looking south toward the Dallas skyline, he didn't want to be in that apartment anymore. It was a chilly morning and there was frost on almost everything, his breath hung heavy in the frigid air, but it wasn't the cold that caused him to shiver. Hope stepped out of the door just after eight, headed to work. Even on a holiday like this it would keep her mind busy and off the breakup. Standing in front of her apartment with the yellow rays of the sun bringing anything but warmth, they said farewell. One last hug was in order before Hope sat in her car and looked beyond into the distance. Chris broke the silence, "So this is it, huh?"

Hope grabbed his hand; her fingers were like ice on his skin, "Don't be like that. We'll see each other again," although that statement would take many months to manifest.

"The terms of that meeting are what worry me."

"Don't talk like that, just don't."

With a nod Chris closed her door and loaded into his own vehicle. He saw her pull away in his mirror, and he followed suit. They headed down the same side of the interstate which ran just in front of the complex until she pulled off and crossed the overpass following the frontage road around and back to the north while he maneuvered his way through downtown. The road before him splayed out into thousands of different opportunities. Chris had no motivation toward or away from any one in particular. How could he choose just one?

Flashback #2 (Moving)

The return trip to Austin after the breakup was a blur and the city was not the same. This is where they were supposed to move after graduation, before everything went to hell, before he had lost sight and dropped the ball. It was to be their new home, not his alone. He couldn't remain here. For a few months he held out, trying to stay the inevitable but by summertime Chris tapped out and moved back north, not really knowing what to do. Opportunity though had something different in mind.

Arriving home, everything was still an unknown. Women could not make him feel anything over the raw nerves. Not knowing where he was headed left Chris confused. He'd heard little out of Hope since the New Year and the silence was deafening, the speculation brutal. Was she happy? Had she found another man?

Chris returned to bartending at night, but it bored him. To pass the time during the day, he began writing. There was no particular reason, but getting his thoughts on paper removed them from rolling around his head and sheet by sheet he began to organize the chaos that fogged his vision. The bar offered no opportunity but what it did was provide freedom, the freedom to follow whatever dream he wanted to chase on any particular day, and chase he did.

Over the span of a year there were two failed businesses, one in construction, a failure he chalked up to inexperience and one in design and manufacturing which the economy drowned before it ever saw infancy. In the meantime he'd managed to maintain Coupland Design. It was his little pet project that gave a name to all the sketches, designs, patents and creative projects that sprang forth. Initially it was no huge success and there was no financial gain, but it helped to formalize things. There were some houses and a church he designed, nothing spectacular. Several patents were drawn up in association with an engineer he'd attended school with but they were pending, it was a lengthy process which took years. Everything changed again the following spring.

Almost a year after leaving Texas a small collection of writings began to form into a cohesive group that roughly resembled a manuscript. Coupland Design would soon be a publisher. The first draft was crap, as they all are, the second didn't improve much but with the help of several friends it was massaged and eventually turned into a piece of work worth publishing. The book was a semi-autobiographical tale of searching through unlimited options and the chaos that limitless freedom brings with it. It took many influences from his life. Chris financed the publishing under Coupland Design, which would soon become Coupland Studios. The book took off almost instantly. The rights were sold to one of the large publishing houses back East for a sum well above the six digit line. After the dust settled from a whirlwind tour and all debts were paid, Chris knew he had to get away. Life, though fruitful, was still spinning out of control. He was going in circles. Heeding the advice from a wise, old friend, Chris chose to leave for desolate west Texas. In the middle of nowhere he would give up everything he had possessed and known, to search for answers. Answers he thought he could find in himself.

On the first day of July that year, Chris Coupland left home for good. Packed only with what was needed, in the same truck he'd driven for almost ten years now, he found a distant town, away from everyone he'd known. After only a week in this new town, living out of a roadside motel, he met his future partner in crime, Ramone.

With the money generated from the publishing, Chris developed several patents and formally established Coupland Studios Incorporated. His ideas, whether architectural, literary or inventive, finally had a formal outlet that could not only manage the expenses but also the income generated. In time there were books, art, architectural designs and product patents, even a board game. Several short stories were circulating amongst the producers out West, but Chris wondered if any film would develop. The biggest project on the table was a contract in negotiation with a furniture producer over a patent that had been filed a few years ago regarding a foot for chairs and stools. It was a simple piece, but inventive. With only three pieces it naturally leveled the seat on an uneven surface if left to rest for just a few seconds.

When Chris began he had a financial goal, that if reached, neither him, nor his mother would ever have to worry about money again, and it was getting close. Cindy Coupland was an integral part of the business machine that Chris and his associates, including Neal had created. She sat on the board, acted as chief financial officer and held power of attorney over the entire business. Chris had no idea and never even entertained the thought of what would happen to the business if his mother left.

Flashback #2 (Ramone)

Ramone Padillo, standing in the local commodities exchange, watching a thunderstorm pass, noticed the stranger the moment he arrived in town but had not yet had the opportunity to meet the young man. Chris pulled up looking for a Coke; parked and leisurely strolled inside in spite of the ensuing downpour. He walked with an air of confidence and a quizzical nature, which Ramone noticed immediately.

With Coke in hand, he took up a position standing next to Ramone, watching the rain, saying nothing. As the storm began to pass, Chris finished the last of his drink with a long gurgle from the straw and turned to introduce himself. "Chris Coupland," he said, extending a hand to the elderly Mexican standing on his left. Ramone gave him a thorough once over, trying to decipher his intentions.

"Ramone Padillo," he responded with a heavy accent. Shaking hands he mentioned, "You're new."

Chris gave a subtle laugh; this man did not miss a lot. "Do I stick out that much?"

"No, but I've lived in the area for more than seventy years. I know who comes and goes around here."

Chris smiled, 'wise man,' he thought, "What do you do, Mr. Padillo?"

"For five more days, I run what's left of the Keller Ranch. Then it will be auctioned off, and I'm being forced into retirement."

The potential immediately came to mind and Chris spoke up, "Is it good land?"

"The best in five counties, I am very proud to call it my home, even if my wife won't let me live there anymore."

Chris nodded, "I have an idea, Ramone. I'll see you in five days."

With that the wheels began turning. The following week Chris drove out to the Keller Ranch following a schematic a store clerk had drawn up for him. After several wrong turns and a dead end, the truck mounted one of the modest hills in the area and before him, in the valley below was revealed the heart of what used to be one of the most prominent cattle ranches in the nation. Broken fence line paralleled the long drive on both sides. Off to the left a windmill, missing several blades, carried on with a lopsided rotation. The lonely remaining blades made a slow climb to the top, almost didn't make it in the soft breeze, and rolled over and swung back down to start the cycle over again. The repetition was amusing. In the valley below, just east of him, surrounded on three sides by gently sloping hills, sat a modest house, two stories, with a wraparound porch that almost matched the house itself in square footage. It was a classic piece of southwestern residential construction, aged by the bitter winters and searing summers. Few places on earth felt the extreme range of the seasons that this territory did, but life was resilient here, and the house reflected this. Chris could almost sense it. Not far from the house, further on to the east was an old shed, clad in sheet metal, rusted out in places, a simple patina in others, the building was dressed in a skirt of tall grasses. It had been many years since this shed had seen any care. To the south of the house and shed, like a monstrous sentinel of the plains stood the faded red barn, broken but standing stoic next to the corrals. It was surrounded by vehicles on the two visible sides. The crowd was already gathering. The truck rolled forward, down the hill and coasted to a stop in the last line of assorted trucks. Chris threw her in park and stepped out. Kicking a few stones around on his way to the barn, he noticed the only sign of livestock left was an unusually small bay quarter horse. It couldn't be over thirteen hands. Mounted atop the mare sat Ramone.

With a slow gait, Ramone corralled the beautiful creature and dismounted with a steady pace. He was surely in no hurry to get the day's proceedings on with. Taking a detour Chris veered off to greet his new acquaintance. Leaning on the fence, watching intently, he gave a shallow nod. Ramone returned the gesture. As soon as the saddle and tack were removed, the old Mexican brushed the animal down and sent her away. He claimed a spot along the fence within arm's reach of Chris.

"That's a beautiful horse, Mr. Padillo."

Pride flashed in the old man's eyes as he responded, "Six generations I've bred that line, and this mare is the finest. I have never seen a quicker or more sure footed animal."

Ramone trailed off letting his comments drift away with the blowing dust. Chris decided to wrap up the short exchange, "I had better get inside before they start selling things off without me."

He was stopped short when Ramone grabbed his arm with a firm grip as he looked the young man in the eye. Chris removed his sunglasses and focused on the deep brown eyes shining from underneath the years of weather beaten skin. "Senior Coupland, I can see that you have big ideas. I don't know if to trust you is a mistake, but I would like to know what you have in mind. This is my home. No matter who holds the deed," he paused, "this is my home."

Chris shot his typical sly, reassuring smile which told the whole story, and Ramone released his grip.

"You have no need to worry, my friend."

With that said, they both made their separate ways to the barn. The auction began with parcels of land, further out, miles away. A few corporations seemed to be interested in the low lying areas. A couple gas companies and one geological service went round and round for several pieces, dividing everything up. Toward the end of the afternoon, after the equipment had been sold off, the last item on the docket was the smallest piece of land in the breakup. Three hundred eighty acres which may not have mineral or natural resources, but it was beautiful. It was the piece they all sat on while deciding the fate of the land around them.

Tucked in the little valley, it held all the buildings and corrals. Bidding began at two hundred an acre and quickly rose above seven hundred. Chris had sat quietly through all these proceedings thus far, watching and picking up on the bidding tells of the others. After a several minutes of bickering over a dollar or two, Chris stood and raised the current bid by over one hundred dollars per acre. Everyone stopped. With three little words Coupland Studios had found a new home.

Payment arrangements were made as the barn began to clear. The deed would transfer on Friday. When all papers were signed, Chris searched for the old Mexican. He found him just outside the large sliding doors on the west wall, studying the ground directly below where he stood. Ramone did not look up.

"Congratulations, senior, what will you do now?"

Chris looked around, "I think the more important question, Mr. Padillo, is what will you do now?"

Ramone agreed to stay on at the ranch with no particular description of duties, but he did not care. Chris saw the jubilation this opportunity brought, even if Ramone did not expressly show it. In time things came to be routine around Coupland Studios. The two men got to know each other while remodeling the old barn into a production shop. Chris fired most of the questions, inquiring about Ramone's family and history with the ranch. His father had worked here years ago. Ramone was born in a small shack behind the house over seventy years ago. His father continued to live there until the day he died several decades before. His mother had passed away when he was very young. Ramone was happy to work side by side with his father growing up, learning the land and the business. The Keller family, who had owned the property before Chris, had taken Ramone in as one of their own. He met his wife when she took a position assisting old Mrs. Keller after she became too ill to keep up with the housework. There had been another house on the property a mile east of the barn where Ramone and his wife Rita had lived for many years. It burned down ten years ago, and Rita had forced Ramone to move into town against his wishes.

He had four children, two were dead, one lived on the West Coast and the other owned and operated a restaurant in Lubbock. There were five grandchildren he knew of, the eldest, Erica, helped around the house. She was a vibrant young woman.

Later on, as fall began to set in, the two men were finishing up the conversion of the barn when a thought occurred to the youngest of the pair. "Ramone, you don't talk a lot, I've come to accept this, but you don't ask many questions either. You don't know anything about me."

"I know what you have told me," the old man said matter-of-factly.

"Don't you wonder about anything?"

The old man stopped hammering, took off his tool belt and sat on a wooden shipping crate left in the middle of the floor. He scratched his head, took a drink from his thermos sitting next to him and finally spoke, "Senior Coupland, no one comes out here with the resources you have, as young as you are. You should be chasing the world, fame, fortune and everything that comes with them. Instead you are here, with me, building a wood shop in the middle of nowhere. You are hiding from something, from what I do not know. If you knew, you would not be out here. Until you know, you cannot explain it to anyone, so if you do not know, then neither can I, so I do not ask."

Chris wrinkled his brow trying to interpret just what exactly the old man was saying. The Mexican offered no more of an explanation; he just sat there studying the work they had completed so far. This was the longest string of words Chris had heard Ramone put together in all the time they'd spent in each other's company. His wisdom came on thick when he had to explain it. He was right though, his insight ran deeper than he ever let on. Chris nodded in agreement, letting the understanding settle in. Until Chris knew just what he was running from or toward, he would stick to his work. The subject was not discussed again for a long time.

As the work passed, the stereo wailed into the autumn afternoon. Music was the only link that Chris had left to the world from which he came. Standing there, in the studio, staring out the front windows, Chris could feel the words sink into his skin.

"Maybe I miss your lovin', maybe I miss your kiss just a little bit, maybe I miss your body, laying right next to mine, maybe I miss your touch, a little too much."

Chris thought of her often. And often it was the music that took him back.

"They talked about Savannah. Sweet home Alabama and how he missed the way she always smiled. Are you coming back soon, by the harvest moon, if I have to walk every mile on my knees."

A song of lost love was one he did not need right now, but this song held so much value that his feet would not carry him any closer to the stereo. And so he dove back into the work that consumed his life. Between the work and alcohol, he could almost forget about her.

6th Street

Walking in the middle of Sixth Street in downtown Austin they looked quite the sight. Coming directly from the gallery, everyone had elected not to waste time changing. Evening dresses and full-on suits, ties and all, may have been a little too classy for this scene. Surrounded by street musicians, college students recently back in town, and hobos, they strolled through the scene. As the humidity of the day faded with the time, jackets moved to the women and the ties loosened. Still fairly lubed up from the reception, the party easily spilled from bar to bar. There were shots and drinks, toasts and boasts from college, and stories, always with the stories. No subject left unmentioned except one. It had been almost two years since the last time everyone got together, and with everyone leaving in the morning how long would it be between this time and the next? It was this unknown that fueled the night.

Standing out on the street, half the team smoked while the others waited, not wanting to leave anyone behind. Hope, who happened to be downwind, took a deep breath, enjoying the nostalgia, "*Oh my god!* I haven't smoked in years, I can't take the temptation." She stepped across the circle and took up post next to Chris.

"Chris, tell me again why I quit."

Not knowing the correct answer he guessed the obvious, "'Cause it's horrible for your health?"

With a look of desperation, "That's not helping."

"Um, because you look so much better without poisoning yourself?" he tried again.

"Thank you," she replied with a coy smile.

The personal attention she afforded him made his face flush. It was something he thought he missed, but now, after everything, it came with mixed feelings. It was Rugby who brought his drifting eyes back to reality. "Okay asshole, you don't have much room to talk. When was the last time you smoked?"

"A long, long time ago," Chris reassured him.

"Yeah, see I just can't believe that, it's… just… not…" He trailed off watching a woman walk into the closest bar.

Neal saw this, "Don't do it, buddy. She looks good from a distance, not so good up close."

Rugby smiled, "I'll take one for the team."

"That would be what, the hundredth one you've taken for the team?" Neal jabbed.

"Well, I don't want anyone else making any bad decisions."

Chris couldn't hold back, "Oh, yeah, leading by example. 'The team' appreciates your effort. I can see the self-help manual now, 'Rugby's guide: What Not To Do."

Kathy offered her insight, "He's not the brightest crayon in the box, but he still writes."

Lacey finished off the round of criticism, "I love you, but you're dumb!"

Rugby tossed his cigarette down, "I'll see y'all on the flip side," and walked in after his prey leaving with a bow, "Ladies and gentlemen I would like to apologize now for anything I may say or do." With that he turned and disappeared through the door.

"Shots?" Neal suggested which drew a lively chorus of agreement. Single file they followed Rugby's lead inside. The first round was bought by the brown guy who offered a toast, "To Mama Coupland. We all miss her and wish she could be here, but I look forward to seeing her on our way home." Everyone tipped their drinks.

The scene was one of general chaos throughout the night. They set up camp at a table in the front of the house just inside a large picture window. No one sat still for long. Treks were made to find drinks or a restroom, sometimes both, though the decision of which to find first was often a difficult one. Rugby had given up on the chase and returned to the table. Kathy and Neal were tearing up the tile on an improvised dance floor in the window next to the table. Neal moved like an erratic animal but probably wouldn't remember it in the morning anyway. Everyone else was gathered around the large table yelling over the jukebox, currently pouring out some local musician proclamation of love for the lone star state.

Hope leaned into the table to make herself audible over the noise of the bar, "What ever happened with the little construction company you two started." She directed toward Chris and Rugby. The two men looked at each other laughing. Chris was trying to find a nice way to say what he wanted when Rugby jumped in.

"Well, it was all going great, on budget and on time. That is, until we decided that Jager-Bomb Thursdays should become a weekly tradition."

Chris's sides began to hurt with laughter, in between spasms he got out, "Hey, everything comes out a half bubble off plumb when you're hung over."

"That's what we named it, 'Half Bubble Off Plumb Construction,'" Rugby added.

Chris nodded, "What would you expect, we had a chef, two line cooks and a hung over bartender. Yeah, it was a huge disaster, but by that point though I'd gotten used to failure. If you want to improve yourself you have to accept that you're going to look foolish and fail for some time. A wise old Mexican taught me that."

Lacey added, "Oh Christopher. You and your wisdom, would you draw me a schematic so I can remember that little gem?"

Chris gave her a sarcastic grin and extended a finger in her direction.

They continued on, reciting tales of tap shoes, a Christmas tree disaster in March, skinny dipping, Rugby hooking up in the parking lot of a local restaurant in the middle of the afternoon, they never ended. The stories varied but every single one held a place dear to them all. While Hope told of the homeless guy who shacked in her tent for a summer, Kathy put her arm around Chris, sitting next to him, "Quit staring. It's obvious and it's not going to do a damn thing for you." Her smoky advice was understandable, but did no good to quell his desires.

"Can't help it," he couldn't, she was a thing of beauty. A word puzzle came to mind. It had been posed to him by the wall of a bathroom stall, in an Irish bar back home. He'd read it, but its true value didn't set in soon enough, She was gone by then.

'(Person) is more than just a pair of (noun)!'

He knew the words that automatically popped into his mind. The funny part was Rugby, who had entered the same stall right after him, came out declaring, "Leah is more than just a pair of tits!" Leah just happened to be the girl he was sleeping with at the time. That little bit of graffiti held quite a lot of wisdom, though it would take several long hard roads before Chris would understand this wisdom.

As last call neared, the scene came close to chaos. Before long the bouncers had tossed Neal out, and everyone else took the hint that maybe it was time to return to the hotel.

"Rollin down a backwoods Tennessee byway, one arm on the wheel, holdin' myLover with the other: a sweet, soft, southern thrill."

"Worked hard all week; got a little jingle on a Tennessee Saturday night. Couldn't feel better: I'm together with my Dixieland delight."

Arm in arm the group ambled down the street as one mass. They didn't need a stereo to sing along to. This was one song they all knew by heart. Sunday night karaoke through college had taught them more than mixology.

"Spend my dollar; parked in a holler 'neath the mountain moonlight; hold her uptight; make a little lovin', a little turtle dovin' on a Mason Dixon night. Fits my life, oh, so right: my Dixieland Delight."

Before long, those who could, skipped down the middle of Sixth. The streetscape was beautiful. The people, the music, it all seemed to have a life of its own. Chris had been here many times before, but the first time was the one that remained most vivid in his mind.

Flashback #3 (Relationshit)

It was the summer before their last year at the University, six years ago, when Chris and Hope had made the eleven hour drive south to Austin. They came here to get away for a week. They came to get some time alone together. They came down to scout places to live after graduation. As Chris thought about that trip everyone walking down Sixth Street faded away, save for Hope. He could see her then, no longer in her black dress from the gallery she wore so well. Six summers before it was just a pair of jeans and a green tank top. It was a look he liked better than the evening dress, she was very casual and it fit her personality. He could even hear the song that Hope had played over and over during the drive down.

"Mile upon mile got no direction, we're all playing the same game. We're all looking for redemption, just afraid to say the name.

So caught up now in pretending, that what we're seeking is the truth. I'm just looking for a happy ending, all I'm looking for is you."

Hope walked just ahead of him, looking back over her shoulder, calling him to keep up. Together they walked hand in hand taking in all the sights and sounds. Austin was a city a world away from where they came. The young couple enjoyed the scenery and each other. It was a happy time for them both. Their love was just beginning, only a few weeks old. In that time they had only spent three days apart. Chris had been out of town with Kathy and Neal on a float trip. When he arrived home, he went straight to Hope's townhouse. Her two roommates were gone for the night, and they would be alone. Eager with anticipation Chris didn't slow to knock at the door and took the stairs three at a time. Hope stood at the top waiting, her hair still damp. Chris took her in his arms holding her as close as he could and kissed her again and again. From those sweet lips came her admiration, "I missed you so much."

Chris gazed at her with his ghostly blue eyes locked on the deep emerald greens of her own, "Well, I didn't want to sound needy, but I missed you too."

"Call me needy then, I don't care."

Her needs were something he would come to love and appreciate, though not soon enough. Chris had no idea at the time how his mindset would be his downfall. His pride was an Achilles heel, for the time being though; they were both happy and unaware.

In the beginning, none of their friends knew, they both decided to keep their intimacy under the radar. Since they worked together, it could complicate things. The thrill of the covert relationship kept everything exciting. They had to leave the city just to have a romantic dinner together. They never arrived or left work together. There were inconveniences, but neither Hope nor Chris minded. That last fall semester flew by like a whirlwind, they both held on for the ride of a lifetime. Chris still couldn't remember any of his classes, he retained little of school, but he remembered Hope. He could see her, sitting across the table at lunch, selling beer in a packed bar or laying out on the couch on Sunday afternoons. It was the only day she could get him to sit still long enough to spend time together, just the two of them. It was their time.

Halloween that year was a particularly exciting time. Hope dressed up as the scarecrow from the Wizard of OZ. There was a Dorothy, tin man and a cowardly lion also but none looked as sexy as she did. Her body was not typical of the knees and elbows that were associated with the hay stuffed figures, it was a voluptuous scarecrow. It all made for a particularly adventurous night.

As fall rolled into winter things became routine. In time friends began to put two and two together. Chris and Hope were closer than any other pair in the group; they always seemed to leave about the same time and if one was out so was the other, if one stayed in neither showed up. By the time either Hope or Chris admitted it, anyone who knew them had it pieced together. No one was surprised.

For Chris everything was a new experience. He'd never loved anyone the way he loved her. He'd never been involved in a relationship as serious as this one had developed into. The commitment and sacrifices scared him. In time he began to have doubts, not about her, but about himself. His inexperience and fear began to push him away. By the time the holiday season came around he was scared, truly in fear of the unknown.

Christmas with Hope's family was a first. They were a loving, if quirky, family and Chris felt welcome, but he never found himself comfortable in their company. This was nothing of their doing. He'd never been family oriented. Chris led a very independent and self gratifying lifestyle; it was not conducive to a family environment. For years he'd been avoiding his own, save for his mother. How would anyone expect him to blend in with someone else's, even if she was the love of his life?

The New Year brought even more firsts to their relationship and with them more worries that fogged Chris's thoughts. Chris began to understand that with this commitment he would be surrendering some of his dreams. Foolishly his foresight was far too shallow to realize which of these alternatives, Hope or his perceived agenda, should carry more weight. By the time March came fuses were becoming shorter. Chris felt suffocated and Hope felt like she was not a priority anymore. When her grandmother died Chris was too busy to attend the funeral with Hope though he could have made the time and both of them knew this. Hope began to see the distance growing between them and when she brought it up Chris would dismiss it all, denying his fears.

Their first big fight came in April. Everyone ended up at Lacey and

Mac's house after the bars closed. This had become a ritual for many of them, and everyone looked forward to it week after week. This particular night had been a long one and Chris was not in the mood to see everyone, yet Hope wanted to go and he wanted to be with her so he conceded.

It was a good night as almost every night was. Lacey broke out the infamous tap shoes and gave an impromptu performance which brought down the house. Throughout the night there was music, dance and drink. When it came time to leave, Hope opted to crash in the guest bedroom. Given the long day it took no time at all for Chris to settle in and feel sleep overcome him.

Hope joined him shortly after; as she crawled into bed she snuggled up behind him and put her arm over his shoulder. "Come play with me," she whispered in his ear.

Chris shifted under the sheets. "Hope, it's been a long day, and I just want to go to sleep," he said pressing his head further into the pillow.

"What the hell, Chris," she blasted to life, "I put myself out there for you all the time and you keep making me feel like a fool. Just once can't you indulge me?"

"Just once can't you let me sleep? It's been a long day, I'm drunk and it's not a good time to have this discussion."

"What is your problem?!"

"My problem is that we live in your world. You wanted to be here, so I'm here with you. You wanted to stay here tonight…"

"You know you can't drive."

"I didn't want to be here in the first place. We're always on your schedule. We always stay at your house and not once have you made any room or even offered to make space for any of my things. It would be nice to have clean clothes in the morning if I'm going to stay the night and why can't we ever stay at my place?" It all came from him so quickly he didn't have time to censor himself.

"Because your place is disgusting, and Rugby is always there."

Chris's fuse burned quickly in the early morning hours, "You know what? I'm... I'm not doing this right now." He shook his head and threw his arms up in surrender, "I don't want to be here, and I don't want to stay in this bed. I'm out." He threw the blanket back across the bed and pounded his feet to the wood flooring.

"Then why did you come over in the first place?" Hope asked pulling herself up in bed.

"Because this is where you were and it was come see you here or nothing, so I bit my tongue and tried to enjoy myself."

"Oh yeah, it really looked like you were enjoying yourself tonight; you wouldn't even sit with me," she accused with a caustic tone.

"It was a one person chair. I didn't feel like snuggling up in front of everyone. I was not in a good mood and you were having a great time, I didn't want to bring your night down with me. After eight hours of class and eight hours of work, I'm ready to call it a night. I've been up for almost twenty-four hours now. I'm sorry if this doesn't fit your schedule." He confessed.

"You never have time for me." She accused.

"Because you expect it whenever you have time. I do not have that luxury." This accusation pushed her over the edge.

"I hold a job and go to class the same as you do. Are you saying your classes are tougher or that you work harder than I do?"

Chris grew frustrated with her assumptions and his exhaustion began to show. "No, not better nor tougher, but I work hard at everything I do, I've never half-assed anything in m life, I run circles around you or anyone else."

"Yeah, you've never half-assed anything except this relationship." The gloves were off now and if this fight continued it would get ugly.

Chris threw in the towel. "I don't have to put up with this right now, we're both drunk, I was pissed off when I got here and you're not doing me any good, now I'm leaving before things get out of hand. I'm going home." Chris pulled his jeans and boots on and threw his shirt over his shoulder. His heels scraped the hardwood floor as he took the five steps from the edge of the bed to the doorway.

Seeing him leaving Hope gave in, "Wait, don't go, don't leave me, I'm sorry." She pleaded rising to her knees.

Chris's stubborn, proud nature showed in all its damning glory. She had called him out and unfortunately she was right, he hadn't given her his all, but his pride would not let him admit defeat, instead he knew that leaving would even the emotional burn in her that he held inside. "I can't, I'll call you later."

Hope cried herself to sleep for the first time that night. Chris didn't see sobriety for two days. When he finally picked himself up off the canvas and swallowed his pride, he called Hope. She was very upset over the whole event. Chris knew she was right, he was not an easy man to love and his pride built a wall no one had yet to breach but she tried.

On a Tuesday afternoon Chris met Hope in her upstairs bedroom as she was getting ready for work. Sitting on her bedroom floor leaning back on her queen sized bed he was open and honest for the first time about the daemons that lived inside him. He apologized and admitted his faults. He confessed the lack of trust he held in others, he told of his fear of being susceptible, of letting her have that much control of him. He couldn't explain from where it all came, that was an abyss he refused to even touch on. For the first time reality set in, he knew at that moment, one day she would leave him and it would be his own fault. He would lose his best friend and felt hopeless to stop it. The only question was when. They made their amends and accepted apologies. That afternoon they made love with a passion that hadn't been seen in months. Hope was late for work.

Flashback #3 (First Failure)

As graduation neared, plans were made and families invited. There were five people who worked at the bar and would be accepting their diplomas at the same time. The three other families present would work as a good buffer between Hope's and Chris's. Hers was not particularly fond of him, and other than his mother, Hope knew nothing of his. The day was a near disaster from the beginning. Hope's party arrived early and Chris's late. No one was really to blame but seeing everyone there at the same time was a turning point. At one time Hope had dreams of accepting a proposal and ring at graduation, before both family and friends. When the day came to pass and it didn't happen she was not shocked, yet it still signaled the beginning of the end for her.

Throughout the summer they both had job interviews and scouting trips were made. The move to Austin was thrown out by this point and Hope made plans to accept a position in Dallas moving there with Lacey and Mac. The summer passed without conflict. As the departure date of August first neared, questions began to arise. How would everything go? Could they make a peaceful split? These questions were never discussed but weighed heavily on both of them. Chris was still dancing with indecision and finally refused an offer in Nebraska, choosing to stay behind.

When July 31st came it was a sorry time. There was a going away party for Hope and Lacey which Chris opted to work through. It was an excuse he'd used many times to avoid intense situations. Everyone was out on the town, violating as many laws as they could get away with. When the bar closed, Chris stopped by Hope's townhouse to say farewell. Stepping through the door for the last time seemed eerie. There had been so many memories made in these walls and they were all that was left. Other than the air mattress Hope slept on and a small TV in the living room, the place was empty. Hope rolled over upon hearing him enter. Chris stepped up the four risers from the entryway.

"Hey you how was your night?" she asked, her voice was rough.

"Busy." He replied as he sat down on the edge of the mattress feeling her rise under his hand as he did. "Did you have a good time tonight?"

"I did, everyone was out, we missed you, but I don't feel so good. I'm not sure what I drank but it didn't settle well."

"Is there anything I can do?"

"No, I'm sure I'll sleep it off. I don't have to leave until after noon tomorrow."

Chris took a deep breath, "I hope you get to feeling better."

"Are you going to stay with me tonight?"

Chris avoided her gaze for a long time, "I don't think so. We've drug out a long goodbye for too long already."

"I should have figured you'd walk away, fine." She rolled away from him.

Chris said nothing; he stood and walked out numb. Hope spent her last night in town alone, in tears.

The heartbreak overcame her, and she gave into her illness. The next day, when she was scheduled to leave the state, Hope retired to her mother's house fighting fatigue and a terrible infection. She fought it off over the course of the next week, but it left her frail and dehydrated. Three days in the hospital and she had recovered fully. These events were only revealed weeks later, no one knew of her illness, Chris didn't understand why she chose to remain isolated throughout but when he finally learned it only added weight to the guilt.

While Hope spent her time healing, both physically and emotionally, Chris spent his time moving, settling into a new home, lost in himself wondering why she'd left so silently. Why hadn't she called? In the confusion both parties expected the other to call before the day was done, yet neither could bring themselves to secede.

Over the next few weeks several points were made clear. First, Hope was leaving and wanted nothing to do with him. Second, Chris had made the wrong decision. It was a huge mistake on his part to let her go and he had to live with this.

As the heartache grew, Chris could not take it anymore. On a breezy September afternoon, sitting on the large back porch he called her for the first time in over a month. The phone rang and rang. And rang. The first time he heard her voice after leaving her stranded alone was that of a voicemail message apologizing for not being able to answer her phone. Chris sat on the bench in the shade of an old oak tree staring at his phone. What would he say when she called back, if she called back. How could he tell her he was wrong? Would she believe him? Did he even have a chance, or had she written him off completely?

He could not remember how long he'd sat there underneath the tree, but finally the ring of his phone focused his attention. It was Hope. Chris answered, still not knowing what to say. He couldn't even recall the conversation now but it lasted for over an hour, catching up. Somehow through sheer luck or her foolishness, he was granted a second chance. One week after that first phone call, Chris drove all night to meet Hope in Dallas for the first time. He arrived just before ten in the morning. She met him at the front door outside her apartment. She wore sweat pants and a wrinkled shirt yet he had never seen her look so beautiful. Their embrace was immediate and solid. In no time at all the passion overtook both of them and again they were united. Again and again, that morning they rediscovered each other. At the end of the 72 hour visit Chris pulled away promising to return in two weeks. Through Hope's advice, he chose to settle in Austin with plans of her joining him toward the end of the year. Two months after Hope left the state, Chris followed her south. Everything he couldn't fit into his truck was sold off, and what did fit stacked above cab level He never looked back. He would not return the same man and she would never join him in Austin.

The family, back in Austin, rounded a corner headed off Sixth Street, together again, amongst their friends, the scene seemed surreal to both Chris and Hope. Their past was so distant yet this night drew both of them back to familiar territory. They were now so far from that time and had made so much of themselves since then, that unfortunately, they could never return.

Hope's Apology

"I'm sorry if I was short with you last night. You and I... What happened between you and me, I just haven't thought about any of it in a long time."

Hope's statement caught Chris off guard. He hadn't seen her walk up beside him. He was leaning on the bed of his truck in the parking lot. They all stood outside the hotel. The bars had kicked them out over two hours ago but no one would be able to sleep yet. It was well past four in the morning, the temperature held just above the dew point and the humidity hung heavy in the air, ready to drop. Chris stood with his legs crossed, his back pressed against the bed of his pickup. He spun the beer bottle in his hands several times before looking up. Beyond the beauty that stood beside him he noticed Neal, drunkenly singing along to Rugby's acoustic versions of all their favorite songs that flowed from a slightly out of tune six-string. Kathy had disappeared some time before, searching for food. The herbal hunger crept up inside him as well. Lacey, sitting opposite of Neal joined the others in the chorus. It was a distantly familiar scene. The night was technically morning by this point, but they powered forward.

Chris nodded pondering her statement. "So, I never cross your mind?"

"Of course you do, just not in that sense," she said as softly as possible. "I'm open to talk now, if you still have anything to say."

"There's so much I feel that I need to say, but I don't know what to say. I've searched for so long for a reason to hate you but I always come up short. I never lied to you, I never cheated on you…"

"You also never showed me the love I deserved," Hope interjected seeing where this line of argument was going.

"I loved you, it was there and you knew it."

"That was the problem, Chris; I needed more than just the thought of it."

Chris knew she was right. "I have to walk off this buzz before it puts me to sleep, would you like to see the riverfront?"

"That sounds nice."

Chris tossed his empty bottle into the bed of the truck and pulled two more from the cooler. He opened one and offered it to Hope.

"Thank you," she said taking the cold, glass longneck in her hand.

They walked side by side, both keeping just enough distance between them so as not to accidentally brush against one another. They spoke of family and friends that one or the other hadn't seen in a long time. With such similar families and upbringings they were once a rock for the other to lean on when the trivial conflicts erupted. Many of those battles had long ceased, both were now in better standing with their fathers, which had been one of the initial issues that built the bond between them. It seemed they were both doing well, though Hope held back when Chris asked her about Jon.

"He's a good man, hard worker, you two are very similar, I think you'd like him." She did not discuss the ongoing drama back in Dallas. It was not his business to know.

Chris too left out any details of Marlene. The talk was unusually formal and only skimmed the surface of any topic.

As they rounded back to the hotel from the south side of the river they crossed the bridge on South Congress. The lights on either side, from the capital down South Congress lit up the sky. As they stepped onto the bridge, Chris found the words he'd recited in his mind so many times before. "I know I was wrong. I never should have let you go in the first place. I know you've moved on, you've made something of yourself and I'm very proud of you and the person you have become. I don't want to write you off as an ex. All I want is to close this gap between us. I want to know I still have a friend, like we used to be, before the fights and heartache. I know you can never forget where we've been, but can we focus on where we could go?" Chris's mind was reeling from everything coming up at once. There was a long silence between them. Hope said nothing.

Chris continued, "You were right you know. If we had stayed together neither of us would be in the place we are now, headed down our respective paths. It would all be different; I can't imagine what you'd be like or what I'd be like for that matter."

Hope thought about this for a while. They stopped walking halfway across the bridge and leaned against the railing. "I don't think you could stand being with me all the time. You love the idea of us being together, but when we were at that point you got scared of the commitment. The sacrifices you would have had to make scared you."

"Yeah," he agreed, "but that was a long time ago."

"Do you still feel like there are things you have to do before you can grow up?"

"There will always be things I feel I have to do, it's who I am. I can't yet understand what I don't know and I don't think I will ever grow up, I don't want to."

Hope was surprised at this revelation; this was not the narrow minded man she used to know.

Chris continued, "Even understanding this, my greatest fear still is not being able to find the passion that we've experienced. No one can come close to touching me in the way you did."

"You'll find it someday, if you let yourself," she replied.

Together they stood on that bridge. Hope looked off into the silent distance, the symphony of the city fading away. "You know there was a time when I would have followed you anywhere."

"I know," Chris agreed with a long pause, "but at the time I was young. I wasn't able to see far enough ahead to understand what exactly that meant. I didn't know what I really wanted stepping out into a new world. To a degree I still don't know." He emptied the bottle he held into the river below, wound back and threw it as far as he could downstream. "Did you know there was a time when I would have married you in a heartbeat?" From the left breast pocket inside his jacket he pulled a ring, a single princess cut diamond set in platinum. "I've carried this with me since I first moved down here. I hoped that you would wear it someday. Now it's just dead weight in my pocket."

Hope smiled; the gesture was noble and flattering, but too late. "Only after you saw that I was capable of leaving you behind."

"Sometimes it takes losing everything to realize what you're doing wrong. And I was stubborn enough that it took those kinds of extreme conditions for me to see what I was doing wrong. My pride hurt you, I never meant for things to go down the way they did, I'm sorry for that."

"Thank you, but I think we're both better off in the big picture. That doesn't mean the passion we had was any less real but it wasn't the right path for both of us."

"Even if I walked the straight and narrow, eventually I'd still lose you."

Hope nodded, saying nothing.

For a long while they stood together in silence letting the night sink in. Hope yawned giving into exhaustion. "I think it's time to turn in, the sun should be up before long. Would you like to walk me to my room?"

Chris smiled, not yet able to surrender to the night. "Go ahead, I can see you all the way in from here. If you need anything just holler."

Hope gave him a hug and a small kiss on his right cheek.

With that, she was gone. Chris stayed, leaning on the railing watching the river pass below, a million diamonds floating in the lunar light, rolling to their own rhythm and song, while he stared at the rock in his hand.

His mind raced. For years he had run scenarios through his head, what would happen if he had his chance to catch up. Would he make peace or pick a fight? Tonight he made peace; there was nothing to fight for anymore. They were different people. Hope had grown into a respectable woman; she had a good thing going for her. Chris refused to accept the fact that some of his greatest days were behind him, he had always looked forward to the bigger and better, more fulfilling things in life but it seems that this chapter had finally drawn to a close. It was time to move on. Still, she was unique to him. Hope was the only woman he had ever let into his unique world of passion and creativity. She understood him unlike anyone else, and for that she would always be closer to her than anyone else.

The Turning Away

Everyone was gone by the time Hope returned to the parking lot outside the hotel. She and Chris had been out for a while. She walked silently down the hall to her room, thoughts of the night and her dilemma back in Dallas hung heavy on her mind. Unlocking the door she strolled over to the drapes. She grasped each side and began to pull them shut but Chris caught her eye. He remained where she left him, leaning on the edge of the bridge below. He was staring at something. She assumed the ring in his hand must be the focus of his attention. Suddenly he stood and reached back, his shoulder cocked to throw the thing away, but Hope drew the curtains closed before he could throw it into the river, she couldn't stand to watch.

Back to Dallas

~

As soon as Hope crawled out of bed the next morning she immediately rushed to the window and threw open the drapes looking directly down toward the bridge. Chris had been standing midway on the downstream side when she last saw him the night before, she half expected to see him still standing there. 'No,' Hope thought, 'of course he was gone.' It was late in the morning, breakfast in the dining room on the ground floor had already been cleared. She didn't know it, but Chris was already halfway home by now, he hadn't slept at all.

Hope dressed and packed quickly. She knocked on the door across the hall but Kathy and Neal were gone, she'd missed them. Being up so late the night before, she'd awaken much later than expected; it seemed she missed everyone but her passenger, Lacey.

As she thought of the tiny dancer, her blonde friend came bouncing down the hallway while Hope was gathering her bags outside her door. "Hey lady, let me grab that one for you," she said reaching for the pull-along. "So, two nights in a row out with the ex, when's the wedding?"

"Never, don't worry about it," Hope replied giving Lacey a disgusting look.

"Oh, c'mon, give me the dirty on last night. What time did you get in?"

Hope gazed at Lacey from the corner of her eye, "There's no 'dirty' about it. We talked, settled some old issues, walked up and down the river, you know, catching up."

"Let me guess, he's still in love with you?"

"Yeah, well it's not that simple. I think he understands now, he took it to heart. Tough love has created more devotion in that man than affection ever could. Whatever he does, he gives everything he's got. Unfortunately, only now have I become the focus in his crosshairs. Somehow I think it's the exact opposite with Jon. He's become a workaholic. Engineering seems to be his priority now. How do I find myself so lucky?"

"I know what's going through your mind, and it's not your fault."

"I know it's not my fault," she said shortly, "This isn't my first battle with a man. I just don't know what's going on. He's more distant now than ever."

"Well, if you need anything, just call, I'm always looking for an excuse to come visit."

The girls stepped off the elevator and through the lobby. Hope's car was just pulling up with a valet behind the wheel. They loaded their bags and climbed in. Rolling across the upper deck, headed north on 35 out of Austin, neither girl said anything until they were more than an hour from the hotel.

The 200 mile drive back to Dallas were the three most grueling hours on any interstate in the nation. The traffic made for a good distraction, there were no breaks the whole way and the roadwork was hell. Just before the 35 east/west split south of the Dallas/Fort Worth metro area, Hope thought of Chris and how envious she was of the open road carrying him home. Damn, why was he still on her mind. The way he spoke of it all last night, she wondered what it was like. He had painted such a beautiful picture, his passion for the Studio impressed her.

Back to the Studio

Chris was several hours out of the hill country and flying across the plateau of West Texas. He put the hammer down. His mind sat peaceful, enjoying the wind blowing in from the open windows. His spirit floated with a lightness and freedom he had long forgotten. His smile came with more ease, like that of a young child who just discovered the opportunity the world offered before him. Things had not worked out in Austin the way he'd thought they would or the way he wanted, they rarely did with regards to Hope, but he understood. The Rolling Stones were wailing over the rush of the morning air.

"You can't always get what you want," echoed the lyrics of Mick Jager. The irony amused Chris, *"but sometimes, you might find, you get what you need."* It was the acumen of a true poet.

Chris mounted the hill just outside of the Studio shortly after high noon as his Shangri-La shimmered in the distance, the old mill still loped at an uneven pace in the breeze. The new windmill just off to the south gracefully rotated, cutting silently through the air. It worked to keep the Studio off the electrical grid.

Ramone had taken to the technology surprisingly quickly. He was now quite efficient at maintaining all of the integrated electronics on the property. In another life Ramone may have been a brilliant engineer. In this life though, the simplicity of the ranch kept his spirit at peace, Chris understood why now. Ramone and his family would do a wonderful job of caring for the Studio when he was gone.

Hope's Burning

Traffic was at a standstill on I-35 East. The journey north through the city had been fine, Lacey made her flight with plenty of time to spare. The trip back south though had become congested from the moment Hope turned off G.W.B. toll road back onto the Interstate. She was stuck in traffic for almost an hour now, but her exit was in sight. Slowly the car crept forward another couple feet. She checked her phone for what seemed like the hundredth time. Her hands were shaking with frustration, between the traffic and the unknown situation at home. Hope sat on the brink of a major breakdown. Starring at her phone she pressed the speed dial for Jon's cell so hard her thumbnail turned white and held the button a little longer than needed as if force him to notice it and answer. The seconds ticked by waiting an eternity for the line to connect. Finally it rang once, twice, three times and again no answer. It felt like a lead brick dropped in the pit of her stomach. His phone was on, it took long enough to ring through, was he ignoring her? The car crawled three feet closer to the exit she so wished she could speed down this instant. The clouds overhead had grown progressively darker since she'd left Lacey outside the airport. By the time her tires crossed the white line to pull off and rocket down the ramp, the drops began to fall. The impending storm put on quite the show of light and sound. She could feel the percussion of the thunder above, rattling all of her senses.

The deluge began as she parked just across the street, the run inside would be a short one. The luggage could wait until later. Hope gave her phone one last look and darted from her car. She made a feeble attempt to divert the bombardment of drops with a book but it did little to help her stay dry. Halfway across the street she surrendered to the monsoons and looked up to the apartment she shared with Jon. There were no lights on but the curtains stood open, which was odd, she'd closed them, she always closed them when no one was home. Was Jon home? There was no light coming from inside as the clouds overhead drowned out the late afternoon sun. Standing in the street a passing car sprayed water across her legs. She quickly ran to the door of her building. She hit the lobby at full stride leaping across the threshold and stopping to shake off what she could. Her hair was dripping and the shirt she wore stuck to her body. The man behind the front desk offered her a towel as she passed. "Thanks, Mike," she said grateful for the gift. As Hope climbed the five flights of stairs she toweled her face. Entering the hallway that led to her apartment, she tossed the towel over her shoulder and dug in her purse to find her keys.

Just inside the door Jon sat on a small bench beside the dining table between the door and the kitchen. When Hope came in he did not stand, he did not make a move. She did not notice him at first but with the flick of a lamp between them his figure lit up and Hope jumped back, startled, her temper flared almost immediately. Her purse dropped to the floor as she could feel the blood rush up to her face, she was pissed. Momentarily taken aback by the surprise, she didn't know what to say first. She knew what she wanted to say, but she bit her tongue to save the inevitable fight for later.

Jon made no motion to initiate anything either. She stared at him, he stared at the floor. Just as Hope could no longer hold back, he spoke up. "How was your trip?" came from his lips as his eyes finally rose to meet hers.

"Where have you been?" she asked ignoring the question. "Is your phone broken? Did you forget how to use it? I've called and called. I seriously thought you might be dead," she stated as her brow began to roll together in anger.

"I'm sorry, I was busy."

"Sorry?! Four days Jon, four days! I seriously thought you might be dead! You couldn't even call to put my mind at ease. When you didn't come home the other night, I didn't know what to think. Where have you been?"

Jon's breath was heavy, she could see his shoulders rise under the suit jacket, "I've been thinking, a lot."

Hope could see it coming, fate had a horrible sense of humor and she knew it. "Thinking about what, Jon?"

"About us, about what we're doing and where we're going with all this."

"So have I. I don't know where you are anymore." She stepped over to him and knelt on the floor in front of him taking his hands in hers. "What's wrong, Jon?"

Jon gathered himself, he sat up straight and looked her in the eye and his gaze did not waver. "I'm not here, that's where I'm at. I'm sorry, Hope, but I'm leaving. I've already made the arrangements; I'll have my stuff out by Monday morning."

With that said he stood, picked his keys up from the table behind him and walked out silently stepping around the distraught and confused woman on the floor. When the door clicked shut, Hope was frozen kneeling on the ground. She could not move. The rain and shadows were her only companions. Hope remained there, until the few tears she allowed to fall ceased and she found the energy to stand. Nettle, her cat, sat in the window behind her watching intently.

When Hope finally gathered herself and stood, she would have to face this empty apartment filled with all the things they had gathered together. Pictures, reminders, beacons, waypoints through their years together, they all looked down on her. As time passed so did the rain.

When she had gained control of herself Hope stood and walked straight to the bed they shared. From the closet in their room, she pulled out a large case and slowly filled it with the things she wished to keep. There were photos of her family, trinkets and gifts from friends and an old shoe box buried in the back of a dresser drawer. It held pictures and letters from years ago. They all had Chris's fingerprints on them, and she could not part with them. Everything went into the case. When it looked like it could hold no more, she zipped it closed. Nettle followed her around the apartment the entire time as she made laps selecting what to take and what to leave. Hope stepped across the hall to leave the cat with the elderly woman who lived there. She often watched after the feline while Hope was out of town. With her last pass through the bedroom, she opened the bedroom window, the small breeze left from the storm made the curtains dance before her. On a small table below the window sat a candle; she lit it, pushed it just under the edge of the window and turned away.

Hope grabbed her one piece of luggage, threw her purse on top and headed out. As her car slowly pulled away from the curb, smoke began to pour out the open window five floors above her. Inside the apartment flames quickly consumed the window coverings easily spilling over to the bedding and bedroom set. From room to room the fire grew. Pictures bubbled in the intense heat and furniture fed the blaze. Everything she no longer wanted or needed was reduced to ash. When Hope passed the city limit sign, the fire department was just getting the blaze under control; there would be nothing they could salvage from the scene.

Through Fort Worth and on to I-20 Hope knew why she was going west. She knew he would understand. She hoped he would be there. Chris always understood, whether he agreed or not, he understood. She needed a friend right now, if she could remember the name of that town.

Flashback #4 (4th of July)

Sometime after dark had fully set in, Hope slowed to a crawl in Sweetwater. Just past the city limit sign, there was a large, cantilever, neon sign encroaching on the edge of the road, half burnt out, half flickering, fighting against the streetlights, that announced the presence of a dirt drive to a motel ahead. She pushed the turn signal up and rolled over the right shoulder of the road, the wheels one by one slipping off the pavement grinding the gravel beneath them as they did. The car sat idling while Hope walked to the office window. The attendant, an elderly woman, rather tall, answered the bell. She had to have come straight from a '50's lifestyle magazine. There was not a hair out of place and her apron seemed so cliché Hope caught a sweet giggle at her appearance. Her beauty was eternal and her heavy drawl comforting as she counted back the change. If it had been anyone else behind the window, Hope may have slept with one eye open, but she had no worry with Aunt Bea watching over her. Hope returned to her car to grab only the two bags she needed.

With her hands full, she bumped the door open to survey the small, quaint room. It was definitely dated from the same era as Aunt Bea down in the office, but it was well cared for and immaculately clean, thank God. Hope unpacked, laying out her clothes for the next day, a tank top would suffice; the heat was legendary out here. Besides, to dress for an impression would be uncalled for. Taking her goodies from the suitcase, Hope strolled over to the sink, flipped on the vanity lights, causing a bulb to burn out in a bright burst, only three remained. She pulled her hair back and washed her face rinsing layers of sweat and tears down the drain. Drying herself she walked to window surveying the scene. Her car stood away from the few others scattered out front of the roadside establishment, staring back at her. Even the Pontiac seemed to be questioning her motives.

Standing in the window, the sharp lights from an all-night truck stop across the highway reassured her as a nightlight would a small child. Staring into the lights, at nothing in particular, a small streak through the night sky caught her eye. Moments later a bright flash burst through drowning out the stars behind it. The brilliant pattern radiated out in all directions. Hope couldn't recall passing any billboard or signs announcing a celebration. Was the fair in town? Maybe they were celebrating a regional holiday or maybe some locals were letting loose, trying to blow off the day's heat and stress. It was almost Friday, is that not reason enough for a celebration? Another shell burst in the air, not as brilliant this time, but the colors were still beautiful against the black curtain of night. The second shell was closely followed by a third and fourth. These people where proud about their show. As the artillery shells continued increasing in number, spewing strontium carbonate into the atmosphere they could not drown out her heavy memories.

Fireworks and the Fourth of July where always a nostalgic time for Hope, though it had been a long time since they induced this intense of a reaction. It was that all-American holiday, years ago that ultimately led her here, to a motel, in West Texas chasing an old flame. That fateful holiday had brought them together. It was a situation both she and Chris would walk away from as completely different people in their own rights.

A phone call woke her that morning, seven years ago, just before noon. It was a holiday, she could sleep in. The phone screamed again. Hope opened her eyes to the shadows of an oak tree filtering through the window her bed laid below. It was nothing out of the ordinary for the wind to blow in any part of Kansas. The phone went off again. Hope threw the down comforter to the side, she was drenched. Again, the phone announced its presence. Rolling to the edge of the bed she reached down to the floor pulling her purse up beside her. It took some digging but buried under pens, a wallet, gum and a pack of smokes she found it. The caller ID said, Chris. Hope answered it just before it kicked to voicemail.

"Hello?" she asked still not fully awake.

"Hey, what time are you coming out?" Chris asked with the fever of impatience in his voice. He was wound up already she could tell.

"I don't know. I have to call Lacey, why, what's up?"

Chris gave a small laugh leading into what was sure to be a nonsensical ramble. "Well, it seems that I have some issues with my ceiling. Apparently there is a leak in the roof. It's been there for a while as far as I can tell but last night's storm broke the camel's back. I woke up this morning and half a sheet of gyp board had fallen down. It's soggy all around it so I know it's been saturated for a while now. I'm not going to call the landlord on a holiday, so I was wondering if you could go by the store and find something to cover the hole before everyone gets out here."

Hope tried to imagine this in her sleep riddled mind. "Wait, your ceiling fell in?"

"Only a small part of it, a four-by-four foot piece, but now I have this big hole and I need something to cover it up. Do you think you can find something for me? I'll pay you back when you get here."

"Yeah, we have to stop by and grab a few things before we come out anyway, I'll see what I can find."

"Great I have to go, call me if you have any questions."

Hope hung up and rolled over on her side. She could just imagine that run down, two bedroom house, now with a hole in the ceiling. It only seemed fitting.

Chris lived five miles out of town in one of the most run down houses she'd ever seen. The landlord should be turned in as a slumlord, but Chris seemed to enjoy it. You could trash that entire place and not lose all of your deposit. It sat just off the four lane highway exiting south of town. The drive way paralleled the highway for almost a quarter mile before terminating right in front of the detached garage. The house itself was buried in the vegetation of a small creek that ran between it and the steep ridge above, only thirty yards out the back door. The green siding allowed it to almost disappear from the view of any passing vehicles. There was not much room inside but plenty outside. It was a seasonal retreat for anyone who knew him.

There were many great occasions for everyone to gather out there but the Fourth of July was unique for Chris. He had been planning this celebration for almost a month now and anyone who knew better did not go home for this holiday. There would be friends, food, fireworks. Hope stretched, squirming in bed thinking of how Chris seemed to work more than party on occasions such as this but that was his business, she would be there soon enough and it would be a day of relaxation.

Hope rolled back to the edge and brought her phone up to see through her blurry eyes, found Lacey's phone number and hit dial. It was hot in her bedroom. Why could they not agree on a setting for the A/C? The line rang twice before the tiny dancer picked up.

"Hey! What are you doing?" came Lacey's greeting from the phone, which was now simply lying across the side of her face.

Hope was not surprised with her energetic greeting. If this woman were ever on any kind of stimulant it would kill her. "I'm lying in bed."

"Well, get up, I have to run to the store before we can leave." Lacey was always rearing to go but typically the last to leave.

"I know. What do you have to pick up?"

Lacey gave a long pause, "I'm thinking about picking up a watermelon. What are you taking?"

"I don't know yet, I'll find something when we get there. Are you ready to go?" Hope asked knowing full well what the answer would be.

"Not quite, I have to get the dog inside, then put on my face and get dressed. I'll be there in half an hour. How does that sound for you?"

Hope was still lying in bed, yet she knew she would end up waiting on her dear friend. "Sure, I'll be here."

They gave their adieus and hung up. Hope slid out of bed and stripped down on her way to the shower. She shaved, washed her hair, brushed her teeth, and clocked the usual mirror time before she was ready to go. An hour had passed since she had spoken with Lacey. Now seated on the curb in front of her townhouse Hope wondered just how long she would have to wait. Surprisingly, just as that thought passed, Lacey's car slid around the corner and ground to a stop right in front of her.

Lacey sat in the driver's seat, pulling her shades down slightly, yelling out the passenger side window, "We're burning daylight, and my beer's getting warm!"

Of course she was always on her own schedule and when it was time to go, according to Lacey, it was time to go. Hope stood and brushed off her shorts, "Okay, one stop at the supermarket and we're out of here."

They rolled through town, windows down, stereo up, singing along. They got rock star parking at the store, front row. Walking inside Hope grabbed onto a cart and pulled a right as soon as they made it in the door. First stop was produce, Lacey picked out several melons opting for a fruit salad, while Hope walked ahead leading the way, looking for posters. Rounding out of the craft aisle they found the stand. There were posters of the current pop icons and cartoon characters. Unrolling one to gauge its size Lacey joked, "Maybe we should get him one with Kelly Clarkson on it, he'd like that."

Hope laughed along, "I don't think that would be up very long. Good try though." Having unrolled a nice scene of some Disney teen, Hope realized that a poster would not be big enough. They rolled it up and tried to stuff it back into the slot from which it came without much success. As they searched the rest of the store aisle by aisle Lacey mentioned, "You know, when I start feeling badly about myself, I just come here. Seeing the cross section of folks who usually occupy this store, I feel so much better walking out."

Hope chuckled, agreeing with her observation, she replied sarcastically, "I know, I'm glad we're so perfect we can sit here and judge everyone else."

Halfway through the homeware department Hope came across some large flags. She opened one and laid it out across the cart. "This is the biggest one they have, it should fit." Lacey consented noting the king sized flag laid out in front of her. With all their goods accumulated, the pair made for the checkout lanes. Expecting the worse Lacey grabbed for a coke on the way. As they emerged from the maze of shelves their worst assumptions proved true. The lines were backed across the four open lanes.

"Great," Lacey exclaimed, "and I'm sure they have the 'A-Team' on staff with today being a holiday and all." Despite the impending frustration, Hope smiled. Today was going to be a good day.

Flashback #4 (The Feast)

It was just shy of an hour and half since they'd left Hope's when the pair turned off the highway onto the narrow drive coasting down past the trees to Chris's 'Jed Clampett' style shack. Halfway down the drive, the prestigious resident came walking out of the garage with no shirt, wearing sandals and cutoff hunting pants. Hope noted, "He can be a real class act sometimes."

"Oh, I'm sure he's having the time of his life right now," Lacey added.

Chris met the girls as they parked and climbed out of the car grabbing what they could. "Afternoon ladies, can I interest either of you in a beer bong?" He held the funnel and tube combination up to draw their attention.

"Not, just, yet... I think we need to get everything unloaded and settled in before we get on the power drinking." Hope gracefully declined; the feeling was mutual amongst both of them. Lacey took all of the drinks into the garage while Hope moved the food and rest of the goods into the house. Stepping in the back door the smell of everything cooking overtook her. It was sweet, savory, sour, it attacked all the senses. The scene was overwhelming. There were five people in a kitchen built for no more than one and a half men. Pots were scattered amongst the stove and surrounding counters. Trays of finger food covered the dining room table and freezer by the back door. Hope took it all in wondering how such amazing food came from four drunk men in a half assed kitchen, but it worked out every time. She made her way to the fridge. It was stuffed already. Trying to get all the fruit in was a puzzle in itself. Thankfully Rugby came to the rescue. "Here, Hope, let me clear some room on the table, and we can cut all that up right now." Saving her the effort, she kicked the fridge shut and set everything on the table. Knowing better than to get in the way in this kitchen, Hope thanked Rugby and Neal for taking care of it all and headed back to the garage. Stepping out onto the weather beaten back porch Duke, Chris's dog, came rounding the back corner of the garage headed straight for the porch and eventually the storm door. Hope, seeing the impending disaster inside slammed the door shut. Duke leapt all three steps at once and slid to a stop across the turf covering the rotted deck of the porch. He eyeballed the door, then Hope, back to the door and back to Hope. Not understanding the why, the dog turned tail and walked back down the steps to join the crowd in the garage, Hope followed suit.

Walking to the garage-turned-drinking-establishment, Hope passed the grill, just heating up beneath the carport, and strolled in through the side door closest to the house. Inside, fans blew trying to keep everyone cool in the humid atmosphere of July. Chris stood by the beer fridge, Will sat at the table with a girl she did not know, and Wendy and Lacey occupied two stools along the length of the bar. Hope picked up her mug; it was oversized to minimize the number of trips to the fridge for refills and bright orange, she didn't want to lose it either. She made her way around the bar to the fridge and there in the freezer labeled 'devil's door' lay her handle of bourbon. Hope filled the mug with ice and went for just a few shots on the first round. Shutting the doors she took up the stool behind the bar facing the girls. "Lacey, can you hand me the coke?"

Wendy got a quizzical look on her face, "I didn't think you drank coke?"

"I don't drink coke, unless there's whiskey in it."

Chris gave her a pat on the back as he shook his head walking off.

With everything secured, the girls settled into catching up, gossiping, and waiting on the food. Chips held off starvation until the grill was hot enough. When the smoke was rolling white the first of several appetizers went on, followed by the main course, Kabobs, along with all the barbecue staples. All said and done, they had a veritable smorgasbord. A few at a time everyone took their turn serving themselves as piece after piece came off the grill. It may have taken a few hours, but by the time everyone had finished almost everything was gone. It made clean up easy. Since the guys cooked the ladies volunteered to clean up, this took all of half an hour.

When everyone had settled in after the early dinner, they broke out the cards and board games. Lacey was all over it. You didn't get in the way of Lacey and games, whether there was drinking involved or not, she was the queen. By now there had to be over two dozen of Hope's closest friends and several others she'd just met that afternoon. It was a good afternoon.

Flashback #4 (The Accident)

As the day passed and the sun began to near the horizon across the four-lane highway and the heat faded with it, talk began to circulate about heading down to the river. There was a shallow crossing several miles from the house. It was an easy drive down five miles of a snaking gravel road. When the debate concluded, half the party elected to go while the others would stay behind awaiting guests who hadn't arrived yet. With volunteers in line to drive, everyone picked a vehicle; there would be four in all making the drive. Chris called shotgun, picking out the second in line, Will's truck. Will drove with Brett squeezing his 220 pound frame in the extended cab behind the passenger seat and Duke rode in the bed. Lacey, Hope, Rugby, and Bobby were in the lead car with two other vehicles following Will. The caravan pulled away and out onto the highway a few hours before sundown promising to return for the fireworks as soon as it got dark. There was only a half mile of highway to traverse before turning off onto the gravel snake. As they made the turn one by one, Will floored the accelerator and slung past Lacey's car. Taking the lead he hauled down the road kicking up dust losing sight of everyone behind them. Hope, riding now in second place tried to make out the stretch ahead through the dust hanging in front of them. As Will pulled away further and further the cloud began to clear and the visibility allowed them to get up to speed, but in no way keeping up with leader.

Rounding the first turn in the road Chris, riding passenger in the bullet, decided it would be a good idea to strap himself in. The truck, loaded down with the three friends and one dog, sped along another mile or so when everything flew out of control. On the far side of a small hill just tall enough to block the oncoming view was a turn a little sharper than Will had expected. Flying over the hill, with the turn just coming into view Will eased off the gas and gently pressed the brake not wanting to skid the truck into the ditch. They had nearly made it out of the curve when the turn became too sharp and the rear wheels lost their grip sliding the back end into the ditch, Will turned into the slide attempting to rotate the vehicle. The result of saving the slide was a vicious veer toward the far side of the road. On his toes, holding his breath, Will over-corrected the steering. The adjustment was too much and the truck dove violently into the ditch. Chris and Brett braced for the worst. As they settled into the channel alongside the road, with the speed now below 70, Chris could catch a few breaths calling out obstacles as he saw them. Ahead there laid a culvert that spanned the gully, reinforced by large limestone boulders. They couldn't steer out, for fear of rolling, so all three held on for what would be one wild ride. Chris watched the whole way in, everything slowing down as the truck slammed into the obstruction. Airbags inflated; there was nothing but sky out the front window. As they rotated end over end the ground came into view and slammed through the windshield. At this point Chris could take no more and shut it all out.

Flashback #4 (The Fear)

The view for the tailing vehicles had cleared sufficiently, though they did not know just how far ahead the lead truck had gotten. As Lacey's car mounted one of the many hills along the way, Rugby noticed the tracks that crossed the road in front of them. He sat up from the back seat leaning between the ladies occupying the front seats. Ahead just as the haze was clearing, he saw the truck; it was mid flip, which in that instant, looked to be spinning on its nose. Rugby couldn't believe what he saw. Yelling out he pointed to the vehicle as it slammed down landing on its wheels. The yell caught Lacey's attention. As she looked down the road, her foot slammed on the brake pedal to avoid running over Duke, standing in the middle of the road. When the car slid to a stop everyone jumped out, Lacey was headed to pick up the stunned dog, that didn't seem to realize what had just happened. Hope and Rugby ran the short sprint to the twisted pile of metal that sat steaming before them. As Hope drew closer, she saw the full extent of the damage. The nose of the Ford was crushed in, the front passenger tire was gone and the rim was crushed. The cab was folded in on the passenger side but the windshield was intact, crushed but hanging on. The bed was bent in relation to the rest of the vehicle and folded in on itself. Rugby surveyed the damage and jumped into the bed of the truck to check on Brett as Hope came up to the passenger side of the cab.

The scene was surreal. The dirt was just settling in the air giving the entire scene a foggy aspect that only enhanced the effect. When she finally got to the door, the metal that had folded and wrinkled like cloth felt as solid as ever under her hands. The door was wedged shut, not budging. Everything it seemed was covered in glass and dirt. Inside the cab Brett was making his way out of the rear window with Rugby's assistance. Will was sprawled out across the front seat with his head in Chris' lap. Both men were dazed and confused.

"Oh my god! Are you guys okay?" Hope asked, the fear showing in her voice.

Chris shook his head checking what joints he could. "Yeah… I think so." He gave himself a once over and when it all seemed functional he turned to Will. Bracing the driver's head in his hands Chris looked him in the eye, "Will… Will, look at me. Are you okay? Can you move?"

Will pried his eyes open and rolled his head from side to side, coughing in the dusty atmosphere, "Yeah, I think I'm good."

"Can you move? Can you get up?"

Will groaned as he rolled onto his side pushing himself up. "Yeah, I can move."

Chris coached him out the window. "Okay, look can you crawl out the window here? Easy, easy, just take your time."

When everyone had gathered around the truck, Brett had made his way out the back window and joined in the effort to help Will through the narrowed passenger side window. With Will safely standing outside, Chris unbuckled his seatbelt taking in the scene around him. The windshield was the only glass left in the truck, but he could barely see through the spider web fractures that stretched across it. The airbags hung limp from the dash. The rearview mirror was gone. The roof of the cab sat barely an inch above his head and angled sharply down to the dash. Dirt covered everything, including himself. With a few deep breaths Chris pulled himself out the passenger window stopping halfway and sat on the edge of the door to survey the exterior. It was a nasty looking scene. With Rugby and Neal behind him, Chris fell back and slid the rest of the way out of the mangled remains of the vehicle.

Hope gave him a once over looking for wounds. Deciding he was free of any major injury, she gave him a hug and brushed some of the glass out of his hair. Chris was usually calm under intense situations but his mind could not catch up with what had just happened. He let go of Hope, "is everyone else fine?"

Looking up at him, "Yeah, everyone's okay, Duke is in Lacey's car," She said reassuring him.

Everyone speculated on what to do next. Neal proposed that they all pack in the three remaining vehicles and head back to the house.

"No, no, we can't do that," Chris rejected, "we can't leave the scene."

Lacey spoke up, "You can't, but we can and we have several liabilities here." Kathy agreed with her. They were right. It was best that those not involved get away before someone showed up.

"Look," Chris directed, "take the dog and get him and Brett back home. We're all fine. There's no need in filling up the police report with ten versions of the same story. I'll stay here with Will until the cops get here, everyone else get out of here. I'll call you when we're done with the police."

Everyone agreed and loaded back up as Chris headed up the road to find the driver.

Hope returned to the small green house with everyone else. Brett and the dog were attended to. There were a few bruises and some scratches on both but nothing they wouldn't walk away from. In time Brett decided to call it a night, and Hope volunteered to drive him back into town. As he was saying farewell, her phone rang. Chris's voice came from the other end of the line "Is everything okay?" she questioned.

"Yeah, we're at the ER. Can you come in and get me? I'm in serious need of a beer and a smoke," he spoke into the lobby phone of the hospital.

"Sure, I'll be right there. I'm going to take Brett into his house, he just wants to go home," she replied.

"No problem, I'll be waiting outside."

As the last few rays of light rolled over the horizon, Hope pulled up driving Lacey's Monte Carlo. She was by herself having just dropped Brett off. Chris stood and slowly walked over to the car. Settled in the passenger seat, Hope gave him the sweetest hello. Laying his head back against the seat he lit the cigarette and took a long draw. "Holy shit, that was insane." The weight of everything just hit him at once. A tear built in his eye but failed to fall. Watching out the window the whole way home, nothing was said. The trees passed silently, their silhouette against the indigo sky flying by. Hope left the radio off, just in case Chris had anything he wanted to say, but he said nothing. Over and over in her mind the scene replayed. She knew it was the best that could have been done given the circumstances, but the sheer recklessness of it all had seemed to change something in Chris. He and Will would never be as close again as they had before that evening.

By the time the car pulled off the four lanes that stretched out in front of his house, Chris had finished his beer and asked for another smoke. Hope pulled the car up to the garage and parked right beside the house. She stepped out and caught the scene inside. Everyone she wanted to see was here, except Brett, but she wanted to have Chris to herself right now. She watched as he walked straight to the devil's door and filled his hands with cold cans trying to play catch up. Everyone had survived and hopefully learned something from the whole deal so it was a good day. Seated at the bar Rugby pulled up a stool next to him while Hope took a seat on the opposing side.

"Man I'm glad you're alright," Rugby noted.

"Me too," Chris said with a sip from the can in his hand. "Thanks for all your help, now let's tie one on."

"I agree," Rugby chimed, "Salute." They both had a smile on their face, tonight would be a good night. Looking over to him her smile grew. It was very comforting to have her closest friends here. They talked about what they had seen and how everything had gone down. Chris had to tell the story a few dozen times that night, always adding a twist to lighten the mood whenever he could.

The rest of the night passed without event. Everything was as it should be, just friends living without a care in the world. Once during the show of explosions in the sky Hope, looking for a seat, sat with Chris in the driveway, friends on either side of them. She leaned back and put her arm around him, he was comfortable. Together there, everyone else was drowned out by her dreams. That evening had been shocking and now, coupled as they always were, something was different and she could feel it in her soul.

Flashback #4 (The Confession)

Eventually the cars began to fade away as so did the guests. Chris saw everyone off as they left. When it came time, Lacey decided that she was headed home and Rugby was along for the ride. Hope wasn't quite ready to leave yet; she didn't really want to leave at all. She told them to leave without her; she would stay and help clean up. Rugby went to town for the night with Lacey, anticipating the situation. They were the last two to depart. Hope and Chris stood in the driveway watching the taillights fade in the distance. They turned and walked side by side through the yard toward the back door. Sliding her exposed toes through the dew laden grass as they strolled in the night, Chris put his arm around her, "Thanks for staying; I don't think I want to be alone tonight."

Hope led the way up the rear steps taking them one by one. The porch light burning brightly was a beacon for every insect within sight. The little pests had taken over the door and light alike, peppering the glass. Hope was the first to reach the storm door holding back the invasion of insects. She quickly swung it open as Chris stepped past her and she followed closely behind. Chris traversed the chairs scattered about the dining room, through to the kitchen. He leaned over the sink and splashed cold water over his face. Pulling a towel from a drawer next to his right knee he wiped himself dry. Hope stood only a few paces inside the back door watching his movements. Standing there, her bare feet rubbing the linoleum feeling the lines and grooves under her soles, her heart was racing, could she do this? If she laid herself out there, it would change everything. 'I have to,' she thought.

Chris stood and walked back toward Hope standing on the far side of the room. "Hope, is everything alright?" He asked noticing her sudden silence and lack of movement. She stood there, curvaceous and beautiful. "Hope?" he asked again.

"Chris... seeing that truck when we came over the hill today, I thought you were dead." Her voice shook, as she reached out and put her arms around him. "It really scared me."

Chris returned the physical attention and reassured her, "It's okay, everyone is fine."

"No, you don't understand." She looked up into his smoky blue eyes as he focused in on her. "I can't lose you; I don't know what I would do. I can't wake up tomorrow without you knowing how I feel." She'd said it. Putting herself out there was one of the scariest things she'd ever done. For just one second she thought the whole thing would be a bust as Chris didn't respond.

Standing there in each other's arms, Chris leaned in and kissed her not saying a word. Her spirit flew, the world was spinning and her heart no longer belonged to her alone. They stood there in an embrace neither had felt before. The cushion of his kiss hung on her lips. Her veins pulsed with adrenaline, the rush of honesty in a new love. The world outside faded away as both gathered themselves neither knowing of how to proceed but eager to see what track it would put them on.

Together, two people, two friends, two lovers crossing a bridge from which they could never return. Hope was lost, entranced by his body surrounding hers. The night was late, the day had been a long one and yet she had never felt so exhilarated. Neither one could bring themselves to call it a night. For all the highs and lows, laughter and tears, it was a good day. From this point on, from that moment, once they let go everything would change. It would be a benchmark from which time would be judged for years to come.

Outside the early morning air permeated the screens, the sweet hum of summertime serenading the new couple. The breeze felt heavy on her skin. Chris felt gritty from all the dirt ripped from the ground earlier. There where speckles of glass shimmering in his hair. Hope reached up to brush out what she could. They both laughed and her fingers slid through the short sandy hair that was kept to a fingers length. Chris reached back and pulled the band letting her ponytail down and Hope shook her head free of the tension. Tucking the left side behind her ear he kissed her again and again. His sweetness surprised her. He had always been kind and caring but she had never thought he could be so gentle. The softness of his lips that searched her from neck to ear and back around to her own lips calmed Hope's nerves and excited her at the same time. She buried her head in his chest as he tightened his embrace; Hope let the security she felt in his arms wash over her. For now, all was right.

Slowly the young pair made their way through the house never allowing their bodies to part. Together they slipped across the floor, bumping from chair to table to doorway. Piece by piece, taking turns, they stripped each other of the clothes that separated them, leaving a trail of forgotten garments strewn through room after room. Eventually, through the kissing and petting, they made it to the shower. The water was barely warm to the touch spraying from the head, Chris reached up and adjusted the direction to better suit two occupants. As he stepped through the sheets of water, Hope watched the dirt and grime cascade down the back of his neck and over his shoulders. The flow traced the left side of his back rippling as it flowed from one muscle to the next. Watching him she found her voice gone. When it was to his liking Chris turned and offered his hand to help her step in. Hope took it, joining him, pressing her skin on his. This new sensation excited her. They stood under the shower washing off the day's stresses and past inhibitions. His hands ran up and down her back causing her to flex, pressing her breasts against him. This thrilled him and she could feel the anticipation building. Hope knew that her mascara would run and with her hair matted and wet now she could only imagine what a sight she made, but it didn't matter. She ran her hand up his arm and neck, grabbing him firmly as she pulled him toward her. He kissed her over and over. His loving nature showed through all the layers. Hope responded vigorously to his advances allowing him unrestricted access to her body. Chris's explorations led into passion. Bundled together the pair learned of each other in new and exciting ways until the eagerness took over.

Chris turned off the water as Hope watched the steam float across the ceiling and out the door. She reached to the cabinet and pulled a large towel from behind the door. With a quick toss they were both wrapped up together, dripping wet. The kisses still came in high frequency whenever the option presented itself. He stepped out first and lifted her over the rim, setting her down before him. Wrapped up they slid across the house to the bed, Chris laid her down, caressing all of her curves with his lips paying careful attention to all the right spots. Her breasts rose and fell in quick succession as her breathing intensified. He slid up to meet her face to face, her eyes locking in on his. Her thighs trembled in anticipation, but he didn't seem to notice as they plunged forward, never looking back. Together they stoked a fire so hot she thought they might burn. The night never ended. They relived the passion of their first time together over and over again. By the time sleep overcame either of them, the sun was up, birds announcing the arrival of a new day and a new life for both lovers.

Hope could not remember what time she awoke the next morning, if indeed it was still morning. She rolled onto her side, sat up on one elbow overlooking the man lying next to her.

The light filtering in through the window illuminated a scene she could never forget. Chris lay there only partially wrapped in the top sheet, as was she. The shadows that cast across his figure and aroused her so much were beautiful. He was striking, all of his features stood out against the dark room. His breathing was deep and rhythmic, the scene was entrancing. She leaned in and pressed her lips against his shoulder then cheek, a soft moan slowly emanated with his next breath.

Hope slid next to him to pull away the sheet that had bunched between them. They lay together most of the day, alternating between rest and exhilaration.

A bright flash and deafening boom brought her back. She was standing in a motel, along a two lane highway lost in West Texas. Staring out the window into the distance, Hope wondered if it were even possible to relive a night like that. Probably not but that didn't matter, she needed a confidante now more than a lover.

New Day

H e seemed to be dreaming, the smell of fresh sheets, the birds chirping, the breeze floating in through the open window, it all seemed surreal. Chris woke up in his own bed, without company. Normally it was a hammock or the breakfast table downstairs in the kitchen. Ramone had asked once how Chris always knew when he would show up for work, early or late. It wasn't that Chris possessed any sixth sense, he just didn't sleep much. Today was different though, last night was different, everything had changed. Lying there he knew where he was going and what he wanted to do, to a small degree.

Chris stretched out across the bed and kicked the sheer top sheet toward the far corner of the mattress. The comforter had long been resigned to the floor below the foot of the bed. Reaching over himself with his right hand he grabbed his watch and blinked several times to clear the morning blurriness from his eyes. It wouldn't be morning for much longer. Chris had slept well past ten. Ramone should be here by now. With a quick peek out of the window, across the second story patio and down toward the barn, Chris spied the old '57. It was parked in its usual spot. It technically wasn't a reserved spot but anyone who knew the Studio knew that you did not park there. Ramone himself was out of sight, but he would be around somewhere making himself productive. Even without being asked, he always had something in his mind he felt needed done.

Rolling back across the large, firm mattress Chris kicked his legs out over the edge sitting up. Sobriety was a beautiful thing. After a scratch of his head and a roll of the shoulders, the day looked even more beautifully. Seated at the edge Chris checked his phone, nothing, good. "Hey buddy," was the greeting following a short whistle as Dingo poked his head in to check on the late riser. The companion took his time stepping over the bed. The scruffy dog didn't look so scruffy anymore. "Did you get a shower and shave?" Chris asked digging his fingers into the sleek coat rubbing vigorously. When Dingo was satisfied with his rub down, he turned and headed back out the door, seeking what, Chris had no idea. Standing and stretching his body, Chris felt more refreshed than he had in a long time. Today was going to be a good day. His back popped loosening up. Taking a towel from the back of the door Chris strolled, lighter on his feet than he had been in a long time, down the hallway and rounded down the stairs to the bathroom for a shower. Along the way he hit play on the stereo by the staircase. It introduced the day with selection from a lone star state native.

"I got a girl back in Fort Worth that means the world to me, her eyes are green, green as the emerald sea."

'Well, it's not Dallas,' Chris thought, 'but close enough.'

"She left me, not so long ago, I headed down to Port Aransas for the Gulf Coast, baby."

He took his time gathering himself, washing away years of stress and obsolete concerns down the drain with his toothpaste. Swiping his hand across the foggy mirror after he'd stepped out of the tub something looked different. The lines on his face were the same. His skin still carried the tone of hours in the sun, but it seemed to be more vivid now. His eyes beamed with life. The smile that emerged came with greater ease than it had in the recent past. Chris had his idea, Ramone may not agree but he would go along with it, he always did.

Chris dressed and headed out the dining room door, over the patio toward the Studio. He glanced into the spray booth as he walked in. Ramone was lacquering a bench bound for Phoenix next week. Chris opened the stereo cabinet on the wall and selected a new playlist. Ramone was cleaning the spray gun of the residue left from his last chore when he heard the music come over the speakers hung strategically throughout the Studio. He knew Senior Coupland was back. This selection was one he hadn't heard before; the pace was beyond anything Ramone would appreciate but it was new; therefore it was better than the same stuff they'd listened to for years now. It was a good sign. Rinsing out the gun and setting it on the rack upside down to dry, the old Mexican closed up all the cans and wiped his hands clean. The rag in his mitts was still hard at work scrubbing as he rounded the passage into the fabrication side.

Atop the work tables beside the panel saw, Chris sat with a coffee pot smiling. "Good morning, did you miss me?"

Ramone caught a small chuckle at the warm greeting, "Oh, senior, very much, very much. It looks like your trip went well."

"It did, it did. The show was beautiful. You wouldn't believe some of the things they did with those projects. Here try this," Chris gestured to the pot next to him. "I found these beans in a small bistro in Austin." He poured a mug for Ramone who picked it up and gently blew across the surface sending steam rolling out and up toward the fans roaring down from the ceiling. Chris continued, "This is supposed to be one of the best roasts to come out of Africa." They both sipped and examined. Chris rolled the hot brew around his mouth warming his tongue. It was a dark rich roast that pleased him very much. The bitterness of the coffee was much less than what he'd expected, and the hearty flavors hung around long after the liquid was gone. The two craftsmen stood there enjoying the company as the morning light rose to the level of midday.

In time Chris gave the unabridged replay of his trip. They discussed some of the reviews the show received. It wasn't all good news. Chris hadn't expected many people to praise the pieces, but the warmth of the overall take on it surprised him. The primary critique was the shock value that the radical disregard for customary practice brought.

Ironically, that was the primary praise also. Ramone could see in his eye as he led into another topic that there was something up his sleeve. Before the boss could pull out the transition in conversation, he had to cover one thing that hung in the air of the rapidly warming Studio. For the first time Ramone asked what he'd never uttered before, "and what about the woman?"

"The woman? You have to be more specific than that," Chris gave him a sly smile.

"You know which woman I'm talking about. The one you have been running from," he said giving his friend a deep glare.

Chris laughed, nodding silently. Finally he spoke, "I'm not running from anyone... not anymore. I've made my peace and now have the answers I wasn't necessarily looking for, but they were the ones I needed." Hope had always known him that way. Taking another sip, his smile remained.

"Good for you, my friend," Ramone said nothing else for a long while. Standing there, his bow legs crossed, left over right with the sleeves of his worn cotton shirt rolled up as far as they would go, and the brim of his old straw hat kicked back. Sipping from the chipped green mug he let the obvious question hang. Chris knew what was coming from the wise old man, and the recess he was given to debate the still unknown answer to the pending query was much appreciated.

When Ramone had taken sufficient time to finish off the new roast, he wiped out his mug and set it on the table next to Chris. "What will you do now?"

There it was and still with no answer, Chris decided that he would have to move forward even if there was no foreseeable goal in mind. They would take it all one step at a time. "Well, first we finish the house. How quickly can we get it done?"

"I make a poor contractor, but with the right people, a solid month."

Chris factored that into the timeline he saw building ahead of him. Okay, one month, we can do this he thought. "I have most of the plans ready; I know the materials I want and where to find them all. Can you find the hands to put it all together?"

Ramone counted to himself. "Si, my family would be pleased to provide all the men you need. Until school begins, I know many who need to stay busy."

"Good." Chris slid off the table and made a quick pace back to the stage and up into the office. From a flat file beneath a large built in desk that held computers, a phone, fax machine and scanner he pulled a stack of large prints and rounded back out to the work table. Pushing two tables together, Chris and Ramone laid out the sheets in ordered number pouring over the drawings meticulously taking note of everything they lacked to get from here to final finish of the residence. The numbers added up fast. They checked and double checked everything. They pored over the documents, tore through the store of materials they had listing everything on site. A few hours later noon had come and passed without either of the tireless inventory clerks noticing.

After regrouping at the tables now established as command central, Chris realized he had eaten nothing all day. This was a bad habit. When completely engrossed in any task, which happened often, personal needs such as eating or sleeping were often set on the back burner and soon forgotten about. Only when his body would ache for what it lacked would he cease and take care of himself. Chris could remember fondly his paternal grandmother complaining of the same ailment. It must run in the family.

"Ramone, go eat. Hell, call it a day. We can regroup on Monday and pick this up, I think we have enough to get started."

"Are you sure, there is a list here…" He was cut off.

"We have plenty of time to work on the list; it'll just keep growing and growing as we go along. Tell your boys and any of their friends we can use all the hands we get, and I'll pay more than fair."

"I know you will, is there anything else you need before I leave?"

Chris thought for a second and shook his head still running scenarios through his mind. "No, I'm good. Go home, spend some time with Rita, I'm going to keep you very busy over the next few weeks so get it in while you can." He said breaking into a smile giving Ramone a solid pat on the back. "Thank you again, I appreciate everything you do."

"I know senior, I will return Monday with the boys."

"Alright, I'll see you then." With that said Ramone turned and headed out into the midday sun disappearing around the corner. After a silent minute with nothing but vague music to keep his mind from spinning out of control, Chris heard Loretta fire to life. When she was rolling hot, Ramone lapped around the drive and took off down the road. What was Chris to do with himself over the weekend? Marlene would be around, hopefully.

Still neglecting to feed himself, Chris dropped enough weights onto the blueprints to ensure they would not blow around and walked out of the Studio turning the stereo a little louder on his way.

"Money can't buy love but it can buy affection and I can't tell the difference anymore."

Chris laughed as he exited the Studio, poetic wisdom often held an edge of humor.

Outside the heat beat everything unmercifully. He was used to it by now and the sweat that almost immediately beaded up on his brow went unnoticed. East of the Studio, by the little metal shed sat a trailer. Chris stomped through the high grass toward it and made a mental note to be sure and mow the yard down next week. Reaching for the lock he almost burnt his hand on the searing metal. His palm was tougher than most and it did no damage but the heat was surprising. Swearing at the little silver guard, he pulled it off, swung the door open and tossed it inside to cool. From the stack of materials inside he pulled a large belt with several full pockets and random tools hanging from it. He checked for his hatchet, threw some pan head roofing nails in one pocket and took down a bundle of shake shingles. There were several spots along the south east slope of the house in need of replacing since the wicked thunderhead that rolled through last month and now was as good a time as any. Sweating through the problems bogging down his mind was always an effective solution.

Walking back up to the house, he set everything down and stripped to his boots and blue jeans. Donning the belt Chris gave all the bags another once over and climbed up a post on the patio, crossed the trusses and hopped onto the roof. Prying at the old weather faded shakes, it did not take long for the sweat to begin pouring from the laborer onto the shingles below him.

Lost

With fog still on the mirror of the bathroom and her hair still damp, Hope packed her bags and headed out the door. She dropped the key off with Aunt Bea and jumped into her car already running allowing the A/C to work out all the built up heat. Checking her mirrors she backed up and pulled forward rounding through the empty parking lot. The popping gravel under the tires announced her departure. Two large rigs hauled past before she swung out onto the shimmering blacktop and floored it. The radio her only company, she drove into nowhere Texas, not knowing exactly where she was headed.

She did know that somewhere west of Abilene not too far off US Highway 180 was Coupland Studios. There was a small town nearby, what was the name of it? The name was... the name was... was it Lane? No, maybe the street name was Lane or it was on a lane. Just then she passed a sign that settled it all. White text on a faded green backing and full of bullet holes said "Lane - 19." That was it. Hope pressed the accelerator a little harder. In little Lane, Texas she stopped off at a gas station to fill up and see if anyone knew where to find Chris. It was a well worn building, missing several letters. "_quit_ Ex__ange" were all that remained. The clerk behind the counter, a middle aged woman whose lines told of a hard life and too many cigarettes, said she knew exactly who Chris Coupland was. He came here often, she said, to gather everything from fertilizer to framing materials. Hope caught a grin thinking of the materials the clerk had selected as a cross section to represent Chris's buying habits. What was he doing out there, growing buildings? The clerk told her how Chris always stopped by on his way in or out, but he hadn't been through in almost a week. She mentioned the 'big show' in Austin he'd been at and didn't know if he'd returned yet but she hoped that it was a good show for him. Hope listened intently, revealing nothing. When the kind woman finished with her recap of his latest buying trends, she asked Hope how she knew of Chris.

Hope replied, just skimming the surface, "We're old friends from college. Do you know how to find his place?"

"Well, you head down 180 here for, oh, 'bout twelve miles and there's a county blacktop that goes south..." Hope lost her there. She tried to follow but after the third try the clerk gave up and drew a map. It was far from being accurate to any scale. The twelve mile stretch was almost as long as the eight mile which was longer for some reason. She could decipher it, that's all that counted. Thanking the woman for her time, Hope excused herself and got back in her car. The clerk stood outside in what little shade the small awning out front provided, cigarette in her lips, and gave a big, vigorous wave as Hope pulled away.

At the twelve mile mark from town, there was no blacktop to her left as there should have been. There were turnoffs at the nine and fourteen mile marks, but none at twelve. Since she was further down the road than she thought, Hope decided to try the fourteen mile turnoff first. A half hour later, she was lost. She had been up and down several roads. North, south, there was nothing recognizable. She pulled over and stepped out to try and vent some frustration before her steering wheel started to swing back at her.

After cursing herself for leaving her GPS at home and kicking up enough dirt, Hope surrendered and pulled out a map she had tucked behind the driver seat. Using a water bottle as a paper weight she unfolded the sheet and spread it across the hood of her car. The hand drawn map didn't make sense. The clerk was the Jackson Pollock of cartography. This lady could not draw a schematic to save herself. The heat, the frustration, it was all taking its toll.

There had been no traffic along this stretch of road the whole time she had stood there, but from behind her she could hear the exhaust of something coming at her from the opposite direction. Standing there on the shoulder, shimmering in the waves of heat she turned to see a rusted red Chevy slow down and pass her by. Another second down the road, it pulled off to the far shoulder, lapping back across both lanes and pulled up alongside her parked car. The truck came to a stop as the driver came into view. "Afternoon, miss, are you okay? Is there anything I can do?" The old man said leaning across the bench seat of his truck. The AM radio played an energetic tune. The lyrics were in Spanish, which Hope did not understand.

Hope walked over to the window as the gentle looking, weathered old man removed his sunglasses. "Hi, um, yeah…" she paused, putting one hand on her hip and holding a water bottle in the other pointing out into nowhere, "I'm lost. I, um, I'm looking for a man named Chris Coupland, he lives out here somewhere. I've never been out this far, I don't really know where he lives. Do you know him?"

A subtle smile spread across his old weathered face. The recognition showed in his features. The subtlety in their mannerisms was very similar, Ramone could see why she had such an influence on the boss.

Hope saw the smile come across the old man's face. It was a caring and reassuring smile. She continued, "I'm looking for his Studio, do you know where it's at?"

"Ah, Senior Coupland," Ramone gave the young lady a thoughtful look not wanting to reveal his hand. "Si, he is a dear friend of mine. I believe he is at home this afternoon. It's easy to find from here. Keep

going the way you are heading four more miles. You will see an old
school house, turn south and follow the road another seven miles, and
you will see a sign that points you east, to the Studio. The gravel road
leads right up to his place. You can't miss it."

Hope let out a sigh of relief and gave the old man a big smile,
"Thank you so much," she said bouncing back to her car to gather her
things.

Free Weekend

Ramone sat watching as she gathered her things to leave and now understood why. This woman was one of the most beautiful creatures he had ever seen. Second only to his loving wife who, ironically, had the same athletic yet voluptuous build when she was younger. He knew he was an old man, but she was stunning, truly gorgeous. Only after Hope had gotten back in her car and pulled away, kicking gravel from the shoulder, did Ramone finally release the brake and lap back around to continue his journey home.

The Mexican smiled thinking of the surprise Chris was in for this afternoon. He was a meticulous man and thought everything out. Ramone had yet to beat him in a game of chess, but there was no way he could see this. With all the excitement her arrival brought, Ramone thought he just might get dressed up tonight and take the wife to Lubbock for a nice dinner, just the two of them. He did not have to be back to work for a few days, why not make a weekend of it. It had been many years since he and the missus had been out together. It was long overdue. The sight of a young, passionate love affected everyone near. You were either inspired or disgusted, Ramone was inspired. He had loved a woman like that at one time and still did. She was there for him every night, his rock, his savior. Those two had that love. They may not realize it or accept it even if they did, but it was there.

A New Pickett Fence

~

Hope followed the gentleman's directions; they were accurate to the tenth of a mile. He was good. Something told her he'd made the trip many times. The old school house stood where he said it would. Most of the wood was rotted out but the stone foundation, the fireplace and chimney, even the bell tower still remained. It could have easily been mistaken for a church, but the old man said it was a school house, and she believed him. There was something in his eyes; Hope just knew that he was a good man. Again, ahead, exactly where the stranger had said, stood an enormous piece of art. It was large, all metal, cutaways and inlays formed the symbols recognizable as letters forming words. After seeing his work in the gallery, she could see Chris's fingerprints all over that sign. It not only gave directions but it also read so much into his style, it was advertising. It read 'Coupland Studios'. The arrow pointed off to the left. Hope followed. The asphalt ended and gravel began shortly after her shift to head east. The sign had said Coupland Studios, it was plural. Was there more than one studio? Hope wondered rolling the options around for a while. She had only heard of this one. Maybe it was just a play on words. She'd spent too much time editing, she was now correcting artistic license.

Before making the eastward turn off the blacktop Hope already had a picture in her head of what Chris's place would look like. Maybe it was a picture of what she wanted more than what she expected, but either way it was serene. She could imagine it just over the next hill. There was a large farm house with lap siding and green shutters. There would be a wide wraparound porch and a large back patio. The lush yard stretched out in front and wrapped around either side. There was a lot of the stereotypical 'house with the white picket fence' that many girls grew up with. Though for Hope that dream died when she had outgrown her hometown. She had always wanted something she could brag about and her space in Dallas had done well to fill that.

While Hope was dreaming of her little picket fence, the Pontiac reached the summit of Chris's little hill west of the Studio. Her initial approach stalled, the view having the same effect on her as it had on Chris several years ago. The valley below was beautiful. What stretched out before her was the closest the physical world had ever come to competing with her own picket fence dream. There was a barn, the split rail fence and the run down windmill sitting opposite the new, sleek wind generator on the other side of the road. There was even a garden, a large garden, to the north of the house. To the south of the two-level residence, across the dirt drive stood the large barn. Between the two structures stood a covered boat, Hope smiled and shook her head, 'only Chris,' she thought. Her eyes, scanning the scene, drifted back to the house. Oh god, the house, it was perfect. From atop the hill she could see the tin roof protecting the porch, the second story balcony above the rear patio that stretched out toward the barn. All the windows were large, unbroken panes. This was surreal; she had to have seen this before. Was it just a dream? Had Chris told her about it all before? No, she didn't think so. They hadn't spoken much since this place had come about. As she followed the dirt drive down and split to the south side of the roundabout, Hope was stunned. She pulled next to the barn and parked. When the car came to a stop she looked up and saw him.

Chris was standing in the rafters of his open air patio behind the house. Hammer in hand his gloves had soaked through with the sweat running down his arms. His tool bags hung low on his hips as he stood up to check out the visitor.

Hope sat in her car feeling the air conditioner blow across her face. She took a deep breath but the cold air did nothing to halt the sweat that began to build on her skin. What was she doing here? What would he have to say about her coming out here? What would she say? In Austin he had professed that he would still be a dear friend. Now she would test his resolve. Turning off the engine, she opened the door. The heat of the afternoon flushed the precious, cool air out almost instantly. Accepting the fate of her overheating, Hope stepped into the searing afternoon. She could see Chris standing in the distance, the sweat of his bare torso shimmering in the light and heat. Seeing him there, his physique, dark and solid, she found herself drawn to him.

Luck v. Timing

Chris had noticed the dust rolling out across the field thinking Ramone had returned or Marlene was making a surprise visit. Either way he took little interest in it initially. But, when that red Pontiac rounded into view near the barn, he stood attentive. Watching as the car parked and just sat there. He'd never seen this car before, but his gut told him who it would be. He had no idea why she'd come, but that would be just his luck. His mother always told him that he was the luckiest man alive, but to offset this gift he was also blessed with the worst timing ever. This was just his kind of luck, and his mother was proven right again. Only Chris would be fortunate enough to have the woman of his dreams seek him out, right after he'd written her off and moved on with his own life. Even if this revelation was very recent he'd already made up his mind, and it was a stubborn mind. Now this.

Chris couldn't move. When Hope stepped out of her car, his assumptions became reality. It had far more of an impact on him than he'd feared. Seeing her standing there, in jeans and a tank top she was everything he wanted and couldn't have. He knew this now, but her showing up here really threw a wrench into his gears. Chris finally pulled his eyes away and slipped the hammer he's almost dropped, back into its loop on his bags. He peeled his gloves off and stuffed them in another bag hanging off his left hip. He unbuckled the belt and dropped it down through the trusses to the patio below and swung down himself.

Brushing off his jeans, he made his way toward her grabbing his shirt, hanging on the post beside the steps.

They met halfway up the yard, both stopped short. Standing there within arm's reach Chris wondered what had brought her out this far. Hope questioned her motives. Neither one of them moved. They were so very close and yet still worlds apart. Chris gave the last three days a quick once over focusing specifically on their interaction. Had he missed something? Had she said anything? No, Hope had been rather clear about her intentions as far as he could remember. Still, she looked different this time around. Her hair, pulled back, lay a little lighter in the soft breeze, her smile a little sweeter and those eyes showed something he could not quite put a finger on, but they were gentler now than he had seen in a very, very long time.

A New Meeting

Hope had spent the last day thinking about what to say, reciting several times to herself what she would say. Standing here now, with Chris standing before her, she drew a blank. The silence stretched into what seemed like eternity. The only sound she could hear was a faint song drifting from the Studio and quickly disappearing in the afternoon air.

"*When I get tied down by the ties that bind, seems like I'm never gonna find the time to do what I need… That's to find me a place where I can think, talk about love and laugh and drink, and there's someone there who cares…*"

Finally, when it seemed neither party could take the tension any more, Hope spoke, finding an emotionally neutral subject to break the ice. "The place looks wonderful, just the way you always said it would," she stated, her eyes remained unwavering.

Her words were an angelic welcome back to reality, "Thank you…" he trailed off. It was all Chris could muster.

"The excitement in your voice when you talked about it all, well, I had a couple of days off and thought I'd come out and see it for myself." It was a believable tale, she thought. Her heart was racing; she wondered if he could see through it. There was a time when she had to spell everything out for him, letter for letter, he could never pick up on a hint and now she stood here feeling completely translucent. Her feelings were correct.

He didn't know why she would come all the way out here, and he was not about to ask her. Right now, he just wanted to enjoy the company and the view. Having her this close, alone, was troubling though. Chris knew the right thing to do, if he could follow through with it would be the question.

"Would you like something to drink?" It was another generic question used to break the silence without breaking any egg shells, not yet anyway.

"That would be nice, thank you."

They walked side by side toward the house, Chris continued on with the small talk. "So, how was your drive?" Posing any question that would avoid the obvious.

"It was good. I slept over in Sweetwater under the watchful care of Aunt Bea, who was a complete sweetheart." The soft accent she had picked up since college was adorable and Chris couldn't help but smile. "They were having some kind of a celebration. It was nice to get away, you know, to spend a little time alone in spite of the fireworks going off all night."

The two of them, feeling the vigor of youth overcome them walked across the yard and up the broad steps to the patio, passing the rear of the house. The patio was large with posts stuck in the enormous slate floor in a regular pattern. Between several of the supports hung cotton hammocks, Hope wondered how many he really needed. The tin roof only extended out halfway down the length of the area. At the corner of the house, that stuck out into the patio, stood a circular, empty fireplace. Chris reached the double French doors which opened into the kitchen. He held one open to allow Hope to step inside before him.

Her first impression of the interior took her breath away. It was beautiful. The overall feel was rough in texture and fine detail. He had done well. Looking around, through one room deep into another she noticed there were still a few rooms to finish. Her mind wondered, trying to imagine what the place would look like when it was all complete. When she turned back into the kitchen, Chris held two large glasses of sweet tea and offered her one.

"Chris, this place looks great," she said after taking a long drink trying to wash the silence from her throat.

"Well, we've still got a long way to go…" he began.

"We?" Hope asked giving Chris an interested look.

"Yeah, I have a good friend working with me. His name is Ramone, he was an old hand here before they broke the ranch up. This place used to be part of one of the largest cattle ranches in the nation. There is a lot of history here. I offered Ramone a position to stay on and lend me an extra pair of hands when I needed them. He usually spends his days doing what he's always done, minor repairs and looking after the animals, unless there is a specific project for him. Even when there's nothing to do, he's here. Ramone is a good man, and he has a good family too, they've really helped me adapt to everything out here. It's a whole different world this far out. Once you exit the hill country, you enter God's country. Ramone is a brilliant old Mexican. His English isn't the greatest but he is a genius. He's naturally taken to many of the sciences I had to work so hard at in school like they were just another book to read and memorize. Then he can turn around and apply those theories to aspects of life I never would have imagined. I sometimes wonder what he would have been capable of if he'd not chosen to spend his life out here."

Hope had drifted off and wasn't fully focused on the discussion at hand. Something that Chris had said made her wonder, "Does this Ramone drive an old beat up red truck?"

Chris's brow wrinkled a little bit, "Yeah," he gave a small chuckle, "how did you know?"

"Coincidently, I think it was your Ramone who directed me here earlier this afternoon. I was lost on the side of a county blacktop and a nice old man headed in the other direction stopped to see if I was okay. He knew you and he knew exactly how to get here, down to the last detail. He knew this drive all too well."

"That would be his wisdom. See, the funny thing about Ramone is that he knows these things, things no one else would have any idea about, but he knows and will never tell. He will make you learn by burning yourself before coaching anyone away from the fire."

"I would like to meet him again. He sounds very interesting."

"He is and if you stick around long enough, you'll get a chance."

That sounded vaguely like an invitation to Hope, but she was not making any plans, not yet.

Chris took both glasses and refilled them before ushering Hope to the back patio where they took up one side of a picnic table. Hope was seated facing out into the yard while Chris sat straddling the bench seat, facing her. She didn't seem the least bit nervous. He watched her hands and feet looking for signs that are universal but there were none. Just then he noticed his right foot was twitching. It was something he suffered with for years, being so high strung he had to vent his energies somehow, but as he grew older the restlessness passed with time. He hadn't seen anything like this reaction in years. What was this woman doing to him?

Dingo

~~~~~

Dingo strolled around the far side of the Studio. Noticing the stranger he picked up his pace, just a little quicker than a stroll. It was still the fastest he'd moved in some time. With a whistle and a few choice words of encouragement from Chris, the brown paws shifted into a new gear.

"Hope, this is Dingo," Chris said introducing the two as he reached down to give the wiry coat a rub. The dog took no notice as all of his attention was directed toward Hope. His tail began to swing vigorously as she reached down to say hello.

"Wow, he looks like Duke, a lot like Duke."

Chris hadn't thought about Duke in a long time. There were several pictures of them together, but they were still boxed up buried under the staircase somewhere. "He's from one of Duke's litters. I chose to keep him because of the resemblance. Unfortunately their personalities though are polar opposite."

"Whatever happened to that poor dog?"

Chris smiled but truthfully he missed his old companion. They had been through a lot together. School, the move to Texas and back, all of the success and failure and finally the move out here, through it all Duke was always there. Loyal and loving he never left Chris's side the whole way. "Long story short, I think he just ran out of miles and lives. That last accident out in front of the little green house, when he got hit, really messed him up. He was never right again. Not long after Dingo here was born, Duke disappeared one night. After a day and a half of looking, I found him on a cold Wednesday afternoon up by the old windmill. Looked like he just laid down and went to sleep, curled up on himself. I don't know how long he'd been there but he wasn't getting back up. He was only ten years old. I don't know what caused it. I buried him the next day, right where I found him." Chris turned and pointed off to the west to the hill Hope had mounted not even an hour before. Talking about it now, with her almost choked him. No one here knew how close he was to that dog except Hope. She would understand the way no one else could.

Hope reached out noticing the sorrow in Chris's voice and put her hand on his knee. "He was a good dog, not all there, but a good dog. I know how much he meant to you."

"Thanks, we were both a little crazy, maybe that's why."

"I don't doubt it."

Chris spoke about the Studio, how it had all come together and some of the work they'd done and people he'd worked with. He told stories of the locals and how life out here was more peaceful, moving along at its own pace. When he'd covered all the bullet points he could think of to sum up the last few years, Hope asked to see the Studio.

"In Austin you had mentioned your best work was left out here, can I see it?" she asked.

Chris nodded, not really wanting to go through another show but he gave in. "Sure, I don't know if I can call it my best work, but it's my favorite." They both stood from the table, leaving their empty glasses behind and started off toward the barn across the way.

The Reason

As Hope walked through the Studio examining some of the more exotic pieces, a chair that looked like a shotgun had been taken to it and several occasional tables that reminded her of the transformers cartoon of their youth, Chris sat in the middle of the large, dusty space on the corner of a table watching her. After covering all of his recent questions, only one remained hanging in the air. Out of the clear blue Chris just opened his mouth and out it came.

"What happened, Hope? What brings you out here now? I thought we did well in Austin, everything was settled."

The question caught her off guard and her eyes immediately snapped from the piece she was admiring to Chris and straight down to the floor. She didn't know exactly what to say. Taking a few steps past a large piece of equipment she could not identify, Hope walked over to the table he was seated on and leaned her hip against the edge for stability. Still avoiding his gaze, she analyzed the tabletop. There were notes, numbers and sketches all over it. No doubt this was a good graphical representation of what she imagined it looked like inside his head. Her fingers ran across the particleboard feeling all the holes and grooves cut into it over time. Chris noticed, those were the tells he was looking for earlier. This may not have been his best decision of the afternoon. About the time Chris began to believe he'd officially shot himself in the foot, Hope spoke up.

"Since we separated you've always told me, every time we had a chance to talk, that you'd always be there for me if I needed you." She let the words sink in. Hope knew that Chris was the only one who could relate to her right now. Even though she was the one who put him through the same situation Jon had inflicted on her, if he was being honest he would understand her plight. He was the only one who could comfort her. "Jon and I have been going through some rough times. When I got home yesterday he was there. It was the first time I'd seen him in almost a week. He didn't have much to say other than the fact that he was leaving. It was not up for discussion, he'd already made up his mind. I felt powerless. I understand now what you went through. I just had to get away."

"Hope, I'm sorry to hear that…"

She interrupted, "No you're not, don't lie to me Chris Coupland."

Chris smiled, she was right. "Okay, no I'm not, but I'm sorry you had to go through all that. You know you didn't have to come all the way out here, you could have just called."

"Actually, I *really* needed to get away for a while. See, I *accidentally* left a candle too close to the drapes before I left," she said sheepishly. "The place went up in flames." Telling someone about it finally made her feel more comfortable with the decision.

A laugh burst out from Chris that surprised them both. "Oh my God, remind me to never piss you off again." This was surprising to him, Hope had never been a violent woman, but he was sure she had her reasons. As Chris contemplated the psychology of her action, Hope continued.

"I know this may be inappropriate and I'm sorry to bother you but…" She trailed off.

Chris, sensing the doubt build inside her picked up, "Don't worry; I'm happy to see you even if it's under poor circumstances. Even if the next time we meet might be in a prison visitation room." There was a sarcastic smile on his face. His attempt at humor did not comfort her. The worry on her face registered with him, "I'm sorry, Hope. Look, you have nothing to worry about," his hand gently laid on top of hers, the warmth was surprising. "As long as you're here, you have nothing to worry about," he reassured her.

The remainder of the afternoon passed before either one knew where it had gone. They moved from place to place, house to studio and back again as more and more conversations were brought up and passed on. Eventually they became friends again, old friends catching up, it was almost like they had no 'ex-anything' standing between them. They discussed work and friends, Chris more work and Hope more friends. They argued about the alma mater, sports, academics and old friends they'd left behind. It was a wonderful afternoon which both parties wished they could extend, like turning on a bulb to fend off the pending sunset and hold the brilliant orb above the horizon until they were ready to surrender. Sooner than wanted though the inevitable came, and they both reluctantly accepted it.

Wildflower

~

Noticing the late hour, as indigo began to wash over everything, Chris realized he was hungry. Hope had noticed the odd noises coming from her stomach some time ago but refused to be the one to put a halt on the afternoon's activities so she just ignored it. When Chris mentioned dinner though she was relieved to know starvation was no longer pending.

They had made their way to the front porch and sat on the park bench debating what should be served for dinner. Chris was a relatively good cook and proud of his food. Hope's greatest culinary achievement was spaghetti. It was something that both had acknowledged a long time ago. In their acquired family, none of the women knew how to or enjoyed cooking. The men on the other hand volunteered and more often than not were experienced and the results were surprising. Hope left the decision up to the chef only objecting to one meal, ever. Chicken cordon bleu was out of the question. There was something about meat stuffed inside more meat that bothered her. Chris called out to the porch as he went through the freezer, pantry and dry goods he had on hand. Checking with his guest, just to make sure, they settled on bone-in pork chops with portabella risotto and sautéed vegetables, whatever looked best in the garden at the time. Chris disappeared into the house again with two handfuls of produce. It would be almost an hour before they would be ready to eat.

Hope took this time to give herself a tour of the property. Walking alone she realized the beauty and serenity of it all. It was hard to gather the whole picture on first impressions, there were too many subtleties to overlook but after studying it all for a short while the details began to set in. She could see the birds that darted past, how the clouds layered as they moved into the distance, the drastic change of color across the sky at dusk, and the ever rotating windmill that despite everything just kept on going round and round in a never ending cycle. She understood why Chris had chosen this place to get away from everything. Here he was left alone with his thoughts.

Hope made her way out toward that old windmill churning in the breeze. As she reached the summit she noticed the stone marker where Duke was laid to rest. Standing beside him she could take in the full panoramic view. Staring out on the never ending horizon surrounding her, she was at peace. Her worries faded with the daylight. She had started over before and for the first time, standing here, she was confident she could do it again.

Taking a break from the chore at hand, Chris came out to the front porch to check on his guest. He stood there running his fingers over the weathered railing, watching. In the distance Hope stood amongst the grasses of the pasture, swaying in the wind, the wildflower of his dreams. He could almost smell her fragrance floating down the hill. He knew someday, someone would come along and give her the life she deserved, but for tonight, if just for tonight she was his again. He did not want to disturb her; she looked so tranquil out there, lost in herself. He needed to call her down for dinner but couldn't bring himself to do it. She would be back in her own time. Chris returned to the kitchen to finish everything and wait patiently.

Eventually Hope came in to check on the progress, surprised to see that dinner was plated and set waiting on her. Apparently she'd been out longer than she thought. They sat, speaking little, enjoying the meal. When both plates had been cleaned and the table cleared, they picked up the conversation from earlier speaking of everything and nothing at all. There was a bottle of Chianti left empty in the kitchen and several amber bottles sitting about the table.

The Plan

"The stars are out in full number tonight, would you like to move this outside?" Chris asked wondering to himself how often she had a chance to enjoy the night sky when surrounded by all the city lights.

"I would like that," Hope said smiling. In the middle of downtown, even on the clearest of evenings, all but the brightest stars were drowned out by the haze and glow of the city. As she took one hammock and settled in, the clarity and number of the tiny, shimmering diamonds overcame her. Lying there she noticed the songs of the night serenading her, it was so peaceful. No cars, no sirens, no yelling, Hope took a deep breath and smiled at nothing in particular.

They both lay spread out in the cotton slings, Chris reached over to her, holding onto the edge of the net embracing Hope and with a gentle nudge rocked them both in a gentle opposing rhythm. Hope lay wondering just who this man was. Chris was no longer the high strung uncontrollable ball of energy she used to know. He seemed more focused and oriented. Something in him had changed and it intrigued her. She had changed much herself, she knew there was little that remained of the small town kid in her but felt her values held true. Chris on the other hand seemed to embrace the simplicity of it all. It couldn't last though, not if she knew him as well as she thought. Their cotton beds swung in quiet rhythm, it almost lulled her to sleep.

"Talk to me," she finally spoke up, fighting off the slumber. "Tell me about your plans. You've always had a plan." She didn't look at him, just the starry night. She couldn't see his reaction; she assumed it would be a thoughtful one.

Chris let her request hang in the air. It seemed to float stagnant on the breeze for the longest time. He knew that eventually he would have to tell her but he didn't want to, not just yet.

"I'm going to finish this house first of all. It will take several weeks, depending on the amount of help I can find."

Hope volunteered her services. "I can help; I'm in no hurry to get back to Dallas."

The thought of Hope hanging around for a while comforted him. "How handy are you with a skill saw?"

She could see the impending sarcasm, "Well, I'm horrible actually, but I love to paint and I look great in overalls."

Chris could see her handling power tools. This might be a bad idea but she was right, it looked good. "Hope, you are more than welcome to stay as long as you would like. I do have to tell you though that as soon as my current projects are done, I'm leaving."

"Where are you going?"

That was a good question. One that Chris had only thought about for less than a day thus far. "I don't really know yet. I might head to the ocean."

"Why the ocean?"

This one Chris knew, "Growing up, geographically as far from any major body of water as anyone can get, I've always wanted to try out my sea legs."

"But you ain't got no legs, Lieutenant Dan," Hope said with a good laugh. It sprouted from a favorite of both of theirs for a long time.

Chris found a chuckle of his own. "I think it would be a great experience. I want to separate myself from the world I know. I have almost everything I could ever want for. The freedom and security that success has brought allows me to do whatever I see fit. Gluttony and sin or charity and compassion, I don't know how it should be handled. So I have a theory, if I remove myself from everything eventually I will be able to look back from a third party point of view and make better decisions."

"How long would you be gone?" Hope asked.

This was an aspect Chris had not touched on yet, "I don't know, it depends on how far I decide to go, a year, maybe more."

They continued rocking, back and forth, back and forth. Dingo came to lay below their new guest. The gas lamps strategically hung throughout the patio cast shifting waves of light across the old friends. Chris rolled his head to the right bringing Hope into view. He could not tell what she was staring at, but she seemed lost. "This is the beautiful part; I've always had a plan. Now, beyond finishing this place, I have none. I've got my passport, and Mother has authority to manage all of my investments and business interests. I'm just going, to wherever the wind takes me. That's it." Chris changed the subject, "What about you? You can't run from the law forever."

She smiled, momentarily wondering how Nettle was doing. Hope also remembered that she might be in a little trouble when she got back home. Arson was a serious charge, but none of that worried her right now. Since she left town she'd had no concern about what she would do when she got home. Her phone had remained off since yesterday evening and it was liberating. "I don't know what I'm going to do. I really don't care right now. I've recently thought about going back to school. Work is boring, and I don't feel like I'm going anywhere with it. Someone forgot to tell me that the newsprint industry is dying. Everything is transitioning to online formats. The opportunities for making a successful career are drying up."

"If you went back, where would you go? What would you study?"

"There are plenty of schools in the metro area. As far as a field of study, I don't know; something that would allow me to work with people, maybe in education."

"Whatever you decide to do, I know you'll be great at it," his words reassured her.

"Thank you," she said feeling the blood rush to her face. Chris had always supported her in any endeavor, just as she had done for him. No matter what condition their relationship was in. It was that unconditional love between them that had brought them back together. It was not always a romantic love but one built on respect, it was a foundation that never wavered between them.

Chris, thinking out loud noted, "Today was a good day, thanks for coming out. It was a surprise, a very good surprise."

Hope agreed, "It was a good day."

She did not want the night to end but as they lay there, silently swinging, sleep came to her easily.

Together Again

Before she could fully wake Chris had her in his arms. Not resisting, she slung her arms around his neck as he carried her inside through the kitchen and up the stairs. She felt comfortable, sensing the gentle sway as he made his way down the hall, feeling his chest rise and fall, her head rested on his shoulder. Chris could feel her breath pulsing across his neck, and it moved him in ways he had not expected. He put his back into the bedroom door and swung around gently laying her down trying to not wake her. When she seemed settled in bed, he returned to the patio picking up the last few bottles strewn throughout the place.

Hope rolled over and sat on the edge of the bed pulling a few loose strands of hair from her face. She stood and looked out into the hallway. Where had Chris gone? She returned to the room and stripped down. Looking through the chest of drawers she saw several familiar pieces that made her laugh. His cutoff hunting pants, now faded and almost worn through were here. Why would Chris have saved these? The summer before that fateful Fourth of July, these had been full length pants. After a few days at a music festival and many drinks along the way, Hope had convinced Chris to let her cut them off. Looking back it was a little dangerous letting her take a sharp knife that close to his ACL after drinking, but neither of them were in their right mind at the time. She pulled the pants out and looked them over. She could almost see through the thin fabric. Hope smiled putting the shorts back. In another drawer there were pictures. Old ones and new ones, several almost brought a tear to her eye. Over time she had thrown out almost everything that had any connection between the old lovers. Now she felt a little guilty. Seeing all of this, Hope realized exactly what they'd had between them. Finally she came across a blue pinstripe button-down that looked large enough to let her roll around through the night. More comfortable now she crawled back into bed, waiting for Chris to return.

Turning off all the lights, he slowly made his way back up the stairs trying his best to remain silent not wanting to wake Hope. When he got back to the bedroom door she was rolled up in the comforter, sleeping soundly in one of his old shirts. She was a sight to behold. Walking silently to the edge of the bed he leaned in and kissed her gently on the cheek. "Goodnight sweetheart," he whispered.

Chris rose slowly taking in her beauty. He stepped back to the hall as quietly as possible and down to the bathroom. He stood in front of the sink looking at himself in the mirror. He hadn't felt like this since the first time they'd fallen into each other's arms. Toothbrush hanging from his mouth he cursed himself for not pushing the issue, but he knew she was a woman scorned and did not want to take advantage of her current situation. He spit, rinsed the remainder of the paste from his mouth and returned to his own room catching a quick glimpse of Hope lying quietly across the hall. The lamp next to his bed put off more light than he'd expected, but Chris didn't hear Hope stir across the hall and hoped it wouldn't bother her. As he unbuttoned the top two buttons and pulled his shirt off, he saw her in the mirror, leaning on the doorjamb behind him. He quickly glanced over his shoulder and shot her a soft smile.

"I thought you were out for the night," Chris said.

Hope looked at him longingly, thinking of the tattoos that covered his arms and shoulders, she recognized some and wondered about the ones she didn't. "Are you afraid?"

The question confused him, "Afraid? Afraid of what?"

"Me," she answered quickly and to the point. "I'm a grown woman, I can handle myself."

Chris felt a little foolish now. "I know that," he said turning toward her.

"Stay with me. If just tonight then it will be just tonight. I want you to hold me the way you used to."

"Hope, I want you so badly, but I'm leaving soon. I don't want to hurt you again."

She stepped into the bedroom and put her arms around his waist, "Not like that. I just want you to stay with me. I don't want to be alone tonight, and I need to know that at least once in my life I have a true unconditional friend."

With that Chris kissed the top of her head and swung her into his bed crawling in as soon as he kicked his jeans to the floor, the buckle of his belt thumping as it impacted the hardwood. They lay there that night, holding each other, never saying a word. Both of them felt the tension and knew they could love each other one last time, but this was perfect just the way they were. Neither one wanted to spoil that.

Day - One

The morning came too soon. Hope woke lying in his arms, she hadn't moved all night. She rubbed his chest, feeling him breathe. She threw her leg over and wrapped an arm across his body burying her face against him. Chris stirred gently, waking to her sweet smell hanging in the morning breeze. His eyes slowly peeled open for a brief second and closed again, not wanting to wake just yet. Together they both tried to stay off the encroaching day to no avail. In time Hope rose, patting his chest to stir Chris to life and jumped out of bed. She headed downstairs, and he soon followed.

Chris made his way toward the kitchen seeking coffee. As he passed through the dining room, he saw Hope outside the large picture windows, beyond the porch that wrapped around three sides of the house. She was hopping across the drive to her car barefooted, she hadn't changed that much. Her hair was blowing in the wind as his shirt billowed. She looked innocent and reminded him of the girl he'd first met back in college. She reached into her car pulling out a few bags, from under the shirt a pair of blue boy shorts peeked out. Chris looked away catching a good chuckle, his mind was wondering and his imagination was taking over. This may be tougher than he had originally thought. Eyebrows raised he took a deep breath and continued into the kitchen. "Come on Coupland, keep it clean," he said to himself.

Hope returned to the house, bags in tow, and headed back up stairs.

As she reached the first step, Chris called from the back of the house, "Coffee?"

"Sure," came her sweet drawl as she took the stairs two at a time.

Chris was seated in the dining room, the backs of his legs sticking to the chair in the morning heat when Hope came around the bottom step. The fine wardrobe she donned for Dallas was retired, for now. In slacks and an old worn out tee confiscated from Chris's dresser, she looked comfortable.

"Nice shirt," he noted wondering if he had to worry about her rummaging through his things. Nope, there was nothing she could find that he wouldn't show her.

"Thanks, I didn't pack for a casual vacation. I didn't really pack for vacation at all, I hope you don't mind," she said, the logo of an old bar stretched across her bust. She tugged at the bottom trying to stretch it out as best she could. The thin cotton didn't hide much.

"No, problem, make yourself at home. It's been a long time since I've had anyone stay over."

Hope wondered what the intention of his statement was, but it shouldn't matter, yet the question still rolled around in her mind.

Chris noted, "That stain on your left shoulder there, that's from you. I remember one morning you woke up at my house late for work. Why you grabbed that ratty old shirt I could never guess, but something got spilled on it at the bar. Damn stain never came out."

Hope smiled; his memory always retained the most obscure details that she'd long forgotten. It was nice to think of the little things from time to time. "So, what do you have planned today?"

Chris leaned back kicking the ladder-back dining chair on its hind legs and thought. "Well, it's Saturday, I have nothing to do and no plans. That's the way most days start around here."

"Well, that's got to be nice."

"Can be, but a lot of times I find myself running circles, not getting much done. Ramone does well at keeping me straight."

"What do you do for fun if there's no work to do?"

"Are you kidding, this is all the fun I can handle. And there's always work to do, it's just a matter of if it's important enough to do now, or can we put it off. There are a few chores I need to get done, beyond that I got nothing."

"Don't let me hold you back," Hope said as she continued on into the kitchen.

"The mugs are on the top shelf on the right side of the sink," Chris called through the open doorway. "I'm going to get dressed."

Hope cleaned the dishes from the night before and wiped down the intriguing countertops. She had just finished when Chris returned, clothed in jeans and a button down shirt, carrying a pair of boots. "Thanks for cleaning up. You didn't have to."

"You remember the deal; if the guys cook we're more than happy to clean up after you."

Chris sat at the small breakfast table and bent down to pull on the worn and cracked ropers. "Well, thank you anyway." With his feet covered he stood. "I'm going to feed, then I need to put a few hours into the studio; would you like to join me?"

"Sure, I'd love to see how all this works."

The Business

They spent the rest of the morning going over drawings, portfolios of old work and pieces still in progress. As Chris settled into his toils, answering questions and firing back his own, Hope assumed control of the stereo, working her way through song after song. Hope sat next to a large fan, slowly churning the air to keep her cool.

Mid afternoon Hope began quizzing the designer on all of his projects, "So, I've seen many of the articles written about your work, but how did all of this come about?"

Chris set down the planer he was cleaning, "It all started with the first book. I was jaded and just thought about what if. What if I had no obligations, no financial debt, what would I do."

"I read the copy you sent me, I didn't know you had it in you."

Chris laughed, "That's the reaction I get most."

"Where did it come from?" Hope wondered.

"You," Chris admitted, not looking up from the joinery he was working on and offering no further explanation.

Hope did not understand, "why me?"

"Do you recall the first time we saw each other after the break up? I was back at the bar and you were back to celebrate another graduation?"

"Yeah," Hope responded mentally filtering through the weekend over six years ago. She could not recall anything particularly eventful.

"Do you remember the fight we had at the bar the morning you left to come back to Texas?"

"Not really, I remember you trying to guilt trip me."

Chris finally pushed aside the planer he had been running over the end grain of a cherry stock. Smiling to himself he looked up at Hope, "Yes, that too, but you also said something that started a chain of dreams. I told you that morning that if I didn't have any responsibilities I wanted to do this or that and you responded by saying that I shouldn't worry about 'if' and just do it. That book was the culmination of my dreams, regardless of responsibilities. Luckily it sold well." Chris set back to work on the plank clamped down before him.

He continued in between strokes, "from there I had the finances to finally file for several patents and when they sold everything began to snowball. The trust was set up and mother assumed control. Since then I've lived every day free of the trivial obligations that dictate most lives. I bought this place, set it up so that Mother and Neal would run the business end, and Ramone and I could keep pumping out ideas and projects."

"Now, you'll never have to go back to the trailer park. Wasn't that your motivation for so long?"

"True." He answered bluntly, "what about you, what drives you?"

Hope turned down the music just slightly, "I'm not so sure anymore. It used to be about building a foundation for a family someday, then for a while I just wanted to prove that I could survive in the city, but now I just don't know." Her response hung in the air as Chris continued working allowing her to ponder. In time Hope took up a pencil and began to sketch alongside the schematics on one of the five tabletops. Chris stopped what he was doing and walked over.

"What are you drawing?"

The pencil stopped moving but Hope did not look up. "I don't know. Nothing I guess. I used to draw all the time but I haven't in years."

"Why not?"

Hope wondered the same thing on occasion but never knew the answer. "I guess I just never take the time."

"That's another reason I came here. There's time for anything. You can do whatever you want out here, within the reasonable limits of the law."

"I can see why you would love it. I don't know if it's the kind of place where I would want to live though. I'm afraid it would get boring."

Chris smiled, "Yeah, there can be some long days and it's definitely not for everyone, but I couldn't imagine being anywhere else right now."

"I couldn't either," she said giving him a sweet smile in return.

The day moved on. Whether they approved or not, the sun set. That night they sat out under the stars again, revealing more of each other. In the early morning hours they retired again to his bed. Lying there, the tension building little by little, but neither wanted to admit to it.

Day - Two

Sunday morning was always spent catching up on the news. The internet was an indispensible utility this far from nowhere. Hope finally picked up her phone and assured everyone she was just fine. Her mother had heard of the fire and so had the Dallas police department. She told both the same tale. She had left that evening for a short vacation and had no idea about the blaze. The fire department had ruled it accidental. The report said she had apparently left a candle burning. Hope claimed negligence and the case was filed under accidental. Hope called her old neighbor to see about Nettle's care and she was reassured that everyone was fine. The Fire department had arrived quickly and the only damage beyond her apartment was the lingering smell of smoke. No harm, no foul.

Chris called his mother, who reported that everything was just the same as it had been the week before. Her position in the corporation was to assure financial stability, and she was spectacular at her job.

Chris also called Neal who stated that the marketing was in line for the digital release scheduled for next month. The plans for the management of the future of the company were discussed at length, interrupted by a long conversation with Kathy and her views of Hope's visit. Neal knew the correct actions to take and Chris trusted his judgment, even if his dictations were made over the garbled order of the brown guy's current sandwich.

When everyone had been reassured of safety and goals, the two old friends mounted a sixteen hand bay mare and Chris narrated a guided tour of the property pointing out every tree by number, one through fourteen. Dingo followed the entire way, the poor mutt seemed as entranced by the new woman as Chris was.

Most of the afternoon was spent reading, Hope selected *"All the Pretty Horses"* by McCarthy while Chris worked on *"Lonesome Dove"* for what seemed like the hundredth time. Dingo roamed the premises eventually settling alongside Hope to pass the day as he always did.

The two sat in silence as the day faded into evening. It was something they had always been able to do. Together, they could sit, comfortable enough to say nothing at all. As darkness set in Hope felt the comfort and finally asked what may have been inappropriate, but she had wondered for too long.

"What about women? Is there someone I should be worried about?"

Chris dog-eared his page, closed the book and set it in his lap. He leaned his head back against the house and didn't look at her. "How am I supposed to answer that?" Chris smiled, there were no secrets between them, just subjects they hadn't discussed yet. "What exactly do you want to know?"

"I was just wondering where your heart is."

It was a simple request but Chris knew that with one slip of the tongue he could hurt her. "I have a friend out here, she's a good girl, it's nothing serious but we try to see each other from time to time. She's an artist, a creator like I am. We help each other out and compare notes a lot."

"Does she ever stay with you?" Hope grew flush knowing that this information was none of her business.

"Yes, occasionally," Chris cursed himself. He could not lie to her. If he did she would be able to read right through it. He wore his heart on his sleeve and hopefully she could recognize now exactly where it lay.

"How many others have you been with since me?" The questions seemed to roll out before she could stop them.

"Hope," he took a deep breath, "it's been over five years, does it really matter?"

"No, but I'm curious. You don't have to tell me. I just... never mind." She felt like a fool.

"Three."

She knew two of the three and the last must be this artist he was talking about. "Four, just to keep it fair."

Chris didn't care. "You opened the can, now tell me about Jon. What happened?"

Hope thought for a long while, coldly she reported, "I wasn't enough for him apparently. I'd thought we were doing fine, but his work was more important than I was and one of his clients too, apparently. I didn't even see it coming until the day I got back from the show. No offense but he turned into everything I thought you would become. I'm glad I was wrong about you."

"You weren't all wrong. I'm still obsessed with my work." At his core Chris knew that the traits which built the rift between them remained, though on a lesser scale, "I know now I can't give someone everything it would take to make a marriage work."

This surprised her, "You don't think you'll ever settle down?"

"No, family and kids are out of the question, for the foreseeable future anyway. It would take more sacrifice than I'd be willing to volunteer right now. It's only rational, I couldn't give anyone the time or effort I believe is needed for a healthy relationship."

"So you're saying that if I wanted to move out here with you, to start a family, you would refuse me?" It was not what she wanted, but the question seemed reasonable.

Chris smiled and raised his brow, "That's a tough one, and I don't think I can answer it. Besides, you don't want to do that. You have too much going for you."

Hope knew this and somehow the insight showed more wisdom in Chris than she would have given him credit for two days ago.

"Come on, we need to go to bed, Ramone will be out early tomorrow with help. We have a lot of work to get done. If you're going to stick around, this could get exciting." His eyes grew wild with anticipation, but Hope did not ask what was at hand. She closed her book and stood, walking through the door he held open before her.

Re-Building

~~~

The next morning Chris was gone by the time Hope woke. The rusted brakes of a fully loaded, large, flatbed truck squealing to a halt made for a miserable wake up call, but she still loved lying in his bed. His pillow still smelled heavily of his scent. She rolled over and buried her face in it. Taking a deep breath she rolled back, smiling like a little girl and bounced out of bed and down the hall. After a quick shower and a search of the closet for something to wear she settled on a pair of her shorts and a tank top stolen from the top drawer of his chest.

Chris and Ramone stood at a table working as generals commanding an army. Ramone had shown up with more help than expected this morning. Over twenty men had responded to the call for work. Almost everyone was related to the Padillo family in one way or another, and the others were several cowboys from surrounding ranches. They divided the work up by experience, building small teams with the most experienced in charge of a specific task. The framing crew would be back from town shortly, the finish carpenters had overtaken most of the shop working on doors and windows and the ground crew, being the most inexperienced, manned the hardest labors. Materials were sorted as they came in from town, several trucks had been sent to Lubbock and Ramone's wife, Rita was just pulling in with two grandchildren to cook for the entire party.

Hope stepped out into the brilliant morning light; shielding her eyes she scanned over the entire property. She was surprised at the efficiency with which these men and boys labored so early in the day. In her shorts and tank top she caught the eye of almost everyone as she worked her way through the mass of materials and vehicles strewn across the lawn and drive, past the boat still sitting proud atop its bracing. Stepping through those large ornate doors to the Studio, she saw Chris. He was standing over a table listening to Ramone give directions in Spanish to several men standing with them. His sleeves were already rolled up and he was rubbing his forehead, the typical thinking posture for him. He noticed her as she entered the cool air of the shop. He stopped rubbing and stood up straight. His eyes lit up, and he waved her over. Hope took the long way around the tables not wanting to interrupt their meeting.

Chris turned away from the meeting to greet her. "Good morning, sunshine, you're running late today."

"Late? I didn't think you ever saw a morning this early," she jabbed back.

"You would be surprised what I can do when there is work to be done." His face beamed with excitement. Work always did this to him. "Give me one second; I want you to meet Ramone."

"We've already met," she reminded him.

Chris rolled his eyes and smiled as Ramone sent everyone to their duties. Hope was looking over the plans and lists spread out across the table before them. They did have a lot of work to do.

"Hope, this is Ramone Padillo, Ramone I'd like you to meet Hope Lawrence."

Ramone extended his hand and Hope shook it. The grip was firm but not forceful.

"I believe we met the other day, Ramone," Hope offered.

"Yes, Ms. Hope, it's good to see you found it here safely." He bowed ever so slightly. "Will you be staying for a while?"

"I think so. I would like to see what you have going on here." She smiled; Ramone had a gentle nature to him that you would not guess on first impressions.

Chris stepped in, "Let me show you." He unrolled a set of plans and went over the details of the house and ground work they had to finish.

Ramone went about overseeing the crews, correcting the little details when needed. Chris walked Hope through the entire site, stopping briefly to inspect the boat in the middle of the yard, now christened *Esperanza,* explaining exactly what had to be done to get it safely stored away. The boat was to be finished as completely as possible and packed away in the loft of the Studio. Beyond that, there were three rooms in the house that needed gutted and refinished. The entire porch was in the process of being removed to make way for a new, larger one. The landscaping around the entire residence was to be pulled up and replaced with a rock garden, and the yard would eventually be extended out even further into the wild grasses. There were doors and windows to be rebuilt or replaced. The little tin shed was being razed and would be the site of a new smokehouse. The corrals would all be torn down, and a new vinyl system would replace them. Even the road would be repaved with white gravel. Everything on the property would either be rebuilt or refinished except for the old windmill on top of the hill. Duke was there, and he would not be disturbed. Dingo joined him on the hill throughout most of the work, trying to avoid the commotion as was his style.

Marlene stopped by late in the afternoon on the first day of work. Little was said after Chris mentioned Hope's arrival, and her plans to stay through the construction. Both women were cordial, with an exchange from a distance as Marlene refused to step out of her truck. Hope understood quickly who the visitor was and kept her distance also. It was a tense moment that passed without event. Marlene left quietly knowing that she had nothing left to offer Chris anymore.

The days went by quickly as walls and buildings came down. Hope enjoyed helping out in the kitchen when she could but preferred to pitch in outside. It had been so long since she'd spent this much time in the sun. Her tan lines were well defined after only a few short days but she did not bother. Chris seemed to enjoy tracing over them at night with his fingers and this pleased her. Hope did wonder if she would ever be able to return to an office or classroom after this. The painting suited her well. She was left to her own most of the time, unless Chris needed a break from his attempts and failures at communicating in Spanish. He enjoyed her company, away from the chaos. It was hard to find time alone for the two of them amongst everything going on. At night, after dinner had been left by the girls, they ate and retired shortly, worn out from the long days. Fourteen hours a day was not uncommon during this time.

Sleep came easily, but it wasn't just exhaustion that drove them in early. There was something comfortable between them, lying together, talking or silence it didn't matter. Both of them knew it wouldn't last long and Hope would soon leave. It was the one subject that they did not talk about.

Ramone's Wisdom

E arly into the third week of work, things had slowed as projects wrapped up. The workforce had dwindled to only six, and Rita sent the food out with Ramone every morning. The day before everything was to wrap up, when putting the finishing touches around the upstairs bathroom, Hope finally caught Ramone while he was installing the faucet.

"Ramone, you don't say much do you?" she inquired standing in the tub painting the trim of the new window that overlooked the north forty.

The wise old Mexican had known this would come sooner or later, "No, Ms. Hope."

"Can I ask you something then?"

"You can ask me anything you want," he said.

Hope paused, wondering what to say. There were so many things she wanted to ask and every one of them she did not need to hear. "You've known Chris better than anyone, what do you think he's doing out here?"

Ramone stopped his work and sat down on the john wiping his hands clean. "He's searching."

Hope didn't understand, "Searching for what?"

"That I don't know. An answer, himself, searching for you, I don't know, I don't think he knows."

"Why would he come out here, there's nothing out here that can answer any of those questions?"

Ramone took a deep breath feeling like he would betray his friendship he reluctantly carried on, "Mr. Coupland's mind is a world in itself. When the world outside does not fit his standard, he will abandon all reality and create his own. He is offered that freedom out here." Ramone had known this for a long time. It was the exact same reason he had never left, yet he felt horrible for speaking of his friend like this. "Until he realizes this he will not find anything, he will go in circles seeking but find nothing to satisfy him."

This made sense to Hope. "Do you think he's a good man?"

"The best I have known, Ms. Hope. He has done more for my family than I could ever have asked for. He's given me more opportunities to better myself beyond anything a cowboy like me ever could imagine. He will be sending my granddaughter to school at a university back north, something we could never afford. He's charitable toward everyone but himself."

Hope didn't understand, "We were talking the other night, and Chris told me he was too selfish to ever have a family or children."

"That's what he sees and he may be selfish in many ways, but where it counts, he will give anyone anything, especially you."

"What has he told you about us?"

Ramone smiled, "Not much, but I can see it. That man is easy to read."

Hope laughed, "I agree. He used to get so mad at me when I told him that too."

Ramone even caught a small chuckle, he had never seen the boss's temper, but Chris had told him some eternal irritants, Hope's observation being one.

"He said you could always push him in a way no one else could," Ramone confessed.

"So, why me? I don't understand it."

Ramone wrestled with a rag, debating how to phrase the answer on the tip of his tongue, "You two complement each other. You two are not soul mates but flames that burn brighter when you are together."

"What do you think I should do?"

"Go, both of you need to go. You are in the same boat as he is, lost, not knowing where you belong. You would not be here if you weren't. In your own time, in your own way, each of you will figure it out, but together you will only push against one another."

Hope knew he was right; she only needed to hear it from someone else. Chris was right about Ramone, he was a very wise man.

"Excuse me Ms. Hope; I need to get back to work."

"Ramone," she said forcing a smile, "thank you."

The old Mexican tipped his hat and stood walking out into the hallway and down the stairs. Hope sat on the edge of the tub leaning back against the wall. She knew he was right but didn't want it to be true. Her eyes watered up, and she took a deep breath and stood. Painting again she took her time knowing that as soon as she was done, she would have to leave. Chris would let her stay as long as she wanted, but she couldn't.

That night she didn't sleep. She laid next to Chris listening to his breathing. It was deep and rhythmic. Chris was no longer a stranger. She felt they understood each other now better than they ever had. They were fighting the same battle to redefine their lives. It had been easy for their parents, graduate, get married, start a family, it was all planned out. Their generation was different. What would she do now? Find her own studio to work things out? She didn't have the resources he had. No, that was not her way. They were different people, and she had to figure it out for herself.

Wrapping Up

As the last day of the build began, Hope rose early and spent the day avoiding Chris. She watched him indirectly from the distance. For most of the morning, she joined Dingo atop the little hill under the old windmill. The breeze pushed her hair off to her right side as she sat beside the young dog watching. Questions ran through her head. For the first time since she arrived here, she had to face her options when she returned to Dallas. There were a few days of vacation time left. Maybe she wouldn't go back at all. Maybe it wasn't too late to enroll for the fall semester. She reached over and rubbed Duke's son. Watching Chris below, she saw the same bartender she first fell in love with working beside the hopeless romantic who'd chased her to Texas. Now the two visions came together and she saw the man she never would have imagined they'd become.

Late in the afternoon when Chris was satisfied with everything and the cleanup was complete, he sent Ramone and his two helpers home with cash in hand. Hope waved from where she stood leaning against the corner of the house on the new front porch as they pulled away.

Chris walked over from the Studio. From under the shade of the tin roof she watched him. His gaze didn't waver from her the entire way. As he came up the steps and leaned on the wall just around the corner from her, they spoke for the first time that day.

"Are you okay? You've been distant," Chris asked, this was about to happen all over again and he knew it.

"Chris, I don't think this is going to work out," Hope said looking down at her crossed legs standing in front of him.

Laughter burst from him as he smiled, "You know we had this conversation already, several years ago." He pulled Hope from the house and took her in his arms. Hers remained interlocked across her chest. "At least I saw this one coming."

She smiled, "I know. I just don't know what to do now."

"Neither do I." Nothing was said for the longest time. They stood there in the afternoon heat, yet neither moved.

Finally Hope spoke up, "Okay, you're making me all sweaty and nasty, I'm going to go clean up."

"Alright, I'll set something out for dinner." Together they walked inside and parted at the staircase. Hope went up to the master bathroom to try the new shower. It had been designed for two and she almost wished he would join her, but that would definitely blow past any line of decency they'd drawn.

Chris went to the kitchen and set out some fish Rugby picked out for him in Austin and some greens for a salad. He ran upstairs to ask Hope if she would rather go into town but stopped short. Just outside the bedroom door he could see her silhouette in the foggy haze of the bathroom. He'd controlled himself for so long he couldn't take it. Slowly he crept to the bathroom door. She was singing a tune he immediately recognized. The lyrics came out softly above the rush of water.

"'Cause a life without the one you love ain't no life at all, and a man and a woman need a little bit more than they can get on a telephone call..."

He stood there lost in dreams and memories that would make most people blush. They had a long past, and it remained vividly in his mind. He could remember every detail of her, every line every curve of her body and it was a beautiful body, even more so now than he could recall.

Hope stood under the raindrop shower head running her fingers through her hair when she heard him call. She was not surprised to hear his voice; she had left the door open.

"Hope?"

She peeked around the seam of the curtain letting her shoulder slip further out than necessary, "Yes?"

Chris stood leaning against the doorjamb, hands in his pockets, looking down to his side averting his gaze, "Um..." he paused not finding the words he needed. Hope noticed the sly grin on his face as he looked up. He was bashful, she had never seen him act like this before and it excited her.

"Never mind," he finally stated as he turned back into the bedroom. Hope smiled as she returned to finish washing.

By the time she was dressed and downstairs, the large barbecue built into the patio in the last week was rolling with smoke and the cedar planks were soaking in the sink. Chris was mixing a dressing on the counter with his back to the door.

"Shower's free," she informed him tossing her last towel over his shoulder.

Chris turned his head quickly, lost in his thoughts. He hadn't heard her come in, "Oh, yeah, um, would you do me a favor?"

"Anything," she replied softly still smiling from earlier. Seeing a new side to him really intrigued her.

"Can you put the salmon on the grill, it should be done about the time I get back."

"No problem."

Chris walked past her on his way out talking quietly to himself, "What the hell was she smiling about?"

Hope could smell him as he passed. The sweat of a long day, a long few weeks, it was something she'd miss, but not tonight.

The Dance

They ate on the patio, testing out the new lighting after the sun had set. When the conversation came to a lull Chris found the opportunity to try the stereo system. They had wired speakers throughout the entire house and patio. It rang out beautifully across the West Texas basin. He came back out with two cocktails; hers, whiskey and coke, his, rye on the rocks. Together they went through song after song, and drink after drink. They laughed at old stories told too many times already and spoke of friends they wished they saw more often. When an acoustic song by Stone LaRue came across the speakers, Chris changed the subject.

"I would ask you for a dance but last time I did that I went down in flames."

Hope got a questioning look on her face, "When was that?"

"At Lacey's wedding, given I was about a dozen whiskeys into it, but if I recall you were occupied at the time."

Laughing at the thought, "You were quite the show that night."

"It was the first time the family was all together since we'd broken up and yeah, I was a little nervous about the whole thing. I'd been drinking since early in the afternoon."

"Well, I guess I owe you a dance then."

The strings played on with a blues slide to them as a new song came across the stereo.

"We got moonlight, all night, Lord I pray on the next star I see tonight, we never lose this thing we found. With you by my side I can do without the city lights, I fly so high when you're around that my feet don't touch the ground."

They met at the far side of the table. Surrounded by lanterns and a sea of stars, they moved as close as could be. From one poetic tune to another, the stereo knew just what was needed.

In time they fell into a hammock together. The gentle rocking helping to calm the nerves and the fire that built between them. Chris hung one foot down to the ground to keep the sling in rhythm with the music. Hope closed her eyes not wanting to sleep but not wanting to face what was coming. Eventually sleep came to her before she knew it. Chris could tell when she had slipped into slumber. She had always had a soft purr when she slept. It came quickly tonight. He could not bring himself to close his eyes. He stayed up, rocking her, running his fingers through her hair as they were serenaded by memories and lost anthems. It was not until darkness began to fade in the east that he softly slipped from beside her and carried her to bed. She was out cold. He gently removed her jeans and slipped into a pair of shorts himself to join her underneath the sheets. When he put an arm around her, she naturally rolled over to him. Chris kissed her softly and took a deep breath giving in to exhaustion.

The Last Day

For the last time, Hope woke up in his arms. Today she would have to leave. She had found what she was seeking when she came out here. It was a good thing and though she knew it could not last forever, it had been amazing for a brief while. Before her emotions got the best of her, she got up and headed to the kitchen. When Chris came to shortly after, he immediately thought she had left already. His heart jumped into his throat. He quickly swapped his shorts for jeans and hopped down the hallway desperately trying to pull them up on the run. He bolted down the stairs three at a time only buttoning his fly when he'd landed on the ground floor and rounded the banister. Chris flew through the dining room and slid to a stop. Outside, on the other side of the drive, sat her fire red Pontiac. He caught his breath and heard a small laugh from the kitchen. He spun around to see Hope standing there covering her mouth, laughing at him. Chris glared at the ceiling feeling foolishly, "I thought you might have left already."

"No, I just got down here myself," she said standing against the counter top, still in her shirt, sans shorts. Her laugh quickly faded away.

Stepping through the doorway, Chris noticed the redness in her eyes and the streak of a tear already fallen down her right cheek. He walked over and she wrapped her arms around him as more tears began to follow. When the last sniff had passed he looked down at her, "Are you okay?"

Hope wiped her eyes on his shoulder, "Yeah, I'll be fine. I just didn't realize how tough this would be."

Chris held her for a long while after, not wanting to let go either, "We will never be down the same road again."

"I know, but you were always there, I always hoped you would be. But now, now I don't know. We're both moving on and I don't know where it's taking us."

"It's taking us wherever we need to be. You have to trust that."

After a long pause Hope finally spoke, "Stay in touch, please."

"I will, and I'll be back before you know it. Things may never be the way they were before but I will always love you, and who knows where tomorrow will take us."

With that said, Hope excused herself to clean up and gather her things. Together they packed their bags. There was not much Chris wanted to take with him, everything he needed was stuffed into one large olive green backpack. Everything else had been put in storage the week before.

When Hope finished she came down to find Chris at the dining room table. He was signing papers, a lot of papers.

"What's all this?" she asked.

Chris signed the last one and stuffed them all in a large envelope. He tossed it on the table, and she noticed written across the front in large script was "Ramone Padillo."

"I'm giving my power over the Studio and land to Ramone while I'm gone and if I don't come back, everything I have down here goes to him and the rest will be split amongst the family."

Shocked, Hope asked, "Christ Chris, where do you think you're going? Is this necessary?"

"I don't know for sure, and no, it's not necessary," he gave her a reassuring smile, "but I want everything in order. Just in case. Come on, I don't want to second guess myself."

Together they gathered their bags and headed out the back door. Chris checked his watch as they crossed the patio. Ramone would be arriving soon and he would rather not be here when the old Mexican showed. Ramone knew exactly what was going on and what needed done.

With both her car and his truck loaded, Chris met Hope at her door. "Thank you sweetheart," he said kissing her atop her head.

"Well," she said sniffling already, "I had to come see it sooner or later."

"No. For everything else, thank you."

With one final hug she sat in her car watching him walk away. Chris stepped up into his truck, and the diesel came to life with a thunderous roar. He pulled away and lapped around the drive. Hope couldn't bring herself to leave. Chris stopped in front of the house just at the base of the hill and looked back.

Hope sat there, "Let's go then." she said to herself. She cleared her eyes and followed his tracks around the yard. Chris waved as she blew by and followed right behind her. Dingo, sitting under the old windmill took off alongside them as they both mounted the hill. He gave chase for a hundred yards and pulled back watching the cloud of dust drift away. At the black top Hope waved and pulled north toward the interstate. Chris sat at the edge for a short second and waved back. Together they headed out in two totally different directions.

Ramone passed Hope a short jog down the highway and waved as she passed. She laid on the horn of her car in response and flew by not looking back. The old Chevy pulled past the windmill before their dust had even settled. Parking in front of the house for the first time he stepped out, kicked the dirt from his boots and walked up the porch and in the front door.

The Getaway

The road stretched out before the dreamer like a never ending river, a therapeutic scenic by-way to nowhere in particular. Distant, lost, he had no real destination. "Sometimes it's not the destination," he could hear Ramone instructing him. Windows down, no radio, just thoughts to pass the time. The man looking back from the rearview mirror seemed to age before his eyes. He was not the young ambitious buck he'd once been. A joke about two bulls sitting atop a hill overlooking a field of heifers came to mind, but he couldn't remember the punch line.

Chris pulled off the gold tinted sunglasses and felt better, felt relieved. His brow may have wrinkled over time by eternal thought and his skin, toned a dark tan by the years in the sun, but his ghostly blue eyes still held on to the vivid youth he felt inside again. From memory his fingers dialed Neal's phone number.

"Chris, what's going on son?" came the usual greeting.

"Neal, I'm going to be leaving the country for a long while. I'm not sure how long and before you ask I don't really know where I'm going either."

"Nothing you say anymore surprises me." Neal responded flatly.

Chris laughed, "You know Mother said the exact same thing when I told her what I was doing."

"Okay," a long pause halted the brown guy's question, "so what are we all supposed to do?"

"Just keep on like you are. Nothing's changed, Mom has full control of the company. If you have any questions call her."

"Are you kidding me? I already talk to her at least three days a week. She's going to learn to love me."

"She loves all of you, no worries." Chris made his adieus and hung up the phone.

He drove on reflecting, exploring ideas, searching areas of his own humanity that had never been touched before. For days he drove, stopping whenever he needed or wanted. There was no schedule or rules and no speed limit either. He already had five tickets from some of the finest judicial districts across the Southwest thus far. On the fifth day he chose to stop and sleep in a real bed for the first time since leaving the Studio.

While sitting outside a motel near Gila Bend, Arizona his phone rang. It was Rugby. Word had gotten around. "Hey buddy," he answered.

"I hear you're leaving," Rugby said. "Kathy and Neal had stopped through and retold the whole story. Where you going, man?"

"To tell you the truth, I don't know yet. I'll let you know when I get there, how's that?"

Rugby yelled something away from the phone in Spanish, "Look, I gotta go but keep me in the loop; I need to know where to go if I have to bail you out, okay?"

"Deal," Chris replied and the line clicked dead. He stood and turned the phone off watching the screen fade to black. He walked in the setting sun, out into the middle of the highway, traffic was infrequent here, and with everything he could muster Chris threw the phone down the highway. A few seconds later the rattle of plastic came back guaranteeing its destruction. "I mean no disrespect old friend but I don't want to have to repeat that conversation." Chris stood watching the heat rise off the blacktop, an old, broken two lane. Many thoughts rattled around his head.

On the way back toward his room, he pulled from the old Ford a folder and pen. The small room wasn't even worth the thirty dollars he had to pay, in advance, cash only. For the first time in years he took a cigarette from a pack he'd bought at his last stop and lit it. To hell with it all. Long term health goals were not of a high priority at this particular moment. Taking a long drag, Chris almost forgot why he'd quit. Two more long pulls and everything came flooding back. With a sip of rye whiskey Chris put pen to paper. He wrote his mother, Ramone and several others, those he thought needed to know where he was. In his last letter the pen stalled, what to write, what to say? One word was all he could force out of the fountain pen and Hope is all it brought. Chris slept little that night; he had a bad case of the traveling jones.

Chasing

The daybreak found Chris in the Laundromat across the street washing his dirty leftovers of the previous week. He had little more than a few pair of jeans and several shirts, and a coat, though he didn't need it yet. Everything easily fit in his backpack. The rest of the space was taken up by other necessities of the road. He sat watching the occasional truck drive by outside. He wore nothing but a pair of boxers sitting atop the dryer that worked over his laundry. As the glare of the morning sun shone through front windows of the empty store, he swore he could see Hope walk by. It was an illusion, a dirty trick his mind played on him. It wasn't the first time he'd seen her. She had been a hitchhiker along the road somewhere near Las Cruces; she was strolling along amongst the plateaus just yesterday. The buzzer of the dryer startled him. He jumped down and got dressed trading his shorts out for jeans; there was no one in the store to offend.

Hope Grows

⌒

Hope's return to Dallas brought up questions, all of which she
answered, truthfully, occasionally omitting a few choice words.
When the dust finally settled there was no personal harm and the
ruling was accidental. The young woman, free of all suspicion, gathered
everything she had to her name, four suitcases and a fire red Pontiac,
and trudged on. The total abandonment of everything that held her back
before meant total liberty to start over, and Hope took full advantage
of the situation.

The young woman had always thought of going back to school,
and now was the perfect opportunity. Someone had failed to inform
her when she was working on her first degree that the print journalism
industry was dying. The digital age was building a coffin that was soon
to bury traditional news formats. Everything was online now and the
Sunday paper was rotting away in recycling bins everywhere. She had
been accepted that fall into a graduate track at a local college to study
speech therapy. The day after enrolling Hope put a deposit down on a
small two bedroom, slab-on-grade home in Los Colinas north of Dallas
proper. It was a quaint red brick home that looked like every other house
in the sub-division. The yard was tiny and the space was limited, but
with every bit of furniture reduced to ashes, it was more room than she
needed.

As the end of the summer neared and Hope finished settling in her new home, she secured a job working at a local hospital not far from the house or campus. On her last trip through the old apartment building downtown to pick up her last stack of mail and turn in her key, she found a letter in the stack of bills waiting for her. The return address was that of Cindy Coupland. She ripped it open. From inside the large manila envelope she pulled a standard size red envelope with a post-it note on the front.

"*Hope, I just received this letter in the mail. I'm assuming it is to be forwarded to you. I wish you the best and good luck with school. Love, Cindy.*"

The red letter was tucked into her purse as she walked out of the lobby. It would wait until she had time to sit down and focus. Her mind ran wild as she drove out of town toward home. Where could he be? What was he doing? The more she thought about it all the heavier her foot became. Soon she was racing up the interstate at nearly triple digit speeds.

When her red Pontiac pulled into her own drive, Hope threw it into park and ran into the house. The residence was still empty with only a few belongings strung throughout, but the living room just inside the front door was completely barren. She dropped her purse just to the left of the door and kicked off her shoes. The stark blue walls surrounded her but she was lost in herself. Hope took a seat on the soft beige carpet along the opposing wall and examined the red envelope. One corner was bent slightly and it had signs of the long course it took to reach her. On the front in the familiar tall, lean script it read '*Hope Lawrence*' followed by Cindy Coupland's address. There was no return address in the upper left corner, only a name, '*Coupland.*'

Hope's fingers delicately brushed over the front and back as she examined the sheath. Gently one finger slid down the length of the envelope to break the seal, and she pulled out the paper from inside. It was written on a rather thin paper that Hope assumed to be vellum, but she was unsure. She quickly read over the correspondence then came back for a second time studying the writing. It began simply enough,

Chris greeted her with *'Sweetheart,'* though he addressed many people with the term. Hope always imagined that it meant more when he was calling to her. The letter moved on to tell of his quick journey through Arizona and Southern California. His description of the Pacific sunset was beautiful, she could almost see it sitting there, landlocked in Los Colinas. From there Chris wrote that he had signed on to a commercial container ship, *The Liberty Phoenix,* headed out across the Pacific. The beast, as he seemed to refer to the vessel was old and rusted. He worked under a short, fat old man who sweated profusely in the tropical summer weather. His occupation was maintenance, and he wrote that he had learned much regarding diesel mechanics. Hope skipped ahead to the line she was looking for. The letter read…

"It seems that you are haunting me. Whether this is intentional or not, I don't know. I have seen you, both dreaming and awake. Just yesterday, on our sixth day at sea, I went topside just after noon to get some fresh air. The air was oppressive. The only breeze was the one stirred up by the ship cutting though the water. My clothes stuck to my body with sweat. I took up post leaning on the stern railing looking out at the seas we'd already passed.

Below me, walking on the glassy surface of the water, I could see you following. Every step you took, drawing closer, sent tiny concentric ripples outward to disappear into the abyss below. You looked up and smiled. You were wearing the negligee that I gave to you our first Christmas together. I always loved the way you wore it, the silky piece fit just right."

Hope set the letter down in her lap and looked up smiling. She shook her head as she rested it on the wall behind her. Speaking out loud to no one at all she noted, "It took you eight years to finally make a compliment on that. Why would I expect anything different?" she wondered as she turned her attention to the point she'd left off.

"One of the straps that kept it from falling off slipped over your shoulder. You didn't even reach for it, I almost pleaded for you to stop but couldn't. Step by step you drew closer. Seeing you there I was reminded of the wildflower I saw standing upon the hill the first night you came to visit the Studio. It was the most beautiful scene I have fought to reserve in all its beauty.

As you neared, you looked up at me and brushed your hair aside, tucking it behind your left ear the way you always do. When your path neared the wake of the ship, the hem of your silk cover began to flutter in the air. You began speaking but I could not hear anything over the wake. As you stepped closer and closer to the wash your image faded away. I wanted so badly to leap overboard, to reach for you..."

Hope smiled, her face felt a little rosy. Even from half a world away he still knew how to flatter her.

The letter went on to tell of the stops they made and the unique people of the South Pacific islands. Chris wrote of the food and cultures. His writing became more excited and fanatic the further he traveled. Eventually he gave his farewell and promised to write again soon as he told of the ship making port in Brisbane, Queensland, Australia. Hope picked up the red envelope and examined the post mark. There it was in black ink, this letter had traveled further than she ever had.

Hope folded the pieces of paper back up and stuffed them in their envelope and slowly rose from the floor, walking back into her room. In the closet, on the top shelf above her suitcases sat the old shoe box. Hope filed this most recent addition to the collection of letters on top of so many others that contained the same familiar script.

Routine

B etween work and school the weeks began to blur for Hope. The holidays came to pass and a new year began. Chris was still absent as winter turned to spring and Hope wrapped up her second semester of classes. She received a letter almost once a month, sometimes less.

Returning to her two bedroom house after completing her final exam of the semester, Hope walked down to her mailbox after parking in front of the house. There was the typical junk mail and bills but buried within all the mess in her hands lay the familiar envelope with Cindy's return address in the corner. Hope walked into the house and as always when she received anything from Cindy, she dropped everything else, settled on her plush couch and tore the manila package. The envelope inside was a cream white with red and blue stripes framing the front and back. Again, no return address, only his signature. The piece was titled for her but addressed to his mother. Hope went over the last few letters she had received. Chris had settled on a large ranch several hundred miles west of Cloncurry, Australia buried deep in the Northern Territory. He talked mostly of work and the lifestyle of the ranch. From his descriptions she could see the ramshackle buildings, the thin cattle and the dusty land that he had fallen in love with.

Hope slowly peeled open the envelope as she had every time before and unfolded the paper. This one actually looked dusty. The ink of Chris's pen had smeared several times. It was a common occurrence for southpaws. Immediately Hope noticed the sketches strewn across the pages. There was one of a dog on the front page in the lower left corner. Underneath it was titled *'Duke II.'* On another page there was a very detailed drawing of a small ramshackle bunk house that had *'Home'* written just above it. There were others that looked more abstract and had no title. It was boredom, and it was not a good sign. Just as every greeting before he began with, *'Sweetheart.'* He wrote of the weather cooling as the southern hemisphere headed into the winter cycle. Hope smiled, she was just as apprehensive of heading into the summer cycle in Texas.

'I just don't know what to expect. I timed it just right that I have been living in a continuous summer since we parted ways ten months ago. Kyle, the teenage orphan who bunks right next to me swears that it's not too bad. I guess it can't be any worse than home, the environments are similar. Unfortunately I'm starting to get that itch again, I don't know if I'll stick around here much longer. I believe it's time to move on.'

Chris never wrote of where he planned to go, Hope doubted that he knew. When she had read through a second time, the papers were repackaged and placed with all the others. When the box was replaced, Hope turned her attention to the suitcases below and began packing. She was leaving the next morning to return home to see the family. Everyone was to meet back at the alma mater. There was no particular reason, just a getaway with familiar faces. After the chaos of the past few months, it was a vacation that Hope dearly needed.

Family Reunion

After the eight hour trip north through Oklahoma and most of Kansas Hope pulled into town as the sun was just beginning to set. The drive in was very scenic if the right roads were taken. She had spoken to Lacey about three hours ago as she crossed the state line. Hope was to meet everyone in the bar district just down the street from the University.

Their old stomping ground where everyone had met closed down long ago. The space was taken over and renovated by another bar owner. It looked completely different and none of the family liked it. The change was inevitable, but it no longer belonged to them. Instead, there was an Irish bar they all used to frequent that they now called home. It was divided into two parts, the larger side had booths and a pool table, the smaller side held only one table in the front window. The last word Hope had received said that the lone front table in the narrow side, known as the alley, would be the place to gather.

Hope parked a block east of the Irish bar and walked down the alley approaching from behind. She turned the corner halfway down the next block and stepped into the patio. Rugby and Kathy stood just outside the door smoking.

"Hey!" Rugby cried as he saw the young woman come around the fence.

Hope wrapped her arms around the chef, "How are you doing?" She released her grip and stepped over to embrace Kathy.

"Eh, you know, strikes and gutters," Rugby responded with a shrug, his typical mindset.

"How was your drive, honey?" Kathy asked with her arms in Hope's.

"It went well, long as ever, but well. Where is everyone else?"

Rugby took one long draw of his cigarette and flicked it over the fence, "They're all inside, let's go say hi." He led the way into the alley side of the establishment. The crowd was thin, but it was early. It would surely fill up as the night wore on.

As the trio passed the bar, Hope laughed to herself. Many years ago, into their junior year of college on St. Patty's Day she had been sitting at this bar with Chris and another. Chris had been out at the bars all day celebrating his favorite holiday and was in no condition to even be in public. Hope had only made it down to meet him late in the evening after her shift back at their bar. Together they drank, sang songs, and told lies as best they could. When it came time to rotate to a new establishment, Hope led the way out the front door she was now approaching. She didn't feel drunk, but apparently her feet felt different that night. She'd tripped just one step from the door. Thankfully the bar had been much busier than it was this night for the door was propped open and she'd rolled down the single step and out onto the sidewalk. It was a small tumble, but one that Chris would never let her forget.

Hope shook her head thinking of all the memories this place held. There were dollar bills, signed and decorated, hung all over the walls. She'd hung one up on the ceiling above the doorway on the far end toward the rear. She'd have to look for it later. There was another that Chris had hung on the wall behind her, but she didn't know exactly where. Even all these years later they had fingerprints all over the place. Just outside and around the corner on the next block over there was a small-hole-in-the-wall joint that had their names etched in the wall. Hope wondered if it was still there. Maybe they would make it over sometime later in the night to find it. Right now though, her attention turned to her friends sitting before her.

Neal stood as Hope approached the table, "Hope, last to show buys. I'll have beer."

"Hug me and shut up," She said ignoring his last statement. Hope had to laugh when Neal let go, "what is on your shorts?"

"Bar-B-Q," he replied with no explanation.

There was not an empty seat at the table, several of the family stood, acting as a barrier against the growing number of patrons. The bar got louder and louder by the hour. Not long after dark they had to yell to be heard above all the noise. The late spring night was too beautiful to miss. In time the party migrated outside to one of the many long picnic tables that spread out across the back patio behind the alley. There was live music, cold drinks and everyone in the world Hope could wish to be surrounded by save for one. The musician, a local boy only Rugby knew by name, played acoustic covers standing in the back corner of the patio.

"I know I got a bad Reputation. And it isn't just talk, talk, talk…"

The talk amongst the table stopped. This song had been in regular rotation on the many late nights the family used to spend together after work. Lacey leaned across the table to address Hope, "Have you heard from our wandering friend lately?"

Hope, lost in song turned to the tiny dancer, "What?"

"What!?" Lacey yelled back mockingly, "I said, have you heard from Chris?"

"Oh! Yeah, I got a letter yesterday afternoon. He's still in Australia working on a cattle ranch. I don't know how much longer he's going to be there. The letter said he was thinking about moving on but it didn't say where."

Rugby picked up on the conversation "The last note I got said he was heading north into Southeast Asia. I don't know when he wrote it. It said the food sucked where he was at."

Kathy finally asked the question that was on all their minds, "How long is he going to be gone?"

"I don't know. I wouldn't expect him back anytime soon though." Hope answered.

"Why won't he call anyone or get in touch or let us know how to find him?" Kathy continued.

Rugby had thought long and hard about that very question, "I asked Mama Coupland the same thing. The best answer we can figure is that Chris has always headed down the road less taken for better or worse," Rugby offered. "If he wants to get away from everything he knows, he's going to take it as far as humanly possible. He said he would write often to let us know he's okay. Give it time; he has to find his own pattern."

Hope added, "From what I have pieced together, I think that he's removing himself from all that is familiar he wants to see his life from an outsiders view. I think it's damn foolish, but you know Chris, he won't learn anything until he screws it all up first. I know he can handle himself and will come away a better person, he always does."

Rugby laughed, "Its funny, Cindy said the exact same thing just the other day."

Neal asked Rugby as he finished his drink, "How often do you see Cindy?"

"I try and make it out to her place at least once a week to make sure everything is going well, and she stops by the restaurant every time she's in town. Two or three times a week usually. I think she uses me as a replacement son while Chris is gone."

"Well we're all happy she has someone near," Lacey added.

"She has no hard feelings in all this. She gets a letter almost every other day, so she knows what's going on all the time, she just can't write back, that's all. Cindy knows Chris better than any of us. She knows what it's all worth in the end. The business keeps her busy most days, she's in Jackson, Mississippi right now visiting a potential business partner but I don't know any details."

For the rest of her time back home, little was said of Chris unless in passing or retelling of stories and lies. The family spent their days seeing old sights and visiting familiar places enjoying the company all the while. When Monday morning came though, Hope headed back south into the Lone Star State. There were summer classes to attend and work to be done.

It would be over a year until they all came together again.

Long Absence

～

Summer that year was hotter than average. Texas baked under an unforgiving sun. It could not get any further removed from the cool, ever present rainfall twelve months before. Hope finished all her classes as the dog days of summer set it. The weather eventually broke into fall, which held off the cold winter chill until late in December that year. Hope finished her third semester of school and had only one left as the frost finally came to the Dallas metro area. Winter passed swiftly and spring came about even quicker. By the time March arrived it was already lush and green. Hope had job interviews lined up and was making preparations for graduation in May.

All of her classes were completed with high marks. Just weeks before her final tests she was hired on at the same medical facility where she had been employed for over a year and a half. Her department was Early Childhood Speech Development. Graduation came and passed, the family and her own kin came down to celebrate. The day that everyone left, in the still May night, Hope paced through her two bedroom house unable to sleep. There was something that bothered her. Several times throughout the weekend she had been asked of Chris's present situation and to be honest with herself, Hope had to admit that she did not know.

As the hours turned to a new day, Hope sat up at her small kitchen table sorting through the box of letters that she had gathered over the years. The box was worn now, ripped in spots and several corners rubbed down to nothing. It looked dirty and disheveled. It was the most unsightly treasure box that she had ever seen. Compared to the presents she'd received from graduation, all neatly wrapped and tied, sitting in the corner beside her, this box looked ugly and worthless. But, if the truth was known she would surrender everything she owned just to guarantee the safety and preservation of this rough case and its contents. The only light in the room was a pendant lamp that hung just over her head which swung slightly as the breeze from the window over her shoulder pushed through the screen to cool the heavy night air. It cast swaying shadows from her hands as she ran them over the box inspecting its integrity. Her bare arms extended well beyond the length of the bathrobe that hung loosely over her shoulders. She sat with one foot snuggled against her and her chin on the exposed knee that rose above table height.

Until this last weekend, when questions about Chris arose, Hope had been too busy to realize the worry. The problem was that it had been almost seven months since she received anything from her old friend and lover. Finally Hope lifted the lid of the shoe box. The hinged edge, well worn and half torn gave no resistance. She watched attentively as the shadowy inside, illuminated by the single light above, revealed all of its contents.

The first letter she removed and unfolded was from June of the previous year. It was just after Chris had left the cattle ranch in Australia. It stated that he was writing from a small transport ship in Malaysia. The letter stated that he'd been at sea for almost a month, working as a laborer for a small Asian man who moved goods and people from island to island throughout Malaysia and Indonesia. They were rarely on the water for more than a day at a time, but it was busy enough that he never left the boat. The letter held precious little of the humor and philosophy that filled many of his previous writings. The tone and language began to change. This letter seemed very cold compared to the others. The complaints, which had were almost nonexistent in the first year of his journey, started to take up more and more space.

Hope replaced that letter. The next one was just after he had arrived in Vietnam. The vocabulary of this letter was much more familiar, much more optimistic. He wrote of the beauty of the countryside, but as he entered more populated areas the tone changed. The level of existence there in Vietnam made him sick the first few days. Chris wrote of children who worked harder than he ever had, for little or nothing.

"Slavery is an idea that most Americans are familiar with from textbooks, but here it is alive and well. The cursed hell which man seems fit to inflict upon his own kind has yet to be extinguished by either law or education."

Eventually after weeks of navigating foreign roads and ghettos, Chris finally made it to the capitol city with little left in his pockets.

The letter told of one afternoon, while sitting on a crate in an open air market in southern Saigon watching the people come and go. He began to question the value of possession.

"The smell here is either enticing or nauseating. At one time I can smell the sweet aroma of duck fat frying in the shop across the street, but when the wind shifts, the air carries the stale odor of sewage and decay. These people seem indifferent. I've studied their actions for days now and despite everything, they all seem to be happy. Their happiness is not tied to land or houses, they are happy just to be outside, to live, to exist. This is a basic necessity of human life that those back home have become so far withdrawn from that their happiness is based on what they own."

Chris went on to tell of the markets and small salons that lined the claustrophobic streets. Eventually he wrote of the pains of hunger that he began to feel at night as the money available to him became scarcer.

"Eventually I took a job as an errand boy for several local 'unofficial' businesses. The work may not exactly be legal, but it is no different than what any other young man here must do to survive."

Hope had read this letter in its entirety many times over. She couldn't finish it, she couldn't bear to imagine Chris in such a condition, instead it was gently folded and placed back in the box with the rest.

On the top of the pile laid the last correspondence she received the previous October.

Rock Bottom

Hope sat at her kitchen table staring at the last letter that she'd received from Chris. She had first read it seven months ago. The papers she pulled from the envelope were dirty and foul smelling still. She could not identify any of the stains that discolored the pages. The ink had run and the papers looked like they had been wet at some point. There were greasy smears all over the pages, some obscuring the words at places, but halfway up the right hand side of the first page she could see a distinctive finger print. Hope didn't know if it was Chris's or not, but she imagined it was. She sat at her dining room table under the single pendant light and studied that print until her eyes became dry and fuzzy. With a deep breath and flickering eyelids, she began to read.

This latest letter was shorter than the rest. Chris's whimsical, drawn out descriptions of the land and people were cut down to short jagged narratives of his surroundings. Even the tall, lean script typically used was thrown out for a scribbling of block letters that didn't always form complete recognizable letters or words. Hope scanned the words lightly not wanting to repeat some portions of the correspondence.

"The first night I couldn't sleep from the pains of hunger, my desperation sunk further than I ever imagined possible. The slums back home and those that fight an ever present war of survival who occupy those decrepit places stand before me in a new light. I have never stolen from those who did not

deserve it from their greed, but the first night I did my idea of a criminal was forever changed. Sheer existence is the mother of motivation."

Hope wondered just how far Chris would sink before he came to his senses. She wished she could run to him, to hold him, to hit him as hard as she could. Her left hand had clenched into a fist as she read the stubborn man's words of the suffering he strove to endure in the name of understanding. The danger immediately came to the front of her mind. It apparently did not register with the bastard who remained so far absent.

"The people, the life, I live in a world of illicit drugs and women. In trade for protection they give me a bed to lay in at night, but often I find my mind lost in a haze and fog from chasing the dragon. I wither in the underbelly of society, the home and life I used to know are only distant memories. Only your ghost keeps me company. I am pushed further down the hole of existence by the burning desire to find the bottom. Ramone's words are all that I hear, 'The edge is only known to those who have gone over it.' He's right. He was always right."

The letter ended abruptly. There was no farewell. Hope sat there until dawn was breaking in the eastern sky reading letter after letter trying to find the pattern, to understand where Chris might be. In time she surrendered. There was no hidden message or code. He wore his heart on his sleeve and even in writing it was still obvious.

Recovery

Hope continued on with her life as anyone would. She started her new career and loved every minute of it. The children brought a light to her life that she never imagined. It was a perfect fit and as the days rolled into weeks the fear for her lost friend began to fade. She still thought of him almost daily, especially late at night as she lay in bed alone; yet the longer he remained absent without any word, the more Hope came to believe that he would survive and once again come out unscathed as he always did, smiling with his blue eyes blazing.

In time, her assumptions were proven true when on a balmy July afternoon, Hope finally received word. She could see the corner of a manila envelope peeking out of her mail box as she pulled into the drive. She immediately parked and ran to the box and pulled the package out, ripping it open revealing a sealed blue envelope. Her hands had none of the gentle nature reserved for the previous letters. She tore through the barrier and unfolded the papers that it held. The script that filled the pages was once again his own. Her heart immediately settled, ever so slightly.

'Sweetheart,' it began just as she'd wanted. Hope ran into the house leaving everything behind. Through the living room she strode scanning over the pages not really reading a single word, just reviewing it all. In the kitchen she leaned back against the countertop and crossed her legs and pulled the first page within view.

"I apologize for my absence and any fret that it may have caused you. There is nothing in my life that I do not regret, for there is nothing you can do to change the past, but if there is a time in my life I would ever like to forget, it would be the last nine months and only those. I have only been imprisoned twice in my life. The first was an overnight stay in Oklahoma for being a drunken nuisance. The last six months would constitute my second visit. For reasons I will have to explain later, I was incarcerated in a mass cell for many months in Vietnam surrounded by more than twenty men, pissing in a bucket, locked in a cell for days at a time. I had finally found the edge. Thankfully at the last second before it was too late, with a final grasp I took hold of reality and pulled myself back. I strove to reach the utter bottom of existence, and I have accomplished just such. It's all up hill from here."

Hope was so relieved to see these words in her hand. Her fury still burned hot inside and wished she could confront him for putting her and all the others who loved this crazy man through such an ordeal.

Suddenly his absence made sense. Someone would have stopped him from the fate he'd endured if any of the family had known his location. She continued on. The letter stated that he'd left Vietnam several weeks ago and was now well established in a Red Cross hospital not far outside of Hong Kong near a village named Renhe.

"I've been hired on for maintenance. I help out when I can. I even assisted in a surgery the other day, holding a light, a simple task but it was my part. They will take any volunteers they can get. They give me a place to lay my head and a fulfilling position.

When I'm not working, my time is spent with the children. The terminal children are the only permanent residents we have, and their sources for daily entertainment are limited, as are all of our resources."

Hope was impressed with his tolerance for the children; it was a trait that she'd never seen in him. His final words gave an optimistic goodbye and a vivid description of the sunrise over the terraced hills that surrounded the Red Cross camp. Hope kissed the papers and took in their scent. She swore to herself that she could still smell the dew laden grass that Chris ran his bare feet through while bidding farewell.

Running

$$\sim$$

Hope ran almost daily now. The physical activity helped to soothe her mind and calm her nerves. Most outings only lasted a mile or so, but on the days when she thought of Chris the miles would begin to grow longer and longer. With headphones blazing Hope pushed into mile four as she passed City Hall and rounded the corner toward the fire station of Lost Colinas. She paid no attention to the music that cycled through while one foot after the other paced down the asphalt.

The morning sun cut through the trees, slowly drowning out the early darkness. Brilliant rays shimmered, reflecting off the thin coating of frost that the night had left. It was the first evidence of the encroaching winter. Early December now, Chris had been absent for three and a half years with no sign of slowing. Hope thought of the sunrises that filled the pages of the letters he sent her. It was always his favorite time of day.

Chris had written regularly since he attended to the maintenance of the Red Cross station outside Renhe, China, though he'd long left there. Hope recalled the note sent from Hong Kong.

"I am presently sitting on the dock of Hong Kong Bay, waiting to board the small sailing vessel 'Proud Mary.' The morning was brisk and dark when I left the medical center. It was difficult to part knowing that none of the children will remain there much longer. I gave each of them something to remember me by, but the compassion that they instilled is the most valuable gift anyone could have ever given me.

The captain of the boat is a tall, lanky gentleman from Scotland. I mistakenly referred to him as British when he introduced himself, a mistake that I was instructed to never make again. William Benjamin is his name and with his wife, Kirsten, they are sailing around the globe. He has offered me a position on board. In return for passage I will work aboard and as William put it, 'will be taught to sail and live as a gentleman.' I don't know what all that entails, but it sounds enticing."

As the fourth mile ended and the fifth began, Hope lapped around the small park on the west edge of town and began to weave her way back toward home. The letters came in from every port the small vessel made. The letter from Mynamar told of the open sea and Chris's longing for the music of home. It was the one thing he confessed that was dearly missed. His next letter was postmarked from India. The script had joked that half the people he met in port claimed to be related to Neal. The food was much better than anything the brown guy had ever made, but Hope was asked not to share that revelation with their old friend. Hope smiled as she recalled the confessions of the night.

"As I lay here, rocking gently in my hammock, surrounded by a horizon that would best West Texas by only a small margin, I think the nights I would have died for you come sunrise just to have you one last time. With only stars and a compass for company I now long for your company. There is no other who will take your place and still I know that I cannot have you. The life you want and where my road may lead will never cross."

Hope began to feel the burning in her lungs as she pushed on further and faster. The message from East Africa told of the ongoing debate between Chris and William.

"The Captain sees it fit to lecture me on the finer points of Scotch Whiskey. For hours we argue the merit of American Rye versus Scotch. It is a never ending battle. I will not concede the victory though someday I hope to settle on a mutual disagreement."

'To the bottom and back and yet still stubborn as hell,' Hope thought to herself as she began mile six.

The most disturbing letter Hope had received since the mangled note from Vietnam was postmarked from South Africa. It was well written but wrinkled and stained with whiskey.

"Hope, never in my life have I feared death until last night. It was a scene I will never forget.

We are currently a few hundred miles south of Madagascar headed to South Africa. The night began calmly enough. A few clouds in the sky but the moon shone brightly casting diamonds out as far as the eye could see. I lay watching the clouds build and just as the last remainder of lunar light vanished, the winds changed and began to pick up. Within the hour the rain fell like bombs on the deck. William came to assist me as a wave crashed into the port side of the small boat rolling the vessel and nearly tossing the lanky Scot into the sea.

The salty spray stung, driven by the fierce winds. More than once I was almost lost overboard. William in a drunken stupor cussed Poseidon. Together we fought for six hours to keep the boat upright. For the first time since leaving Texas, I doubted that I would return.

The storm finally relented with the rising of the sun. Kirsten came topside not long ago to relieve us of our watch, yet neither can retire. Clad in soaked pants and nothing else, together, the captain and I, sit here as I am writing this, passing the bottle back and forth as the sun rotates higher above us. There is no argument about the spirit this morning. We must be quite the pair, William, clean shaven, tall, lean and proper and I, weeks from a razor, short, stocky and tattooed. Together we sit only watching, thankful."

Turning the last corner and sprinting to her drive Hope stopped short of the front door to catch her breath in the cool morning air. Standing there, invigorated, she wondered where her old friend was at that moment.

Searching

Winter passed with the ferocity of an immature feline. There was not much more than the occasional hard freeze. This spring day was brisk for late March. It had been cold enough in the morning to warrant a heavy coat but now, in the middle of the afternoon, it was no longer needed. Hope was walking through downtown to meet friends for lunch when she stopped at the corner of Commerce Street and South Austin Street in downtown Dallas. She preferred walking when the weather was nice. She took the time to watch people, searching for something, she didn't know exactly what, but she enjoyed watching. Across the street strolled a man, 'It couldn't be,' Hope thought to herself. The traffic lights changed, and the man stopped a stone's throw away from her. She could only see his profile from the side as she stood across the street. When the walk signal turned over, she moved at a faster pace than usual, and from behind his left shoulder Hope called out.

"Chris!" No answer. Again she called. "Chris!"

Drawing closer, as she rounded the side of this man, she realized it wasn't him. There was a distinctive scar above Chris's right eye that this man did not have and his eyes were a much darker blue. Beyond that the resemblance between this man and her old friend was uncanny. "Oh, I'm sorry; I thought you were someone else," Hope confessed. She laughed at herself and walked on down the sidewalk drawing closer to the cafe.

When Hope returned home, she found another manila envelope and another letter. This one was from Timbuktu. Chris had written her before telling of his departure from William and Kirsten. He'd joined a convoy headed into the sub-Sahara. Since the beginning of the year, he'd been in the desolate desert outpost, almost three months now. Hope changed into a pair of sweat pants and ran into the living room jumping over the back of the couch. The paper in her hand told of the water resource management that had occupied the weary traveler. Still more and more Chris spoke longingly of home. Hope wondered if this meant that his return would be sooner rather than later. He gave details of the goat herders and sandstorms that defined the landscape. On the last page the script spelled out Chris's intent.

"As soon as I finish this letter and it is sent your way along with the many others that are destined for familiar faces, I intend to head for Europe. Starting with Sicily and up through Italy, across the mainland and eventually, in time, back across the Atlantic. I have no time frame yet."

Hope sighed; she walked into the kitchen and laid the letter on the table as she sat down to finish compiling her resume. She had thought for a long time of going to Europe herself. She had been introduced by a colleague to a business based out of Spain that hired Americans to teach English to their international partners. When her resume was finished, she would submit her application for the position. If everything went well she may just meet her old friend overseas.

The Call

Hope began to pack for her move to Europe as June became July. She'd sold off everything that couldn't be carried or shipped. When morning came that first day of July, she woke on an air mattress in her living room. She lay by herself, staring at the walls recalling the first day she'd moved into this house and everything that had changed since. In all that time not once had Chris been home. It was just shy of four full years now since he left. Surrounded by everything she owned in this one room, Hope looked over to the battered box that was now overflowing with papers and envelopes. The hinged lid would not close anymore without fear of tearing the final scrap that kept it connected.

Laying there she could see the beaches of Sicily and the image of Chris attempting to surf with the young man he'd met on the island. The sketches of the fountains and historical sites of Rome had been filed away in a portfolio. There were some truly beautiful renderings that did not show a single sign of the smudges that cursed his writing. As Chris made his way north through Tuscany he'd sent back recipes he thought Hope might enjoy, encouraging her to diversify her culinary ability. She had attempted several with varying degrees of success.

When she finally rose and shook the sleep from her head she quickly changed and brushed her teeth. Lacing up her running shoes she took to the streets of Los Colinas. Hope still had over a week before she had to fly out but already the excitement and her nerves began to build.

She would miss the sights of this quaint suburb, yet she was excited to explore her new home. With her return home, after a long stretch she stripped down and headed to the shower.

On the way she checked her phone sitting on the white tile of the kitchen counter. There were fourteen missed calls. 'Fourteen?' she thought. 'How long was I gone? It couldn't have been more than an hour and a half.' Scrolling down through the list every call came from the same number. Rugby.

The phone barely rang once when Rugby picked up, "Hope, where's Chris?"

"I don't know Rugby. Germany somewhere."

The man on the other end of the phone sounded distraught, almost out of breath and his voice came through thin, "Is that the best you got?"

Hope wrapped a towel tightly around her body and headed for the living room. "Let me look here. What's going on Rugby?"

As she dug through the box looking for the latest post she'd received Rugby began to explain, "I got a call about four this morning from Cindy. She was in real pain so I drove out to her house and she could barely walk. Her appendix ruptured sometime late last night or early this morning. No one knows for sure. She just got out of surgery but the doctor doesn't know if they got to it in time. They're afraid she's septic. I don't know if she's going to make it."

Hope sat down in the middle of the living room floor, message in hand. She didn't want to believe what she was hearing. "Oh my god! I don't know what to say."

"Just tell me where to find Chris."

Hope unfolded the papers and quickly scanned through the writing. Mumbling to no one in particular she worked her way down page after page, "Bavaria, Czech Republic... There's something here about Trier. No, wait," She read from the letter,

"I've found the my new home in a small mountain town just a stone's throw away from the Belgian border and less than an hours' drive from

the French border. This place isn't a town or even a village. It's a hamlet. Exactly five families occupy the municipality, forty-three people total.

I've rented a room from the Hess family. It's just a small one room cottage they rent out as a bed and breakfast, just up the road from their own house of six. I've paid up front for three months and have settled in to enjoy the countryside.

Integration into the tight knit community has been surprisingly easy. The loyalty amongst and within the families here is rarely seen in Western culture anymore. These people live, work, cook, eat and play together. It's very reminiscent of our acquired family back home.

The Hess family operates a very diverse agricultural operation. They work hard and drink harder. Their kin across the road run a small brewery. The product is some of the best cereal malt beverages I have ever tasted."

"That's the best I have, Rugby."

With an audible deep breath, "Okay, thanks Hope."

"Rugby," Hope ordered, "find him."

Retrieval

C hris Coupland had been adrift upon the sea of humanity and almost completely around the world in four years.

Chris did his best to spend his time in productive ways. He worked with the Hess sons to repair buildings, clear the undergrowth, and supply the family with firewood for winter. Even with a brewery across the street and the encouragement to drink from the family he refrained, partaking only on rare occasion. He spent most of his day thinking about both of his families. It was only in this close knit environment that Chris began to realize what he had left behind. He often questioned why he had to take the long way around the world just to enter the same environment, to see this family mimic his own, and only then realize that this close association is what he wanted. For the first time in almost four years, he became homesick for those he had abandoned.

On a beautiful Tuesday afternoon when the noon sky shone with a darker, more vivid blue than he could have ever described, Chris swung his axe with more and more efficiency while he dreamed of being home. When enough cords were split the axe was planted in the stump that played the part of the cutting block. Chris picked his jacket off the small pine that stood just out of arms reach. He pulled it on as he turned from the days chores and began the two mile trek toward his small cottage. It was a good day, but his soul was restless. There was something in the air he could not pin down, he walked with a quicker pace than he had in years.

As Chris reached the center of town, where two narrow blacktop roads met, he saw up the hill in front of him a strange but familiar face. The young man who approached him wore blue jeans with a black tee and a pair of sandals. This stranger carried a small pack over his right shoulder. When Chris stopped to focus on the face, his feet automatically started again in a gait that he hadn't expected. Running up the road his assumptions proved true. As the figure came close Chris yelled out, "Rugby!"

The two strangers wrapped each other in their arms and Chris embraced his old friend longer than he'd held anyone in years. His scent was familiar even this far removed. Rugby's beard buried into his brother's neck. When they finally released each other, the pair remained coupled while Rugby gripped Chris's shoulders and the opposite grasped his arms.

"My *god* man, it's good to see you!" Rugby exclaimed.

"I was just thinking of you… and everyone else," Chris confessed staring at the older, yet familiar face. "I have missed you sorely, my friend. I was just about to peel off the road here into the brewery, join me. I know it's been a long trip, you must need a drink."

Rugby gave a shrug of his shoulders, "Hey, why wouldn't I?"

The pair walked side by side into the Backhause family brewery. The owners had known Chris for some time but never in an occasion to drink. Tonight would be different. The two old friends back together would do their best to drain the tanks and rotate the stock.

The pair swapped stories and told exaggerations of the things they had seen. Rugby related the sin and debauchery of the food service industry. He spoke of innovative and new ways to offend people. Chris told of the lands and places he'd seen. Eventually the question of Rugby's appearance here in a foreign land came to the young designer's mind.

As he rotated his mug of beer in his hand, Chris finally asked, "So, I can't imagine you showing up for no reason or even a good reason."

Rugby looked down at his beer. Chris watched as his friend shook the mug in his right hand several times and saw the foam lining slowly slide down. "Your mother's sick," Rugby said as he took a draw from the foam left behind. He ran his tongue across his lips, "Her appendix ruptured. The cards are not in her favor."

Chris couldn't decipher the words that he'd just heard. "What?" he questioned.

"Mama Coupland may not make it much longer."

Chris was at a loss for words. He stared at his mug as the weight of consequences came over him.

With a heavy mind Chris stood to leave as the last of the Backhause clan was picking up stools. The duo stumbled out into the center of the hamlet where the two blacktop roads met and into the light of the single street lamp that illuminated the intersection. It was just after midnight and the insects of the summer were their only company.

In the chill of the German night, Chris stopped under the light. Rubbing his head he finally spoke, "Have you seen her?"

Rugby, stepped past the lost son, and turned with a face of anger that Chris had never seen, "I've seen her several times a week since you left the country. I drove her to the hospital the night she got sick. I sat with shaking hands in the cold, sterile waiting room while she went through surgery. I was by her side when she woke the day after. You're not going to like what you see. I just want you to be ready. I saw her last two days ago. She was looking better than expected, but it was not pretty."

Chris stood in the light of the lone street light, his eyes swelling with remorse, "Thank you for being there. I would never expect you to cover for me…"

Rugby cut him off, "Hey, *fuck you man*, don't you ever think I'm covering for you. I loved Cindy as much as anyone. We are family no matter the relation. I was there because I wanted to be there, but I wish you would have come home sooner."

Chris stuttered, "I'm… I'm sorry. I never thought how my absence would impact my mother or anyone else…"

Rugby let loose a rage that Chris had seen only a select few times before in all their years together. He was usually a very calm and collected individual, "*Listen*, I know you think you have been through some drama, but whatever it is that traumatized you so badly, you have no idea of the shit you are about to step into. Do you think you can handle this? What are you going to do this time? Hike through Antarctica? I'm sure it's great that you can chase whatever dream you want but have you once, just once, thought about how your absence affected everyone you left behind? We all get a letter every once in a while? You're okay, *great*, but what the hell are we supposed to do when something goes wrong? What was I supposed to do? Your mother asked me find you, what was I supposed to tell her? I had to lie to her. I had to tell her we found you. I told her you were on your way or that you'd be home soon, anything to keep her hopes up, to keep her going for just *one more day*." Rugby dropped the bottle he was carrying and immediately planted a right hook aside Chris' foggy head.

Chris hadn't seen it coming. The knuckles dug in behind his left eye in his soft temple. The blow sent a blinding flashes of light though his sight that erased the night. The distraught son dropped to the asphalt ground burying his left cheek into the loose gravel. The pain did not immediately set in.

"*Goddamnitt!*" Rugby swore as he stood above the downed man shaking the pain from his hand, "Where the hell have you been?"

The right side of Chris' face began to sear with pain, and his gut wrenched. There was nothing he could say in defense. Rugby was right, and it would be his cross to bear.

Chris rolled over with an audible moan. He had no pride left. The anger he felt inside burst forth as he began to rise. Suddenly he dove toward Rugby taking them both to the asphalt with as much force as he could muster. The pair wrestled there beneath the light until both exhausted every bit of strength they had left. Chris could not recall exactly who he was fighting, but Rugby bested him in the long haul.

When the dust settled the pair sat side by side, leaning back against the light pole on the corner of the intersection. Rugby reached out and snagged the bottle he'd dropped earlier and pried the cap off with his lighter. After a long draw from the long neck he passed the bottle to his panting brother.

Chris took the bottle, had a drink himself and passed it back. "I have to see her," he said staring out at nothing in particular.

"The plane leaves at eight a.m." Rugby said into the night.

Return

～～

Chris hadn't slept in almost two and a half days as the large 747 cruised in the moonless night somewhere far above the Atlantic. Rugby sat two seats over in the sparsely populated transport. Chris thought he looked like a sleeping lumberjack in his wool cap and beard. Even with all the adrenaline and emotions pulsing through his veins, Chris's eyes became heavy. In time his head began to sag to the side and before he knew the lights were out. The cheap pillow and blanket the stewardess tucked around him went unnoticed. There was no waking him now.

Rugby had to shake Chris to life. He was groggy and didn't fully come around until after he walked out of the terminal. It was early in Atlanta, and there was work to do. Leaving security would be a pain in the ass, to go through it all again, but the pay phones were outside the secure area. His green bag, worn thin and patched together in several places, seemed to pull down his left shoulder as he trudged his way through the airport. Chris's heels drug on the smooth flooring as he made his way to the bank of phones, just out of sight of his checkpoint. Chris stood in the airport; his head against the phone, his bag was sliding down his shoulder when he heard the line finally connect with Neal's cell phone.

"This's Neal," his voice was so familiar and comforting.

"Have you seen Mom recently?" Chris's voice was rough and guttural.

Neal whispered something away from the phone, "Yeah," he said softly, "Kathy and I are here at the hospital right now."

Chris asked the question that he did not want, "How is she doing?"

There was a long pause on the line, "I can't say man, she's been in and out of consciousness for the last 24 hours. She was awake and coherent last night but she's been out since then, all I can tell you is get here quick."

"Okay, we should be there by noon. Is Hope there?" Chris wondered.

Neal crunched down on something and mumbled through the food, "No, she will be flying in tomorrow morning."

"Alright, thanks, Neal." Chris laid the receiver of the phone across his shoulder, slapped the lever on the box, swiped his phone card again and dialed again.

The line rang with no answer.

Finally, after an eternity, the message that had remained the same for years came on, "Hi. This is Hope, I'm sorry I missed your call but if you leave me a message I'll call you right back." Beep.

Chris stood there letting her angelic voice settle. He took a deep breath and spoke, "Hope, it's Chris. Rugby and I are in Atlanta on our way home. I'll call you when we get there." He hung up the phone and stormed back to find Rugby and a bite to eat. An hour after landing the pair was airborne again. Seated amongst strangers, separated from his traveling partner by two seats and a dozen rows, Chris pounded a single serving bottle of whiskey and was out cold before they reached cruising altitude.

The landing startled him to life. Chris didn't even feel like the sleep even put a dent in the drag that he felt weighing him down. Being this close to home though, brought a rush of emotion pushing his body into top gear. Rugby was off the plane ahead of him. The first step off the terminal was polite and in pace with the crowd but the second broke free in a dead run. Moving as fast as his boots would allow, through the crowd with Rugby in close second, they burst through the doors and Chris stopped. His chest was heaving. He looked around, "Which way?" he asked turning around to find his friend but as he did Rugby blew past him.

"This way," Rugby yelled back as he headed across the drive and into the parking lot.

The pair raced for a hundred yards, down a flight of stairs and into the underground garage. With his boots slapping the concrete floor, after the second turn, Chris saw Rugby's white blazer. The driver beat him there by only a few seconds. Panting and out of breath, he tossed the green pack in the back seat and settled into the passenger seat in front.

Rugby turned the key violently, and the engine roared to life. The vehicle backed up suddenly and without ever coming to a complete stop, the he kicked it into drive and they raced out of the garage.

Little was said as Rugby pushed the old SUV to its limits flying down the interstate. In just under an hour and a half they turned off the highway and cut through town heading straight for the hospital.

Censure

～～

Rugby slid the vehicle to a stop just outside the double set of sliding doors that led into the facility. Chris jumped out and ran as Rugby shouted from behind him, "Fifth floor. Room Five Fifty-Three," as he climbed out and followed his friend.

The sliding doors could not open fast enough. As soon as they spread far enough for Chris to slide in sideways, he pushed his way through. He sprinted past the front desk, "Stairs!" he yelled as he blew past the nurse seated there.

"Left!" she yelled back.

Chris slammed through the door and took the steps three at a time, five stories worth, by three he was panting. His legs burned and sweat began to bead up across his brow. As he made the last turn in the staircase he ran with everything he had to the landing just above him. The door into the corridor violently swung open and Chris slid through. He looked left, then right. He was becoming frantic. A nurse rounded a corner down the hall to his right. "Five Fifty-Three!" was all he could catch between gasps for air. The nurse pointed the other way straight down the hall in the opposite direction. He immediately turned to his left pivoting on his toes and took off as fast as his boots on the vinyl floor would accelerate him. As he slid to a stop in the hallway that ran perpendicular to the corridor he saw everyone standing around. He had seen none of them in almost five years, some longer. The sobs were

audible; Chris could see the tears from twenty feet away. Members of
both his mother's family and his own stood lining down the hallway.
Kathy and Neal were closest. Chris was four steps down the hallway
when Rugby pulled up alongside him.

Kathy reached out and put her arms around Chris as he passed,
"I'm so sorry, honey," she said with wet eyes as her smoky voice cracked.
"It's too late."

Chris immediately pulled away and looked down the hall at the
open door.

Neal grabbed him by the arm reading the son's mind. "They've
already taken her."

Chris pulled as hard as he could but Neal only gripped him tighter.
Rugby came up from behind and took a hold of the other arm. They
tried to be gentle, but Chris fought. He scrambled and swung in a feeble
attempt to break their grasp. It took everything the two men had to
restrain him. Chris thrashed wildly, screaming like a madman, every
vein from his neck up bulged with pressure and his face flooded with
emotion. He was fire red, his mouth dry, his eyes bloodshot, he screamed,
cursing himself, cursing God and anyone else within range. Equipment
was smashed, doors kicked in and walls assaulted the entire way out into
the stairwell. Step by step Neal and Rugby drug Chris down to the lobby
and through the front doors. Only when they reached daylight did Chris
relent. When his escorts let go he dropped straight to the ground. The
aching pain of his knees striking concrete went unnoticed.

In time everyone exited the hospital passing by the fallen son. Kathy
was the only one to stop, if only briefly to kiss him on top of his head.

Chris could not remember how long he remained there in front of the
hospital, but when he finally stood and took account of his surroundings
the only person he saw was Rugby. He was leaning back against his
vehicle in the parking lot across the lawn. As Chris approached his
patient friend he offered the distraught man a pull from his lit cigarette.
Through his shaky lips Chris drew in the smoke and slowly exhaled
watching the white carcinogen float away on the summer breeze.

Rugby held an envelope. He handed it to Chris. "The day she was recovering from surgery, as I sat by her bed. I watched Cindy pen this. I don't know what it says nor do I want to, but you have to read it, she made me promise."

Chris took the letter and watched his friend walk around the front of the vehicle and climb in the driver's seat. Chris seated himself, and they drove over to Rugby's house.

Cindy's Sway

Chris would spend his first night back in the country at Rugby's place. He lived in the same college town where they had met not quite fourteen years before.

The afternoon was getting late when the duo pulled into the alley beside the large blue house. The entire first floor was a limestone foundation a foot and a half thick. The second story was a stick frame with blue lap siding. Rugby parked behind the house to the west. Chris stepped out, the gravel of the small drive, just off the alleyway, crunched under his boots. He pulled his bag from the rear seat and finally it happened. The one remaining intact strap ripped loose and the bag rolled out onto the gravel, bursting open and spilling its contents. Chris's temper flared immediately and he wanted to punt the damn thing across the alley. When he realized the situation, his anger turned to humor. That bag made it home, not one step further, but it made it. Chris stood staring down at the pea green backpack. It was dirty, weathered and in pieces. He laughed for the first time in days. Rugby came around the vehicle to see what was so funny. Rounding the rear standing at the edge of the alley he saw Chris, the bag on the ground, and the strap he still held in his hand. He voiced what Chris was thinking, "Well, it made it."

"Barely," Chris added beginning to laugh harder. He bent down and gathered everything and carried it all around to the front of the house. The ancient residence had a large porch in the same style as the limestone foundation. It sat three feet above the yard below. Kathy and Neal, now joined by Lacey all greeted them as the duo came around the corner of the house. Chris sat down on the rock ledge that ran around the open air porch. Rugby went inside. The tiny dancer sat down next to the designer and put her arm around him.

His gracious host returned a short while later with a round of beers. Everyone took one, Rugby handed one to Chris and took a seat on the opposite side with his back against one of the two pillars that supported the gabled end projecting out from the house sheltering the stone outcropping below. One can popped open, followed shortly by the second and so on. Chris offered a toast, "To Mom."

Everyone tipped their drink, "To Mom," they agreed. The five of them sat there for hours swapping stories. Chris recited where he'd been and what he'd seen while Rugby gave all the details of the life of an entrepreneur. Everyone had their turn. The air was heavier than usual and the laughter thinner, nonexistent in Chris, though he was more comfortable now in the company of friends.

Rugby was the last to get his fill of tall tales and beer; he excused himself and followed the others inside. Chris remained.

"Can you turn on the porch light when you go?" Chris asked. He was not ready to sleep, not quite yet. It was July, it was still eighty degrees at midnight. It was beautiful, and Chris wanted to soak it all in.

"Sure," Rugby replied, "goodnight."

"'Night," Chris called as the brilliant light erased the darkness and shadows of the porch.

The son who came home too late sat on the porch, alone with his thoughts. He tilted his head back to drain what was left in the warm can he held and placed the shell on the floor below him with the others. Chris pulled the tattered remains of his bag over and tossed open the top flap; he reached inside and pulled out the letter his mother had written him. He studied it. '*Christopher,*' was all it said on the envelope. He traced the lettering with his finger. The loops and lines looked so graceful. 'Mother wasn't as weak as everyone believed, she carried a steady hand until the end,' he thought to himself. The envelope turned over and over in his hands. He was unsure if he could open it. What would it say? Gently he slid his finger underneath the sealed fold and pried it open. Inside was a single piece of paper, the same color as the envelope. It was written in jet-black ink. Chris's eyes followed the graceful flowing script.

Christopher,

Alright, now it's my turn, so pay attention.

I love you, I always have and always will. Do not ever forget that. I wish that you could be here and I miss you dearly, but I understand you have always lived with your own rhythm and I harbor no hard feelings. I know you will try to blame yourself for not being here. Don't.

There is nothing you could have done. Don't beat yourself up over this and no matter what anyone says, I believe that what you are doing must be done. If I have to let my only son go free throughout the world for it to be a better place, then so be it. You have made me a very proud mother. I love you,

Mom

Chris studied the letter, reading it time and time again until he fell asleep there on the front porch atop a limestone bed. He was so exhausted it didn't matter where he slept. At sometime during the night he must have crept inside because Chris woke up on the living room couch just inside the front door but he had no recollection of this.

The Funeral

⁓

I t was an abnormally cool Friday afternoon when Chris gathered amongst friends and family in the cemetery to bury his mother. Lacey made the long trip out. Neal and Kathy lived only an hour and a half drive down the Interstate and stood with the group also. Surrounded by ancient trees, the casket sat before the mourners. The slightest breeze ruffled the canopies that had been placed for the graveside service. Underneath the largest of the three shelters, Chris sat hand in hand with Hope who had flown in the day before. His suit fit a little tighter than he remembered. This was the first time he'd worn it since his last trip to Austin. Rita Padillo had sent it overnight and apologized for not having it cleaned first. He could almost smell the faint aroma of beer and stale smoke still lingering in the fabric. This was not the most appropriate thought, considering the circumstances but it helped to lighten his mood.

Together, everyone recited prayers, one of Cindy's longest and dearest friends gave the eulogy and flowers were placed on the casket as everyone departed. Slowly as the mourners filed past Chris shook hands with most, and embraced others as they expressed their sorrow and support. He knew or recognized almost everyone there. Some of the younger kids had grown so much since he'd last seen them, it was shocking. Still, there were others present he did not recognize at all but shook hands with just the same. Chris's father attended the services. It was the first time since college that the two men stood next to each other. Rugby noted how much Chris had grown to resemble his father, in physical appearance anyway. They spent most of their time away from the rest of their relatives, getting reacquainted. Eventually even the family began to leave, followed closely by his peers who had come to show their support. Before long, only Chris and Rugby remained behind. Chris did not want to leave his mother's side.

Rugby finally convinced him that they had to head back into town. It took several tries but Chris relented eventually. Side by side, the only two left on the hallow ground, they walked across the cemetery toward Rugby's vehicle waiting to carry them away from this grief. When they were within fifty yards of the SUV Rugby asked, "Do you have any smokes?" searching his pockets.

Chris patted himself down and reached inside his jacket pulling a pack from the breast pocket. "Mother would kill me if she knew I was still smoking," Chris said handing the pack over to Rugby.

"Maybe she's still in line to meet St. Peter. If she's not settled in the Promised Land just yet, maybe she won't notice," Rugby offered, handing Chris back his beaten pack of smokes.

With the pack in hand he reached into his pocket again, deeper this time feeling for a lighter. He felt one buried at the bottom. Pulling it out a slip of paper came with it. Chris lit his cigarette and handed the lighter to Rugby. Unfolding the paper he realized instantly what he was holding.

Chris had searched for hours looking for the note Hope had slipped him the night of the gallery opening. He had surrendered, accepting the loss a long time ago but he still wondered about it. Here it had been all this time, buried under two business cards, one lighter and several packs of matches. What secrets did it hold? Chris stopped walking and stood in the field of granite markers staring at the folded piece of paper in his hand. He took a long haul from the smoke and held it, slowly releasing the smoke as he looked down.

"Chris, are you okay? Rugby asked noticing his lack of locomotion. "What's that?"

Chris looked up from his hand, shot Rugby a look of surprise, and set his gaze back on the note. "It's a note Hope wrote me years ago. I thought I'd lost it. I looked for this thing forever."

"What's it say?"

"I don't know, I never had the chance to read it."

"Then don't, burn it man, you don't need to go back there. It's all whiskey under the bridge. How many miles did it take you to get away from that place?"

"I don't know I'm still counting," Chris replied in a flat tone still focused on the note. It was an automatic reply he'd responded with for so long now it just came out. Rugby realized the dilemma and strolled off toward the SUV leaving Chris to stand alone. He'd seen enough of this duel.

Standing alone on amongst the trees and stones, Chris unfolded the note.

Chris,

I'm sorry for the way things turned out. I know you and I had something that few people in the world are lucky enough to find. If I could live it all over again and again for a lifetime I would. I know now that we can neither return, nor would it ever be the same. Please remember I still love you and no matter how long or how far apart we wind up, I always will.

Love, Hope

Chris folded the note and put it back from where he found it. He made a quick pace to catch up. Rugby, leaning with his elbows on the hood of his vehicle, questioned, "Going down to Dallas aren't you?"

Chris put on his sunglasses to cut out the glare of the midday sun and shot his old friend a big smile as he opened the passenger side door and stepped in. With one last drag, Rugby threw the cigarette to the ground. "This is a bad idea for the both of you," he yelled through the window as he stood and stepped to the door.

Chris nodded. When Rugby sat down and started the vehicle Chris agreed with him, "She said she needed a ride home."

"Well, whatever you have in mind you better get on it. She flies out in a few days."

Chris was surprised, "What?! Flying out to where? Hope didn't say anything about leaving."

This time it was Rugby's turn to sport a big grin, "That's best left between you and her."

Photographs

Hope drifted through the house of Cindy Coupland. It was a modest three bedroom, which in refusing all of Chris' offerings, Cindy chose to remain. The late mother had always preferred the simpler, rural conditions from which she came. Hope walked down the narrow hallway that split the residence looking over the pictures, framed and hung, covering the walls on either side of her almost entirely. There were photos of Cindy's family, most of whom Hope did not recognize. Scattered throughout the length of the corridor set against the beige walls were pictures of Chris at all ages. Hope pulled one in particular off the wall. Her old friend couldn't have been older than two years, the brim of a straw hat pulled down almost covering his blue eyes that gazed off into the distance. She knew that look well. Replacing the picture Hope moved further down the hall. In the latter snapshots she picked out Rugby in a dozen, Neal and Lance in a few and herself in one. This particular picture hung directly across the hall from the door leading into Cindy's bedroom. Hope stared at the scene from a decade ago, at graduation. Cindy caught her and Chris, standing arm in arm on the patio of the bar. God! Hope noticed how young she looked, as did Chris. The miles and memories that connecter her to that time could not be counted. Her fingers delicately crossed her own image as a smile developed.

Hope couldn't tell how long she had been standing in the hallway, but she had not noticed Lacy approach. When she looked toward the opposing end of the hallway just off the living room, the blonde stood in just the same fashion as herself, gazing at a photo. When Hope reached her side a solemn tear rolled off Lacey's soft face, yet she was smiling. Hope had overlooked this picture. It was a group shot of the acquired family. Everyone was on the large stone porch of Rugby's house. On the third step up, Hope was seated next to Cindy with Lacey and Kathy on the other side, the boys stood above them. It was taken in their last year of school on a Sunday afternoon. Hope remembered it clearly.

Hope reached out and took hold of her old friend. She could feel the tightness build as she swallowed holding back the tears.

Breaking the silence, Lacey finally spoke, "are you sure you still want to leave us?"

"Yes," Hope said softly. "It's only a four year contract."

The Homestead

⌒

Chris rode the twenty miles from the cemetery to his childhood home in silence as Rugby drove, scanning the radio time and time again searching for something that suited him. Nothing did. When the vehicle pulled off the blacktop and onto to lengthy drive, Chris lost all sight of the day. He stepped out just as the wheels came to a halt. Standing in the drive of his mother's house for the first time in over half a decade, Chris's feet could not move. As the sights and sounds of the cool, overcast afternoon collided with the warm, loving memories of his childhood. A stiff breeze kept what little comfort he felt upon his return from sinking in. Bumps rose in waves across his skin. Chris's left foot spun where he stood digging the sole of his boot through the top layer of river rock. His eyes, faded in time, sunk beneath a furrowed brow, scanned the scene. The line of cars in front of him, over a dozen strong, disappeared. He imagined the land as his childhood had imprinted it. He could see his rusted red bicycle, years gone, laying in the middle of the drive twenty yards ahead. To the right, hanging from the solemn, massive black walnut tree, a stones' throw away from the front porch and halfway between himself and the old barn clad in gaping slats, was his old tire swing. It hung, suspended from the largest branch by the first lariat his maternal grandfather had given him. The swing had long ago fallen when as a young boy he had spun it a little too tight. When the lasso snapped the young boy shed a tear for the first time that he could now remember. His hurt was not from the pain of the fall but from the destruction of his prized lasso.

There in the drive Chris could hear his mother calling from Twenty-Five years ago, calling him in. Surrounded by the odd coolness of the summer air, Chris could recall sitting just inside of the storm door, looking out across the yard as his mother's call came again and again. His memory said he was eight years old but at a few years past thirty now, Chris could not recall for sure his age. He could remember vividly the rays of light that passed through the glass of the door before his young eyes. Chris's focus had been solely on the tiny particles of dust that drifted in the soft light. The boys mind shifted, dreaming as it always had, and always would. It questioned all that was unknown in his isolated world. What was smaller than the small particles before him? His ten fingers and ten toes felt warm in the light. He could count by tens now in extreme multiples, yet he questioned why it was all based on tens. What if he only had eight fingers and toes, would he then count by eights to reach numbers beyond his imagination?

In a short time his mother's calling drew nearer and she approached the entry in which he now sat. When she joined him on the floor, sitting behind the young boy, embracing him with her entire body, his attention was drawn to the saint that held him tight. Chris could feel her comfort and warmth enveloping him.

A gust of wind, frigid as the cold gray rock that marked his mother's grave jolted him back to reality. The sky was overcast, the light was hazy, the rocks under his boots sharp and jagged. A warming call from a young cousin was the only cushion against a harsh, cold truth.

Chris stepped forward, back into reality, as fast as he could, short of a jog, to embrace his young kin. The cheers and kisses that covered his face where the warm welcome he needed. As Chris carried the youngest of his blood relation, and hand in hand with another, he strode ever closer to the house. Twenty yards away he saw Hope emerge from the front door with another of his cousins in her arms. She always did take fondly to children. Having both families here for support buffered the guilt.

Standing in the kitchen, plate in hand, surrounded by relatives and friends alike, talk turned to business. Leaning back on the counter Hope finally asked, "What will you do with the estate?"

When he finished chewing, Chris finally answered, "I'm not sure. Talked to the lawyer yesterday, I could liquidate it, sell it maybe, or give it away. I don't need it and mom's not using it. I don't know, haven't thought about it much."

Lacey asked from across the room, "What are you going to do?"

A sly grin spread across the designer's face, "This I've thought long and hard about. I think it's time I returned to Austin. I want to expand the studio and need to be closer to an urban setting to make it grow."

Rugby stepped to the sink behind Chris, with his empty plate, "what do you have in mind."

"Well," Chris continued, "I want to build Coupland Studios into a multifaceted firm. I want you, Rugby, and you too," he said pointing to Lacey, "to move down to Austin if you want. I want all of you to join me. I'm going to put together a studio where designers, artists, craftsmen of all trades can sit around a big table and approach problems together. Writers, draftsmen, illustrators can work on projects together. Mechanics, painters, everyone is welcome. If say, a cabinet maker had a problem with a hinge, the steel worker in the shop next door may have an answer."

Neal had come to stand in the doorway, "Those are some pretty ambitious plans son."

"And you too, you have to move with me if you want to keep your job."

The brown guy smiled and nodded contemplating the offer. He turned around back into the dining room, "Baby, we're movin' to Austin."

"As the studio grows and more resources become available more positions will open up. I have the business plan detailed in my journal." Chris could feel the blood rush to his face as the excitement and anticipation of finally expressing his idea to everyone. "It's going to be a wild ride."

To Dallas

⁓

As the crowd began to thin, Chris slipped out the back door and marched up the hill to the shed that sat back in a grove of oak trees. He unlocked the large door and swung it open, Before him sat the first truck he ever owned, a two-tone '69 Chevy C-10. Several laps were made to inspect the vehicle before Chris climbed inside and fired it up. The engine he'd rebuilt through junior high roared to life. The exhaust rattled the walls. As he pulled away from the shed and down the hill, Hope came walking around the corner of the house with her bags in hand. She dropped them both and stuck out a thumb. The truck stopped just short of her, kicking up dust that continued out past the house and toward the end of the drive.

Chris loaded the bags into the bed of the truck.

"Leaving so soon?" Kathy asked from the front porch.

"I'm sorry, Hope's flight leaves first thing in the morning," he apologized.

"Call us when you get there."

Chris nodded, "Yes, ma'am."

The family gathered in the front yard and made arrangements to discuss moving and the restructuring of Coupland Studios. After saying goodbye, both Hope and Chris climbed into the cab. He dropped the transmission into drive and pulled out across the gravel road leading out into nowhere. It was only eight hours to Dallas and they needed every minute of it to catch up.

As the vehicle pulled onto the interstate headed southbound on I-35, Chris finally asked the question that had been on his mind all afternoon. "So, where are you going?"

"Spain," Hope answered with no explanation.

Chris removed his sunglasses and eyed the beauty sitting next to him. "Excuse me? Spain? Why Spain? What do those Spaniards got that I don't?"

"I have a position teaching English with an international business. The company is based out of Spain. So I figure I'm young, I have nothing holding me back so, why not? You of all people should understand."

Chris replaced his gold tinted sunglasses, having no room to speak he just smiled.

There was very little silence as the truck carried the pair south into Oklahoma. Just north of the state capitol the sun finally ducked below the horizon. Chris removed his sunglasses and tossed them on the dash. The glare of the sun faded away and dusk settled in. He could feel the excitement build the closer they got to their destination. Chris spoke of the people and places he'd seen. He told of his busted knuckles on the *Liberty Phoenix*. He described the short portly old man who taught him so much. How the mechanic's bushy black mustache almost entirely engulfed his lips and how his greasy hair was always matted to his head.

Chris recalled the heat of the cattle ranch in the Northern Territory. He spoke highly of the young man he befriended, Kyle, and the mischief he always seemed to find himself in. He told all encompassing lifestyle that the ranch took on. His revelation of the sheer exhaustion the work produced was laced with much pride.

Chris' mood became somber as he spoke of Vietnam and the sin that engulfed him He gave little detail, but pry as she might Hope finally pulled a confession from him. "My imprisonment saved my life," he said in a flat tone, staring out at the road ahead, avoiding eye contact though he felt her gaze.

"Little of my time in Vietnam was within the legal scope of the law."
Chris shivered, bringing up memories he'd rather not see, but as always,
he was honest with Hope.

"It was early one morning, before dawn I know, but I had been
unaware of day or time for weeks at that point. I was lost in a haze of
alcohol and drugs that I don't even know the name of." He swallowed
hard, "First thing I remember is chaos, people running up and down
the hall that connected all the little rooms of the brothel I was living
in. A man in tactical gear stormed through the door and smoked me
with a club. I woke up in a rank prison some time later. It was dark,
musty and cold. The stench of humanity was choking. There were
twenty men, give or take, in that cell. Some days we ate, some not. I
didn't fight it at first, but when men began leaving and not returning
I began to worry." Chris shook his head looking out across the road
ahead of him.

"Finally, when one of the men I used to run favors for found me,
strings were pulled and I was released. I don't know if I would have made
it out if it weren't for that man. He may have run a shady operation, but
he was a good man. I went directly to the brothel for the last time to
find my things, if I had any. Luckily the Madam had saved them for me.
She let me clean up before I left the country. The bathroom was small,
the floor and walls were covered in dingy white tile. The porcelain was
stained and chipped and the neon blue light above the mirror cast a
vicious light." Chris looked at himself in the rearview mirror.

"I don't know how long I stood there looking at myself in the broken
mirror that hung on the wall. I hadn't seen my own face for over half a
year. I had a six month beard and hair almost down to my shoulders. I
was a ghost of the man that I remembered."

Hope sat in the passenger seat trying to imagine the scene; she had
never seen him with hair any longer that finger width, and never with a
full beard. "What in the hell were you thinking? You had money, why
couldn't get in touch with the consulate?"

Chris shook the idea off, "No, that wasn't the point. Money would have undermined everything I was trying to do. And this was about humanity, not government."

"You stubborn sonofabitch."

Nodding, "I know. But I walked away a better man, which was the point."

From there Chris told of his journey into China as the mile markers flew by. His voice cracked just once as he told Hope of the children at the Red Cross station.

It took nearly an hour to fully describe Captain William and his wife Kiersten. The night of the storm still remained clear in his mind, though the following morning was a little hazy. Chris admitted that he did miss the peaceful nights swinging in the hammock to the roll of the sea.

Hope spoke of her classes and work, the people she'd met and how she'd read and saved every letter. She told Chris of all the times he'd missed. Driving down the split, four lane interstate his mind wandered.

Finally, in a lull of conversation Hope asked what no one had yet, "We all had our reasons to justify why you were absent for so long. I guess what I'm trying to say is, what is the real reason, how do you justify it to yourself?"

"The only explanation I have is this: this world, the one that all of humanity has to share, I knew nothing of. It wasn't until Australia that I understood toil and hard work. Vietnam taught me humility and the true meaning of poverty and pain. In China I found compassion that I swore I would never know or understand. William taught me that true class never goes out of style. In Timbuktu I saw the true resolve of the human spirit. In the Muslims of northern Africa I was shown love from what everyone believes is the enemy. They're not, they love and weep just like the rest of us. In Sicily, the young surfer Chicco taught me not only to surf but to have passion for something that does not harbor money or power. He was devoted to surfing just for the act of surfing. Italy introduced me to an unbridled passion for human talent.

The Hess family loved me as one of their own and proved that the love for family still exists. I can't say that I practice all of this faithfully, few men ever could, but now I understand."

As Chris spoke Hope sat with her bare feet on the dash, feeling the movement of the truck, listening intently.

Finally Chris admitted, "Everything I went through, voluntary or not, was an education, one more block that filled the emptiness I carried around for so long. Even Mother's death taught me the consequences of indirect action. Everything you do or don't do impacts the people you come into contact with directly or indirectly every day."

Hope said nothing. Chris let the words hang in the cab of the Chevy.

Hope eventually caved into the silence, still with nothing to say, she turned on the radio and worked the dial, settling on a country station. A song Chris hadn't heard in years came through the speakers.

"Miss my chance, I lost my turn. My ship sank, I crashed and burned. Broke your heart then I let myself down. Lost the fight, I lost the game. Now there's only me to blame. If you wonder where I am, check the lost and found."

Chris smiled and nodded as the chorus came around again. He looked over to the woman sitting next to him. In the glow of the dashboard lights her beauty was striking. Her bare feet on the dash made her look young and innocent again. She either did not notice his gaze or chose not to react but it was not until Hope yelled out, "Chris!" that he focused on the road again. The truck had drifted halfway into the other lane.

"Oops," He said with a small laugh.

"Some things just never change I guess," Hope offered.

When the song ended their conversation picked up again covering almost every detail of the past four years. It was a long ride, but Chris appreciated the time to catch up. He counted down the miles to his exit. Finally, just after nine, the truck pulled off the Interstate onto the municipal streets of Los Colinas. It was a relatively new addition to the metropolitan area. The civic buildings were not yet weathered by time and the elements. The streets remained smooth and black. Past City Hall, through several intersections, Hope directed him through a maze of houses that all looked the same. From the eye of a designer it was the most disgusting thing he'd ever seen. Eventually the truck pulled up in front of 1314 Spanish Oaks just after eleven at night.

Chris turned off the engine and sat back resting for a second. This long on the road, it would be painful to step out. There were several injuries in his past that would make the first step out uncomfortable. It was something he'd dealt with for years but it had also been years since he spent this much time driving. Hope led the way out of the truck and up the yard carrying her bags. Chris slowly opened the door and stepped out. His hip popped and pain shot up from his ankle as his foot hit the ground. Slamming the door shut, he grabbed his bag from the bed and followed Hope inside.

One Last Night

The interior was bare. No furniture, no pictures on the walls. Hope walked through turning on lights as she passed from room to room. Chris followed her. The entire place was empty, no table or chairs, no couch in the living room, no bed, nothing. The only signs that anyone lived in the house were three suitcases in the bedroom, two towels hung in the bathroom and several cups that sat next to the sink in the kitchen. Hope excused herself to change into a pair of boxer shorts and a tank top while Chris remained, wandering through the house.

"Do you want something to eat?" Hope asked with her phone pressed to her ear.

"No, thank you."

"Hey," she spoke into the phone, "we just made it…" She walked back through the kitchen and turned toward the bedroom. Chris remembered his bag in the truck and ran out across the front yard to grab it. When he returned to the house, Hope was standing at the front door. She opened it as he mounted the one step that led up the porch. "Wow, there for a second I thought you ran off again."

Chris laughed, "Not at all, I just remembered something I didn't want to forget." Walking into the kitchen he tossed the battered bag on the island in the middle. Untying the cord that held it shut, his hand pulled out a small book, bound in leather. It was stained and cracked.

Several pages hung out further than they should. Hope pulled a bottle of wine from the cupboard beside the sink.

Holding the bottle and two plastic cups, "I was saving this for my last night here; care to share it with me?"

"Wine with story time, are you trying to seduce me, Mrs. Robinson?" Chris said heading into the living room. Behind him, Hope hesitated and smiled, it was flattering.

She didn't know what to say. "No, you're safe from my awkward sexual advances for the evening."

Chris pressed his back against the wall facing the front door and slid down to sit on the floor. Hope joined him, taking a seat next to her guest. The journal, when opened, randomly fell to a page that described the etiquette lessons Captain William had been leading. Chris read the passage aloud, reminiscing on the Captain's theory on the need for cuff links when at all possible.

Sitting there, on the floor of her living room surrounded by those blue walls Hope knew she still loved this man, but they could never make a life together. He didn't want a family, she did. He was a dreamer, and she considered herself a realist. Their history would always be the bond that kept them close but neither could understand why this made loving someone else so difficult. Chris saw the turmoil he'd fought for so long surface in her eyes.

"There was always something about you that I don't think I'll ever find in anyone else," he confessed. "You were good to me, the best friend I've ever had, without expecting anything in return. Well, until we began sleeping together. After that, everything changed. In time, I just wanted my friend back. I couldn't keep both of you. You made the decision I couldn't. I do not regret crossing the line to lovers. If we'd stayed plutonic I don't know where either of us would be right now."

Hope had thought the same thing many times over. "Are you saying I'm the reason you moved out West or why you've been gone for four years?"

"In the beginning, yes," he confessed. "After we separated I was lost. I was free of any commitment to hold me back. Until that point I'd always had a plan, albeit an often changing one. When I left Dallas that morning, I saw so many options in front of me with no priority to push me toward one or away from another it scared the hell out of me. Worse than anything I'd seen before."

"I can't really believe you," Hope accused. "There was always an underlying motive. You never do anything without it getting you closer to an ultimate goal."

Chris nodded, "You're correct, to a degree."

"You thought I would be impressed by your success and worldly experience and decide that it was all a mistake and come running back to you."

Chris nodded let out a small chuckle as a smile began to appear as she spoke. "True. If I had pleaded and begged, promising you the world, would you have denied me?"

Hope thought long over the question, "I would have stayed at the Studio if you would have asked me." The night grew long but she could not sleep with Chris so close. "Why didn't you? For so long you acted like that was all you wanted."

"I took a page from your playbook. You wouldn't have been happy there for long and I wouldn't be happy here. I finally knew that to let you go, for both of us, I had to get away from everything I'd ever known. That's why I left the country. For a long time after, I still questioned my decision and cursed myself. I couldn't get you out of my head. Then I realized that there is a world out there beyond you or I and everything shifted again."

Hope felt comfortable with her head resting on his shoulder. She shifted onto her right hip, moving closer to the new man beside her, and placed a hand on his stomach feeling him twitch when she did. "Not hearing from you for so long almost drove me crazy. I worried about you more than a sane woman should."

"Now you know how I felt leaving Texas the first time, you wouldn't even talk to me, I had no idea what condition you were in."

Hope laughed softly, "Trying to give me a taste of my own medicine?"

"No, not at all, it was unintentional. I was lost in my own world. Unfortunately it hurt several people other than you," Chris admitted.

Hope could feel her heart beat beginning to race remembering how she felt in the weeks after leaving Coupland Studios. The more time that passed, the more she longed to have him back until she could take no more. Finally she had to forget about it all and move on. But here he was again. It was a vicious tango they'd danced for too long. The pair sat in silence. Hope counted his heartbeats to keep her mind from wandering where it should not. Eventually her mind drifted. She recalled everything that had brought them from that fateful Thursday night at the bar to this empty living room floor. The many nights spent drinking, laughing, and leaning on each other flooded back.

Surrender

〜〜

Sitting there, with all their memories, Hope could imagine him the morning after they'd first made love, after they both woke up. She sat on the back porch of that little green house wearing nothing but his bed sheet as he played with Duke. She recalled singing karaoke on Sunday night, the afterhours amongst friends, skinny dipping outside her townhouse, their first trip to Austin together, all of it came to her.

He leaned in and kissed the top of her head. She could smell him and it was the same earthly scent he'd always had.

"Hope," Chris said.

She pulled her head off him, pushing herself up to his level. In those ghostly blue eyes she could read his soul. She could see the same man she'd known for so long but something was different. They held a compassion and understanding that she had never seen in him before. This was not a thin veil; he didn't wear his heart on his sleeve for her to read tonight. He was handing it to her. She said nothing.

"I'm no saint. I've seen many women for many different reasons," he admitted, "but I have only ever been in love with one. I have nothing left to confess, no pride, no dignity, all I can offer you is my love."

This was more than she could handle. Her walls came crashing down and her heart exploded. She could feel the heat building inside of her. She placed a hand on his chest; his breath was becoming shorter and quicker. She studied his features. Beneath the surface, beyond the lines and scars, behind the day old stubble she saw the young man she fell in love with on that fateful July night reappear. "Chris…" Two roads stretched out in front of her. Hope could not decide which path to take. "I'm leaving in a few hours."

"I know, and I would never let you stay, but I'm not leaving you alone again," Chris spoke in confession to the heartbroken girl he'd once abandoned. He leaned in and kissed her. His lips held the sweet taste she longed for. His arm pulled her closer as she shifted, further closing the space between them.

Hope could feel the passion in his embrace. Years of chaos melted away. She let the young woman trapped inside her for so long take over. She couldn't resist it anymore. Her hips rolled over his, pulling Chris up to his knees with her. Piece by piece, together, they removed every barrier they had built between them. Hope leaned back pulling him down with her, never letting their lips part.

Their passion flared. The remainder of the night was spent in a world all their own. Everything else melted away. Together they relived their youth. Hours flew by and neither one stopped to sleep, if the fervor ceased, reality would have returned to them. By sunrise they were exhausted, yet they still held each other in a lovers' dance.

Flight or Fight

The morning sun was in its infancy when they parted for the last time. Hope showered quickly. Chris dressed, leaving her scent embedded in his skin. He was sitting outside the front door when she came out carrying everything that she would be taking with her. Chris took two of the three suitcases and waited while she locked up, dropping the key in the mailbox at the end of the drive. Together they walked to the old Chevy parked along the curb. All three suitcases went into the bed of the truck along with the green bag that had made it so many miles. Hope stood beside the truck, arms crossed. She eyed her chauffeur up and down, "I'm a Texan now, and I don't get in a truck unless the door is opened."

Chris laughed opening the passenger door as Hope slid into the truck and sat down. When she was settled he closed the door, jogged around the front, and climbed in behind the wheel. They would be cutting it close. Traffic should be light this early on a Saturday but you could never tell.

"So, are you going to come visit me in Spain?" Hope asked as they pulled away from the curb.

Chris took a deep breath; his smile had been tattooed on his face since they finally pulled each other off the floor this morning. "I will try."

Chris thought about this for most of the way to the airport. "You know you have a job at the Studio, with the family, if you ever decide to return," he said as they pulled up to the airport. He put the truck in park and turned to her. "Just keep that in mind."

She nodded, understanding. Chris reached down into his bag. From underneath layers of old clothes, he pulled a small box wrapped in brown paper and held it out to Hope. "Here, this is for you but you have to promise me that you won't open it until you get in the air."

She took the package and inspected it. She shook it a couple of times listening to how it responded. "What is it?"

"I'm not going to ruin the surprise; you'll just have to wait."

She smiled, "Thank you." She sat looking into those eyes of his. There were none other like them, "So this is it, huh?"

"Yeah," he replied, "this is it."

Hope crawled across the bench seat of the wide cab and kissed him. Chris hugged her with one hand and the other slid down the side of her face. When their lips finally parted, Hope whispered, "Goodbye." She was afraid if she said it too loudly that she would have to accept it as the truth. Chris could say nothing, not wanting to acknowledge the end. She crawled back to her door and opened it, stepping down from the seat. A baggage handler came to the door and helped her with the luggage. Chris watched silently from the truck as she walked away. Just before Hope entered the airport, she stopped and turned slightly. Looking back over her left shoulder, she blew him a kiss and smiled. She was glowing and as beautiful as ever. Leaning on the wheel, Chris waved and threw the truck into drive.

Takeoff

~~~

Hope sat, checking her watch in seat 13C. She was eager to leave but the airline was not cooperating. The longer the wait in such a cramped, tight place the more miserable she became. Was she doing the right thing? Chris was who he was but maybe she could change his mind. Sitting in the window seat she began to feel trapped by the two passengers who had filled the seats between her and the aisle. It had to be the nerves. She was leaving her entire family, life and culture behind to spread her wings. The idea excited her and nauseated her at the same time. Added to that was her fear of motion sickness and it was almost more than she could bear. Suddenly she remembered the box Chris had given her. Her fears fell aside as she became distracted. Hope pulled her bag from below the seat and dug for the box.

The small package was two inches on all sides, tiny enough to sit in the palm of her hand. It was wrapped in plain brown paper and sealed with clear packing tape. There was no label, address, not even a name on it. She inspected all sides and picked at one of the folds that the tape had missed. The paper peeled away easily revealing a wooden box. It was blood red. The paper fell to the floor of the cabin and Hope turned the present over. On the top was inlaid one of the most intricate rose patterns she'd ever seen. It looked like it was pieced together with individual grains in the wood. The lighter inlay shimmered with a pearl luminescence against the sun.

The tiny silver latch flipped open easily with the flick of her fingernail. She pried the lid open. The box split into two even halves. The hinges hid in the amazing craftsmanship, the box looked so refined, yet it was sturdy. On the underside of the lid something was painted in a script she didn't recognize. In the bottom half, under a small tissue, was a note. Hope recognized the few words that looked up at her. It was her handwriting. Hope picked up the note and unfolded it. This was the same scrap of paper she had slipped Chris the night of the opening in Austin. The words remained clear in her mind, yet she read them again. There was something written on the back. The note flipped in her hand and Hope read the familiar long cursive writing that filled the letters in the shoebox packed in her luggage. Beyond the piece of paper in her hand a ray of light caught her eye. In the bottom of the box sat the princess cut diamond that had ridden for so long in Chris's pocket. The sunlight split into brilliant cascades of color as it struck the icy carbon. Hope picked it out of its masterfully crafted case and set the box in her lap. She examined the piece of jewelry. It slid past the first knuckle of her ring finger but she dared not push it further for she may never want to remove it. As the morning sun rose out of view above the window to her left, the light caught the radiance glistening in the ring on her left hand. The diamond was beautiful; it shimmered as she rolled it back and forth on her finger. The digits of her opposing hand slowly ran across the stone. She pulled it off and grasped it firmly in her palm. Her attention turned toward the message that accompanied it. The paper was worn thin but it still held together.

Hope,

Please take this. It has seen many miles with me, but has always been yours, it belongs with you. I could neither sell it nor ever stand to see another woman have it. Keep it, pawn it, or lose it along your travels wherever they may take you. I would hope you keep it as a reminder of everything we were and are.

With love, Chris

A smile grew as she read over the note again. As the jet rose into the air, a tear fell silently, spotting the old paper in her hand. Hope repacked the box, kissed it gently and carefully layered it in her bag, wrapped in an old shirt.

A New Sun

The morning sun in the city could never compare to the glow over a never ending horizon. The giant orange orb sat above the outcroppings of high rises and the sound of exhaust from the commercial jets screaming overhead all mixed to paint a beautiful scene. Amidst all the chaos that makes up Dallas there were six acres of space that sat open just outside the southeast corner of the Dallas/Fort Worth Airport. Chris lay across the hood of the truck, still warm from this morning's drive, parked in the middle of the tiny field. His hands were locked behind his head propped against the windshield. His days of chasing lost dreams and wanted fantasies were over. He lay amidst reality, accepting of everything that had put him here. From this morning he would move on. To Austin, to the family.

'I've already missed too many birthdays, anniversaries and reunions,' he thought to himself.

Chris remained stretched across the hood of the old truck. The engine had cooled as the radiant heat dissipated. It had been his faults that were the catalyst for the events that eventually brought him here on this morning. He had run from commitment and daemons, chased ghosts and dreams. Now what would he do? Overhead a very large airliner rumbled no more than 100 feet above the ground. The wash that followed the roar was exhilarating. His sea legs were strong, maybe now he could try out his wings. The thunder of the four massive engines passed and faded into the distance revealing the sounds of the city that surrounded him. Chris didn't know specifically which plane Hope was supposed to be on but it was now a half hour past her departure time. He assured himself that it would be safe to leave. She was surely gone by now and once again nothing held him back. He slowly crawled off the truck. The previous night's passions had left him battered and sore. He climbed into the cab and put the flame to the engine. The radio came to life. He turned it up as loud as it could go.

"*I'm going to Galleywinter, the place where all the cowboys ride, the place where all the outlaws ride away from the men who want to kill them for what they've done...*"

When he was happy with the settings, he threw it into drive and spun the tires, kicking up dust. The rear end spun around rotating the Chevy on its front axle. Chris shot out across the empty lot.

Afterward

Chris's hands instinctively knew the all the turns and stops to make along the entire route westward to the Studio. It was like riding a bicycle. As Hope was strolling through the terminals at LaGuardia, on a lengthy layover before she jumped the pond, Chris was turning off the blacktop. He put his weight into the accelerator, kicking up dust. When he jumped over the last hill, his foot let off and he coasted down into the valley. Passing the windmills, several dogs gave chase, led by Dingo. Ramone's old, reliable truck sat in front of the house. It was still working apparently, Chris was surprised. Alongside it a soft-top Cadillac and a late model Charger were parked. Rolling down the hill he surveyed the scene. The house was just as he'd left it. The grounds though looked alive and brilliant with color. Mrs. Padillo possessed a much greener thumb than he had. The yard was filled with quaint ornaments: an old bathtub with flowers in it, several wrought iron chairs, brilliant in their patina, and several magnificently constructed mills and chimes that rotated in the wind. Ramone seemed to have mastered his metallurgy.

As Chris was parking his truck, Ramone came out of the Studio wiping his hands with an old rag. His face lit up when he saw who the driver was. He tucked the rag into his left pocket; it hung past his knee and swung with the rhythm of his gait. After a warm greeting from Dingo, the two men met in the white gravel drive and embraced as old friends do.

"Come, Senior Coupland, tell me of the world, I have many questions."

They toured the Studio and surrounding land together catching up. Ramone had taken well to the design and production industry. His furniture was very popular amongst the southwestern region of the country and production was in full force. Several of the younger Padillo family had joined the Studio to help out. Efficiency had improved and they had all adapted well. Rounding the back side of the studio, strolling through the tall grasses with Dingo and three of his offspring in tail, Chris noticed the house. In the lowering light of the day, the windows shimmered, the shadows of the posts cast across the patio.

After dinner with the Padillos, Chris sat atop the hill under the old windmill, next to Duke's stone with Dingo between his legs. Ramone stood behind him, just off to his right leaning against the steel structure. "You might want to be careful old man, push that thing to hard and it just might come crashing down."

Ramone chuckled and pulled a blade of grass from the ground, "You worry too much and things that you need not worry about."

Chris rubbed his old companion, "Somebody has to look after you."

"My wife does a fine job of that," Ramone replied without hesitation. "What will you do now?"

Chris ran his hands up and down the sides of his furry companion. "I'm moving the operation to Austin. Several friends are joining me." He squinted in the setting sun, "I want to diversify the Studio, hire on more craftsmen, all with different skill sets and see what we can come up with."

Ramone said nothing. Chris knew what was on the tip of the old man's tongue.

"I want you to stay on here if it fits you. This land is yours, always was, but if you wish to join me in Austin, you are more than welcome."

From behind him the old Mexican cleared his throat. "I am an old man, I cannot afford to pay you for this."

Chris nodded, "Don't worry about that. We'll work something out." He leaned down and growled at Dingo, "And yes, you are pretty old," he added with a laugh.

Ramone reached down and slapped the young man on the back of his head in passing, "I'm not too old whip you. Come on, I have a wife to tend to."

Chris laughed, "And I have a boat to tend to but somehow I think you're going to enjoy your night better than I am," but the old man was already headed down the hill at a good trot. Rising with considerable effort, his joints cracked, showing the miles he had been through. Standing under the old windmill, his eyes surveyed the scene. He would miss this place dearly. It was his Eden that had seen him through the roughest of years. Part of him did not want to leave, to surrender the youthful abandon that had marked his time on this land but deep inside something pushed his soul to move forward. Chris held his head low as he rolled it from side to side, shaking all the inhibition from his mind. "Alright Dingo, let's do this," he spoke to the dog as his feet carried him down the hill, through the tall grassed and toward the studio.

The next morning, after a sleepless night of meticulously unpacking the refinished boat and putting on the last few touches it needed, Chris pulled away in the '69 Chevy, Dingo riding shotgun, focusing out on the road ahead, with the boat in tow. There were many stops to make along the way, many people he needed to catch up with and make amends.

Two weeks after departing the Studio, Chris finally had the *Esperanza* on the waters of Lake Travis. It was a Sunday afternoon; a light breeze was slowly pushing the beautiful vessel across the waves. The shore line was drawing closer and closer. He might have to steer sometime before sundown, but for now Chris was content to lay back with his feet propped on the brass railing that glowed in the afternoon light. With his sunglasses on, he pulled his old hat brim down one more notch and leaned back, beer in hand, enjoying the motion of the water. It was nothing like the open ocean aboard the *Proud Mary,* but it was the best this area had to offer.

Rugby came up from the small quarters below with one can fresh from the ice for himself and one for his old friend. He tossed the second at Chris who was jarred back to reality when the icy road soda landed on his stomach. "So, what's the plan?"

Chris put his feet on the deck and straightened his wide brimmed, straw hat, "Who needs a plan?"

"Touché."

"Neal and Kathy are supposed to be coming back to the beach with Lacey soon. We need to find them, but beyond that, I really don't care."

Rugby took a seat on the opposite side of the vessel, "Apathy, it's about time you found some."

"Just trying not to worry, that's all."

"So, when will the Studio be up and running?"

Chris cracked the cold can in his hand, "I'm not sure, I try not to worry about a schedule. Lacey's getting paid to keep us all on time, you'll have to ask her."

"Does this mean I have to do what she says now?"

Nodding with a laugh, "We all do."

Rugby raised his brow and shook his head, "Shit."

The duo floated along the gently rolling ripples for most of the afternoon, rising only to change the stereo or drinks. As the sun settled gently on the horizon, Rugby finally asked, "Did you ever find what you were looking for?"

Chris sat back with a big grin beneath his straw hat, "I don't think I ever will, don't want to. Some dreams aren't at the destination... they're in the journey."

The Gift

H ope stood in a small, family jewelry store in Santiago de
Compostela, Spain. She had been in the country for just
over three and a half years. Standing in the shop just off the main
thoroughfare she thought of her old friends.

She pulled a slip of paper from her purse and handed it to the elderly
gentleman standing behind the counter. He adjusted his glasses, read
over the receipt and nodded as he turned and headed into the back of
the store. Hope surveyed the merchandise inside the counter before
her. They were brilliant, handmade pieces. This family had operated
their business for hundreds of years and was famous throughout the
Mediterranean for their quality and attention to detail.

Hope heard from Chris occasionally, he had yet to make it for a
visit, but she thought of him almost every day. Sometimes she thought
of what might have been, but never in wanting, only wondering.

The old man returned with a small box. Handing it over to Hope,
he thanked her for her business and wished her the best of luck. She
smiled sweetly and excused herself. She walked the streets enjoying the
late May weather. The local businesses bustled with excitement. Life
moved at a slower pace but it was more passionate. The people were
very polite and loving. Her fears of the new land had quickly dissipated
when she got to know the city.

Her home was almost two miles toward the outside of the city. Hope enjoyed every step of the walk but couldn't get home soon enough. She followed the stone walk through the front gate and across the garden that worked to dampen the heat of the summer that was building. The vines that scaled the garden walls and the sides of the house popped with beautiful, aromatic flowers. Hope picked up a few of the toys left scattered around as she walked toward the double doors leading into the sitting room. Just a step inside the residence, she set the toys beside the door and called out, "I'm home!"

From around the corner she heard the tiny footsteps on the tile floor. Hope placed her purse on the couch and bent down as her daughter rounded the corner running as fast as she could. Her sandy brown locks that spiraled down to her shoulders bounced as she opened her arms reaching for her mother. Hope wrapped her arms around the child as they rolled across the floor laughing. They swapped kisses and giggles. "Happy birthday, sweetheart," she offered lying on her back in the middle of the room. Her daughter let loose of her neck and sat up on her stomach. "Here honey, I got something for you." Her daughter's eyes widened with anticipation as she drew her hands to her mouth in a feeble attempt to retain an excited gasp. Hope laid the small box from the jeweler across her chest and opened it. From the satin case she pulled a platinum chain that held at its bottom a small pendant. Set in the pendant was a familiar princess cut diamond.

Hope reached out and hung the stone around her daughter's neck. The little one reached up with her small, delicate fingers and examined the pendant. The light shattered through the diamond and cast vibrant rays across her soft round cheeks. She looked from the ornament to her mother, "Pretty, Mama." Her smile brought out dimples that could melt any heart.

Hope smiled, gazing at her daughter. She was three years old today and already the most beautiful child in the world. Hope was lost, staring into her ghostly blue eyes that radiated with love. She could see the innocence and wild passion in her baby's eyes. She was once again reminded of her long lost friend and lover, and the last gift he gave her.

The Music

The music tracks referenced throughout this novel were chosen for differing reasons, both personal and common experiences amongst friends. The following is a list of the songs which provide a list of those songs selected in the novel, and still provide a soundtrack to my experiences and the stories they hold. The music is cited out of respect and appreciation for the artists that created these songs. The music they create puts a tangible, palpable essence to the emotion which they convey. I only hope that if any of the musicians happen to read this book understand the great debt I owe them in how they helped to develop and translate my own thoughts and observations into this literary project. The songs here are listed by section and are as follows.

West Texas –

Somewhere Down In Texas by Jason Boland

This song is by far my personal favorite. The tone of this song carries the same pace and emotions of what I see in where I want to go. It is the soundtrack to my fondest memories and dreams at the same time.

The Last Word –

Here's to the Night by Eve 6

A personal favorite of mine for its ability to recognize the transition from what has been to what is coming, this song carries a strong beat that has the ability to pulse with the emotion it conveys.

Apprehension –

Standing Outside the Fire by Garth Brooks

One of the most recognizable of all artists in the novel, this song is one that at any time creates a positive, motivational atmosphere. I have never been a fan of emotional, motivational speeches. Most rants of such nature are cliché and choking, but in this song, with the power that the music portrays, there is uniqueness in its message and how it is told.

Flashback #2 (Ramone)

Alabama (the New Version) by Cross Canadian Ragweed

The powerhouse. The one juggernaut. The song that no matter where I am, or where I have gone, it always takes me back to that time when we were all young and hadn't a care in the world beyond the day we lived in. It is one that is held dear for both musical appreciation and nostalgic retreat. Plus I have followed Cross Canadian Ragweed for year now, from the clubs to the stages which put them in front of thousands of people and I have never once been disappointed.

6th St. –

Dixieland Delight by Alabama

This song was always a staple of Sunday night karaoke. We all knew it by heart and it is one that always brought smiles. It's reflection of country nights in the summertime were a common thread that many relate to. We may have been far from Dixie, but the lyrics still rang true.

Flashback #3 (Rlationshit)

Wave on Wave by Pat Green

This is a song which, in timing and beautifully crafted lyrics, paints a vivd portrait. This is one song that in its storytelling matched my own love at the time. Pat Green is hands down the greatest of the Texas troubadours. If not for the ground that he broke to gain the attention from the rest of the country much of the American Public would be naïve to the talent that calls the Lone Star State home.

Back to the Studio –

You Can't Always Get What You Want by The Rolling Stones

This classic staple is one that everyone should know. If you do not, I feel sorry for the classic rock and roll which you have missed out on. The most popular song cited here, it is self explanatory. Ironically, the context in which it is used it taken directly from my personal experience. The radio can be a therapist, if you find the right station.

New Day –

Donnelly Drive and *North on 35* both by The Kyle Bennett Band

Both of these selections are reflections of my experiences as I transitioned from school, the move to Texas and my eventual return. The former is especially true in regards to the green eyed girl. It will always live in a particular moment for me.

A New Meeting –

Somewhere Down In Texas by Jason Boland

Again, the repeat of this song shows the deep connection I have with the scene and emotion conveyed in it. The song as a whole is a beautiful piece, though the specific lines are ones that strike a chord.

Wrapping Up –

Watching Fireworks Alone by Pete Gile

This artist is a local favorite of mine who also graduated from Kansas State. I have heard him play in bar after bar and he tells some great stories. His songs are rural and honest and I appreciate all he does to remain true to the roots of western country music. There is more truth and honesty in one line of his music than all that may come out of Nashville in any given year. This selection is a nod to Pete, and a show of my gratitude for the many, many hours of entertainment he has provided both myself and all the others throughout the years.

The Dance –

My Feet Don't Touch the Ground by Brandon Jenkins

This song is an absolutely amazing story of how respect and love for one person can completely alter the priorities of someone. A lesson I picked up on far later than I should have. It is beautifully written, though to be honest, the first version I ever heard and immediately fell in love with was a cover performed by Stoney LaRue, the blues edge he puts to the song only strengthens the emotions portrayed.

Family Reunion –

Bad Reputation by Freedy Johnston

A great nod to the late nights and the sin the boys and I used to actively seek. The 90's rock sound is unique to most of the selections provided here, but the song is nostalgic.

To Dallas –

Lost and Found by The Randy Rogers Band

Amazing song. The story told here directly reflects much of how I once felt when thinking of the mistakes made in the past. I do not dwell and I have no regrets, but once and a while it's nice to remember.

A New Sun –

Galleywinter by Pat Green

The second selection from Pat Green, this song tells of dreams and wanted fantasies from a man of all ages. I relate closely with the dreamer described in this song and love the beautiful pictures painted within the music. I may not know exactly where I'm headed but I know that in the end, I want to go to Galleywinter.

Other songs relative to the material –

St. Elmo's Fire by John Parr

Wildflower by The Great Divide

Wonderwall by Oasis

Friends in Low Places by Garth Brooks

Later On by The Kyle Bennett Band

Girl in Red by Eli Young Band

Oklahoma Girl by Eli Young Band

Circle the Sun by Pete Gile

Barefeet on the Dash by Jackson Taylor Band
Three Days by Pat Green
Texas on My Mind by Pat Green
Oklahoma Breakdown by Stoney LaRue
Lighthouse Keeper by Cross Canadian Ragweed

I could go on and on with more and more music, but these songs are the most relevant to the stories conveyed. There are many other stories and much more music to go around but that is for another time. I would like to thank you for taking the time to invest in this work. It is a first attempt and the next will be better.

Regards,

Jake Hessman

May 17, 2010

Jake Hessman always had a knack for words. The energetic designer graduated from the College of Architecture, Planning, and Design at Kansas State University in May of 2007. After a short stay in Austin, Texas the author moved to Lawrence, Kansas. He is currently attending the University of Kansas.